Praise for *Perennials*

"This highly anticipated coming-of-age novel from Mandy Berman delivers the perfect sunny trifecta: summer camp drama, growing pains, and the enduring power of female friendships." —*Redbook*

"Mandy Berman delivers a duffel full of drama in her debut." —*Vanity Fair*

"A coming-of-age tale set at a New England summer camp = soon-to-be classic." —*Domino*

"Horseback riding, arts and crafts, illicit parties . . . spend part of your summer at Camp Marigold in the Berkshires via Berman's absorbing and moving debut novel-in-stories." —*Newsday*

"If you have a mini freak-out when someone says 'summer's almost over' . . . this is the read for you. It's about two girls who meet at summer camp and come back as counselors years later. Think: *Wet Hot American Summer* meets *The Parent Trap* meets your last summer beach read." —*The Skimm*

"Berman's debut recalls the beloved teen and adult novels of Judy Blume, both in topic and prose style: simple, powerful, unafraid to confront serious issues." —*Kirkus Reviews*

"If coming-of-age tales always get you, you won't be able to put this one down—it involves a female friendship between two campers who become counselors at Camp Marigold who must confront their past to move forward as adults." —*The Knot*

"Berman's command of prose is astounding. The more you read, the more difficult it is to believe that this is a debut novel. . . . Charged with hope, longing, an unexpected sensuality, and a bruised tenderness, *Perennials* is a book you should most definitely put near the top of your reading list." —*Pop Dust*

"*Perennials* centers on two girls who met as campers but are reunited as camp counselors once they're in college. As the summer progresses, they begin to grow apart—keeping secrets from one another, avoiding conversations about things they need to talk about—all culminating in one fateful event that makes them put everything on the table." —*PopSugar*

"Berman entices readers with this coming-of-age tale of two girls. . . . This story of facing life's difficulties is most memorable because of Berman's excellently crafted, multifaceted characters." —*Publishers Weekly*

"A full cast of well-drawn characters, a soup of issues and crossing storylines, and a setting right out of the Summer Reading Playbook—summer camp—are just some of the draws of this debut coming-of-age tale." —*Library Journal*

"Berman is at her most insightful when exploring the awkward unfurling of female adolescence. . . . *Perennials* is a sharp meditation on the changing female body, and the ways in which such changes are often involuntary and unwanted. . . . [She] skillfully captures the details and rituals of camp. It's a place where freedom from the roles young people play at home lets them become who they are. And where, for those who return year after year, a girl can retrace her steps, see all the parts of herself past and present, with the occasional glimpse into the future." —J. COURTNEY SULLIVAN, *The New York Times Book Review*

"In *Perennials*, Mandy Berman explores the inner worlds of girls attending a summer camp together—a place where the rules don't always apply. Weathering love affairs, escaping crumbling friendships, and even surviving the loss of one of their own, this cohort of girls grows into women in the span of one short summer—and you'll be glad for the chance to eavesdrop every step of the way." —MIRANDA BEVERLY-WHITTEMORE, *New York Times* bestselling author of *June* and *Bittersweet*

"Mandy Berman has remade the American summer camp narrative, ditching the usual clichés and getting in close with her characters and their various states of emotional and economic precariousness. *Perennials* is a sharp, crushingly observant, and empathetic debut, full of wit and tragedy, and good for all seasons." —SAM LIPSYTE, author of *The Fun Parts* and *The Ask*

RANDOM HOUSE

NEW YORK

Perennials

A Novel

Mandy Berman

2018 Random House Trade Paperback Edition

Copyright © 2017 by Mandy Berman

Published in the United States by Random House, an imprint and division of Penguin Random House LLC, New York.

RANDOM HOUSE and the HOUSE colophon are registered trademarks of Penguin Random House LLC.

Originally published in hardcover in the United States by Random House, an imprint and division of Penguin Random House LLC, in 2017

LIBRARY OF CONGRESS CATALOGING-IN-PUBLICATION DATA
Names: Berman, Mandy, author.
Title: Perennials: a novel / Mandy Berman.
Description: New York: Random House, 2017.
Identifiers: LCCN 2016028144 | ISBN 9780399589331 |
ISBN 9780399589324 (ebook)
Subjects: LCSH: Girls—Fiction. | Female friendship—Fiction.
Classification: LCC PS3602.E75864 P47 2017 | DDC 813/.6—dc23
LC record available at https://lccn.loc.gov/2016028144

Printed in the United States of America on acid-free paper

randomhousebooks.com

2 4 6 8 9 7 5 3 1

Book design by Dana Leigh Blanchette
Title-page and part-title art: © iStockphoto.com

For my parents

*And for Eleanor: May you hold on to
your girlhood as long as you can*

She would not say of any one in the world now that they were this or were that. She felt very young; at the same time unspeakably aged.

—VIRGINIA WOOLF,
Mrs. Dalloway

2000

1

Denise was supposed to drive Rachel to camp that morning, but she was hungover. Rachel had heard her come in late the night before, her heels clacking in the entryway of their apartment before she exhaled loudly and trod barefoot into the kitchen. Then came the slamming of cupboard doors and rustling through boxes; the crackling of plastic; the cereal tinkling into the bowl; the repetitive crunching. Denise had had a date with a tax lawyer who took her for French food in the Village. Most of her dates didn't leave the Upper West Side on the weekends, and neither did she.

Rachel imagined the night went something like this: They split a bottle of expensive wine. Denise tried not to drink it too fast, but they were done with it before finishing their entrées, and she was relieved when he suggested another. She went home with him but didn't sleep there; she sobered up enough to remember she needed to take Rachel to Connecticut early the next morning.

When Rachel went out into the living room at seven, Denise's mouth was wide open like a cartoon fish's. Dark purple eye shadow was smeared over her closed eyelids. She hadn't bothered to pull out the couch. People always said Rachel and Denise looked alike; often it was a pickup line from a guy—that they looked more like sisters than mother and daughter. But aside from the same dark, wavy hair, Rachel never saw the resemblance.

"Mom," she whispered.

Denise swallowed, then sighed, like she was in the middle of a nice dream.

"Mom," Rachel said again, stroking the top of her mother's head. Denise groaned and put the pillow over her face.

On the ride there, with her Dunkin' Donuts iced coffee, Denise started to wake up. They sang Pat Benatar; Denise had one hand on the steering wheel, and the other dangled out the window, holding a cigarette. They didn't need directions. This was Rachel's fourth summer at camp, and they knew the route by heart now—a straight shot up the Taconic, a winding parkway that could be so unpredictable Rachel sometimes worried her mom wouldn't make a turn in time and they'd end up smashed against a concrete boulder on the side of the road.

Rachel always got the feeling when they pulled into camp that time hadn't moved since the previous summer. Everything was exactly the same: the wooden Camp Marigold sign with the fading painted orange flowers; the smells of the horse manure from the barn and cut grass from the athletic fields. In the months leading up to camp opening, she would think maybe the grass wouldn't be as green. Maybe some building would be painted a different color. Maybe they'd fixed that one broken rail on the fence around the horse arena.

But none of that ever happened. Time didn't touch Camp Marigold, and that was what was so perfect about it.

They pulled into the circle of platform tents in the girls' Hemlock section, where the thirteen-year-olds stayed, and lugged Rachel's trunk from the back of the rental car. Counselors were greeting parents, helping them carry trunks and shopping bags filled with magazines and snacks, and girls Rachel knew well, girls with whom she'd compared nipples in their tents and stolen ice cream from the dining hall in the middle of the night, were hugging each other, holding hands, and gleefully yelling her name.

Denise put her arm around Rachel. "Happy, baby?"

Fiona ran over and embraced Rachel. "I saved you a bunk!" she said. She led Rachel into tent three. Their bunks were always at the top, head-to-head—best for late-night whispers after lights-out.

Fiona Larkin, Rachel's best friend at camp, was a nosy but brutally loyal girl from a big family in Westchester. It was Fiona's fifth summer at Marigold. She had already unpacked her own things and was now helping Rachel to unpack hers, taking items out of her trunk and organizing her cubby in a way Rachel would never be able to maintain.

Fiona stood with one hand on her hip, a box of Tampax raised in the other, and a questioning expression on her face.

"What?" Rachel asked. "Isn't it obvious?" She stood back and let Fiona appraise her. The changes were small, but there: slightly wider hips, and breasts in a real, underwire bra, size 34B.

"You need to tell me these things!" Fiona said.

"Sweetie"—Denise, who was tucking Rachel's mosquito net into the bunk, was shaking her head at Fiona—"it's nothing to be jealous about."

A few months earlier, Rachel had been home alone, lying on the couch watching a movie and eating Chips Ahoy! cookies. At a commercial she had gone to the bathroom and been shocked to see brown in her underwear. For a minute, she thought it had something to do with the cookies, like she had somehow gotten the chocolate on herself. But then she realized. No one ever mentioned it could be brown.

The next morning, Denise kissed her on the forehead. "I'm glad we got you those pads."

"I used one of your tampons."

"Really?" She cocked her head to the side.

Rachel shrugged. "It wasn't that hard."

"You shouldn't be going into my things, Rachel."

"The pad was so bulky."

"Why didn't you call me?" her mom asked.

"You were on a date."

"You can interrupt for something like *this*."

Denise turned around to put on some coffee. As she was

reaching for the ground coffee in the cabinet above her head, she paused with her hand there and turned to Rachel again.

"Are you having sex?"

"Mom. God."

"It's not impossible," she said.

"There's not even anyone I want to have sex with."

"*Want* to? I don't care if you want to or not. You're thirteen fucking years old."

"I didn't mean it like that."

"I don't know how you figured out the tampon so easy."

"There's an instruction manual, Mom. I can read."

"Don't be smart."

"I'm not."

"You know you have to be careful about these things now."

"I know what getting your period means."

"Don't be such a smartass, Rachel. I'm being serious." She poured water into the coffeemaker. "And you might want to start watching what you eat. No more full boxes of Chips Ahoy! in one sitting."

Fiona and Rachel thought it was weird that some girls were new to sleepaway camp at this age, as if they had been afraid to be away from home before now. One of the new girls cried quietly at night as if no one could hear her. Another was a tomboy who just played sports all day. Their counselor was from Poland, and Rachel and Fiona made fun of her accent when she left for the staff lodge after lights-out.

Fiona was the one who had convinced Rachel to take horseback riding, and then Rachel had convinced her dad to pay the extra money for it. Her dad wasn't around much anymore, but she knew she could still ask him for things. She knew at that age, though she didn't have the words for it, that she was using him and that she was allowed to. That, because he was the one who wasn't always there, she could ask for the things she wanted, and he would give them to her.

Riding was the first activity of the day, and Fiona and Rachel went down to the stables together after breakfast, walking arm in arm. Rachel got to ride only a few times throughout the year, when she was able to get her dad to take her out of the city, which wasn't often, so while Fiona was going on about boys—"Matthew Dawson was staring at you today at flag raising, Rachel. Didn't you see him?"—Rachel was thinking about Micah.

Most everyone else hated riding Micah. "His stubbornness is inconceivably annoying," their riding teacher used to say, making it obvious that she wanted to trade him in for a younger, more obedient horse. It was all the better for Rachel. He and Rachel had a sort of understanding that she'd never thought she could have with an animal, and when she got back each summer, she swore he had missed her.

He was a dark brown dun with a gleaming coat. When she saw him again, she hugged his neck and trailed her fingers down his mane. He let out a *neigh* by blowing out his lips, and Rachel laughed.

She and Fiona saddled and mounted their horses. Rachel and Micah remembered each other's rhythm as they cantered. She lifted off the saddle for one beat, stayed down for two. The air smelled like dry dirt and dandelions. She looked over at Fiona, whose face was clenched. She seemed nervous about what would happen next, her hands in tiny fists on the reins as if she would lose control of her horse if she let them slack even slightly.

Fiona rode a lot throughout the year; she lived just a short drive from a fancy stable. Rachel's mom had taken Rachel on Metro-North the previous fall to sleep over at Fiona's house in Larchmont, even though Rachel had insisted she could go alone. Fiona had a younger sister and an older brother, and they each had their own bedroom in their big house that looked the same as all the other big houses on the street. Inside there were freshly vacuumed carpets and a yellow Lab and parents who kissed each other on the cheek. There were brownies sitting warm and fresh on the counter like on those shows on Nick at Nite, and Fiona's mom was wearing an apron and cutting up vegetables and boiling water in the open kitchen. She asked Denise if she wanted to stay for a cup of tea, but Denise said no, she really had to be going. With her eyeliner and her cigarette breath, she didn't belong in that kitchen.

Then, when Fiona came to Rachel's apartment around Christmastime, Fiona's mom had stood in the doorway and looked inside with her mouth puckered like she'd just tasted something sour.

"You'll be here the whole time?" she'd asked Denise. Denise lied and said she would be. Later, after drinking a glass of white wine in the bathroom while she got ready for a date, she winked at Fiona, saying, "This is our little secret." And Rachel could tell how much Fiona loved being able to have a secret from her mother. When the girls were alone, Rachel showed Fiona her room; then they ordered Chinese food with the twenty dollars her mom had left for them and watched *The Real World*. At the commercial, Fiona asked where Rachel's mom slept.

"Here," Rachel said, patting the couch they were sitting on.

"You mean there's only the one bedroom?"

"Yeah. Obviously."

"Wow," Fiona said. "She must really love you."

Rachel's dad paid for the apartment; her mom was a secretary. Fiona clearly had no idea how expensive a two bedroom in Manhattan was.

When *The Real World* was at commercial, Rachel asked Fiona, "Want to watch something crazy?"

She clicked through the channel guide and found Showtime, which she sometimes put on late at night when she was by herself. She clicked on the title of the movie that was playing, *Animal Instinct*. Immediately an image popped up of two people leaning against the bars of a cage in a zoo. The guy had no shirt on and was wearing army green shorts. The girl had on much shorter shorts and a matching army green, button-down shirt, which was open, showing a black lacy bra, and her legs were wrapped around his waist. He was holding her up around him with his strong arms.

"Ew!" Fiona said. "What is this, Rachel?"

Rachel giggled. "Look at her huge boobs," she said, and at that moment, the guy opened the front of the girl's bra with his finger and thumb, and out they popped, these two giant things with two giant brown disks for nipples. Rachel's nipples were small and pink, like little bull's-eyes.

Fiona put a hand over her eyes.

"What are you so afraid of?" Rachel asked.

"This is so weird, Rachel," she said, her eyes still covered. "Please, just change the channel."

"Whatever," Rachel said. She turned back to *The Real World,* and they watched the rest of the episode in silence.

On the first Friday night of camp, they had a coed dance. Rachel wore a sequined, royal blue halter dress and silver heels with skinny straps. Fiona was in something flowered and paisley and flat, bone white sandals, because her mom wouldn't let her wear heels yet.

The dance was on the tennis courts in the boys' section of camp, with the girls standing on one side and the boys on the other until one of the boys made the first move. The previous summer, Rachel had been the first girl to be asked to dance. She knew that that sort of thing polarized people: There were girls who clung closer to her because of it and others who recoiled from her. She did wonder, in her limited, thirteen-year-old way, if Fiona only stayed friends with her because of what was, to Fiona, social capital.

That night it was Matthew Dawson, the tallest Hemlock boy, who breached the divide and tapped Rachel on the shoulder.

He was almost a foot taller than her, so anytime he tried

to talk as they danced—Who was in her tent this summer? Did she like this song?—he had to bend his head down, and she had to tilt hers up in a way that quickly became too tiresome to maintain. Soon they were dancing in relieved silence. Rachel could see Fiona and the other girls standing over in their circle looking at them. Matthew was in all the plays, and he was always the lead. That summer he was going to be Willy Wonka in *Charlie and the Chocolate Factory*. He had all these big features: big eyes, big nose, big lips, big ears. During afternoon open, the free period on the flag lawn after lunch, he'd pretend to be a monster with the little Maple kids, picking them up and running around with them above his head.

A slow song came on, and Rachel was happy to see Geoff Mendelson ask Fiona to dance. Matthew moved in closer and put his arms around Rachel's waist. She clasped her arms tighter around his neck, and he crouched down, swaying with his knees in a sort of half bend. The positioning was awkward but made Rachel feel like she was being taken care of.

He cleared his throat. "Are you having a good time?" he asked, his eyes going wide with the question.

"Yeah. Are you?"

"Yeah," he said. "It's always a fun night."

She tucked a piece of hair behind her ear and then put her arm back on his shoulder.

"You look really pretty," he said, swallowing.

Now everyone was dancing in a clump, coupled up and

swaying to the song. Matthew moved his arms tighter around her waist and crouched more.

"Funny how so many of us are camp regulars now," he said. "When did we get so old?"

"Thirteen is not very old."

"Summer of 2000," he said. "The world was supposed to blow up by now."

"The real millennium isn't until 2001."

"Well, good," he said. "We have another six months."

By mid-July, the days were very hot, and the flies were worse than ever, but this didn't deter Rachel from riding. She took good care of Micah, and she was often the more thirsty and tired of the two. She made sure they stopped a lot to give him water on trail rides and took it easy, just trotting and cantering, no galloping. They were stuck together, so they had to move together. She was controlling him to move forward, but he was equally controlling her. There was a strength there that was almost scary but comforting at the same time. Some days the riding counselor let Rachel stay through lunch, when she would help straighten up the barn and feed the horses, and she would linger too long at Micah's stall, feeding him extra hay and carrots when the counselor wasn't watching.

Matthew started hanging around Rachel more: in the morning when the campers walked from the flag to breakfast, on the lawn during free period, in front of the dining

hall after lunch. "How's your day going?" he'd ask, and Rachel would tell him about riding and tennis and swimming
or whatever else had happened that day. He talked about the
play a lot.

"It's getting really good, I think," he'd say. "I hope you're
excited for it."

Rachel was excited to see him in it. People started talking
about them like they were a pair.

"What base have you gotten to with him?" Fiona whispered one night after lights-out.

"No base," Rachel said.

"Don't lie to me, Rachel! I'm your best camp friend."

"I'm not lying. No base."

She sighed. "Well, tell me as soon as you do get to one,
okay?"

Fiona seemed ready to tell Rachel all her secrets at any
moment.

"How far have you gone?" Fiona whispered in the bunk.
"Like, ever?"

"I don't know," Rachel said. "Not far."

She sighed again. "You're so private sometimes."

In the city, kids saw things early; they learned the names
of sex positions and underground drugs, and for many, it
was not long before they tried them. And though Rachel
knew things, she was something of a late bloomer in the
Manhattan middle school social scene.

"You mean you don't get horny?" Karla once asked. Karla
was Rachel's best friend at school; Karla had met her boy-

friend, Joe, who was in high school, late at night when they were both smoking weed in Riverside Park.

"I don't think you can be horny if you've never even done it," Rachel had said.

In the spring, Karla and Rachel had gone to Joe's apartment for a party, because his parents were never home. There were bottles and smoke everywhere, and there was loud rap music playing. Rachel sat on the couch between Karla and Kevin, Joe's younger brother. Kevin passed her a bottle of Bacardi, and she took a huge sip of it and swallowed. Kevin said, "Daaaaaamn, girl," and Rachel pretended it tasted like water even though inside, her lungs felt like they were tearing apart from each other. But the rush to her head was good, and it made her care less about where she was and about Kevin's arm clamped tight around her shoulder. She didn't remember how or when he started to kiss her, but she knew they were doing so right there in front of everyone.

The next day, Karla called her. "Kevin told Joe he had a great time with you last night."

"That's weird," Rachel said. "We hardly did anything."

"Yeah. He knows you're playing hard to get."

"I'm not meaning to."

"Well, meaning to or not," she said, "keep it up. It's working."

On Visitors' Day, Denise drove up in a rental car again and brought Rachel a bagel from their favorite neighborhood deli. Fiona's family showed up to see her—her parents and her younger sister and their yellow Lab; her older brother was away at lacrosse camp. They had a picnic lunch together, Rachel's and Fiona's families; Mrs. Larkin had made chocolate-and-vanilla sandwich cookies, which weren't as good as regular Oreos.

After lunch, Rachel's mom took her to CVS to buy some toiletries; Fiona's thirteenth birthday was coming up the following week, so the Larkins went out for a "birthday surprise." Rachel filled up the shopping cart with necessities like toothpaste and bug spray, but also cans of Pringles, boxes of sugary cereal, and Pixy Stix, which she'd heard were fun to snort, while Denise wasn't looking. At the register, Rachel expected her mom to tell her to put all the junk food items back—partly because they weren't necessities and partly because Rachel wasn't supposed to eat that stuff anymore—but Denise was in a good mood. She smiled and didn't say a word, except to order a pack of Newport Lights from the guy behind the counter.

They drove back to camp with the windows open. Their relationship felt different in the country, all the stresses of city life left behind. There was no smog, no subways or sirens. Here it was just Denise and Rachel pared down, mother and daughter driving along a country road.

The unspoken element, of course, was that Rachel's dad made all this country ease possible. But he was the one with another family. He was the one who had left. This was, as they understood it, their due.

They parked next to the horse stables, and when they got out of the car, Rachel saw Fiona brushing a sandy-haired mare that wasn't one of the Camp Marigold horses. The rest of the Larkins surrounded them; Mrs. Larkin was taking pictures.

Rachel approached the fence of the arena, and Denise followed behind her with the CVS bags in her hands. When Fiona saw Rachel, she stopped brushing the horse and ran toward her friend.

She leaned against the fence, breathless. "They got me a horse, Rachel! Can you believe it? Her name is Josie. And you can ride her whenever you want."

Rachel looked up at her mom. Denise shoved the CVS bags into Rachel's arms and took the pack of Newports from her back pocket. She pulled one out and lit it right there. She took a long drag.

She wasn't allowed to smoke at camp. But Rachel decided not to say anything.

Charlie and the Chocolate Factory went on that night so the parents could see it, but Denise had already driven home to beat Sunday night traffic. The show was pretty bad, but Matthew had real talent, a way of dominating the entire stage.

At the end of the show, he came over to hug Rachel. He was sweating and had orange makeup on his face that she hadn't noticed from the audience. He smelled like he needed to put on more deodorant, but she liked it. It was a long hug, their bodies closer than they had ever been, and she felt small and safe in it. She pulled away because otherwise she might have stayed for a long time.

"What'd you think?" he asked.

"You were great." Over Matthew's shoulder, Rachel saw Fiona watching them. "Do you want to meet up later?" Rachel asked.

His eyebrows went up, and he looked around the auditorium with all the kids and counselors laughing and buzzing.

"You mean sneak out?" he whispered.

"Yeah."

She knew that inside he was terrified and thrilled like her. She could tell by the way his nostrils were flaring and how his eyes had taken on a crazy wideness.

He slowly nodded. "Okay."

Later, after lights-out, it wasn't hard for Rachel to keep herself awake. Her pulse hammered against the flesh of her throat; her limbs were electric, tingling. When her watch said twelve-forty-five, she peeled up the mosquito net and climbed, very quietly, down on top of her trunk and then onto the wooden floor of the tent. She slipped on her flip-flops and tiptoed out of the back of the tent and stopped at the bathroom. She took her hair out of its bun and fluffed it around her face. She put on lip gloss and smacked her lips together. She pinched her cheeks to make them rosy.

She tiptoed out of girls' camp and all the way down the gravel road, which eventually ended at the stables. It was so quiet and so hard to see at night that she had to move very slowly, so she didn't trip over a hidden root or a loose stone. Her eyes started to adjust to the dark, and she could see the rectangular wooden performing arts building ahead. They'd agreed to meet in the woods behind it.

When she walked around to the back of the building, a dead leaf crunched under her foot, and she paused. She saw a tall figure and held her breath as she moved closer.

"Hey," Matthew said. She moved toward him and saw he was also in his pajamas, flannel drawstring pants and a Camp Marigold hoodie.

They walked into the woods without talking. Marigold felt different at night: dark and scary but in a good way. Like it was uncharted territory. Like it was impossible there were hundreds of kids and counselors sleeping in their bunks in the very same camp.

Matthew slowed and stopped at a spot between two trees.

"This is good," he said and took off his backpack. Then he pulled a blanket out of it and spread it over the flat part of the ground. He was very careful to flatten and even it out just so.

They sat down on the blanket at the same time. They looked at their feet.

"I was really happy that you invited me out here," he finally said.

"Oh," she said. "How come?"

"Well, I've always had a crush on you." His voice cracked on the word "always," and he cleared his throat. "Well, not always. But you know. For a long time."

Just the edges of their kneecaps were touching.

"How long?" she asked.

He thought about it for a minute. "Since Buckeye summer, I think," he said. "Yeah, that was it. You were green team captain that year, weren't you?"

"I think so."

"You were. I remember you were standing in front of all the Buckeye girls at the pool before a swim race and leading a green team cheer. We were at the athletic shed playing four square, but I saw you all the way over at the pool in your green shorts and green paint under your eyes and your hair in two braids. I couldn't hear what you were yelling, but it didn't matter because everyone was listening to you and watching you. You were really, really in charge of all those girls."

"That's funny," she said. "I don't remember that."

"Anyway." He cleared his throat again. "I just am trying to say that I like you, Rachel." Before she could say anything back, he leaned in and pressed his mouth against hers. Then his tongue pushed its way into her mouth, poking and prodding as if it was going to find something in there.

They kissed like that for several minutes. She could tell Matthew thought that was what he was supposed to do. She didn't really know at the time exactly what you were supposed to do, but she knew it couldn't be that.

She finally pulled away to take a breath. He was panting.

"Are you okay?" he asked.

"I'm fine," she said, which he took as "Let's keep going," and he went back in. This time, though, he rolled over on top of her. He pressed down into her, and she could feel his penis, erect and hard, poking the bottom of her stomach. He was slobbering, grunting, a different person from the one she thought she was starting to get to know. But as he moved down slightly, it started to feel right—not quite as good as when she was riding Micah, but a hint of it. They stayed that way for a long time, their bodies heating up inside their flannel pajamas, until she also began to feel like a different person.

Then in the midst of all the grinding and grunting, Matthew reached a hand up her pajama top, and as soon as he cupped his hand around her breast and squeezed, he went, "*Oh,*" and his body convulsed against hers.

"Sorry," he said, glancing down at himself, and it took her a moment to understand what had happened.

They lay on the blanket looking up at the stars for a few minutes until Rachel said, "We should probably go back now." They walked out of the woods not touching and got to the hill separating the boys' and girls' camps. He went in to give her a hug goodbye.

"You're supposed to kiss me good night," she said, and he did, dutifully.

Rachel was so tired in the morning that Fiona had to shake her awake.

"What's wrong with you, Rachel?" she asked.

Rachel groaned. She could barely keep her eyes open as they walked to the showers.

"You're seriously acting so weird," Fiona said when they were getting dressed and Rachel was practically silent.

"I just didn't sleep that well last night," Rachel said.

"Whatever," Fiona said, suspicious.

At flag raising, Rachel looked over at Matthew as he was yawning. He caught her glance and smiled with half his mouth, like he wasn't sure if he was supposed to or not.

Rachel offered a mischievous smile back, then flipped her hair behind her. She grabbed Fiona's arm, and they walked arm in arm to the dining room. He followed behind them the whole way. Rachel had never liked coffee before, but at breakfast she was so tired that she decided she wanted a cup. In the dining hall, boys and girls sat on opposite sides, but as Rachel went up to the coffee station in the middle—which was supposed to be for counselors only—Matthew came rushing toward her.

"Hey," he said conspiratorially. "Are you allowed to be up here?"

"I don't know," Rachel said without an iota of worry.

"Let me get it for you," he said, taking the cup from her.

"Skim milk, two Sweet'N Lows," Rachel said, which was the way her mom fixed hers.

He handed the coffee and the Sweet'N Low packets to Rachel and said, "Want to sit together on the lawn during free period?"

He was just a boy again—nervous and human. Whatever he had been the night before, in the middle of all the sweating and heaving, that was not who Rachel was looking at now. Now he was a boy who would do whatever she wanted.

Fiona could have her stupid horse.

"Maybe," Rachel said, and turned away, flipping her hair behind her once more.

When she got back and sat down at the table, Fiona leaned against her. She had been watching. "Did something happen with him last night?"

"Maybe," she said.

"What did you guys do?"

"None of your business," Rachel said, stirring the Sweet'N Low into her coffee.

The excitement on Fiona's face fell away. "That'll give you cancer," she said about the Sweet'N Low.

"See if I care," Rachel said, and took a scalding sip.

2

Denise smoked one cigarette after another on the drive home, lighting each new one with the butt from the last. She felt a stronger urge to smoke in the country than she did in the city, as if it were the clean air that didn't belong in her lungs. She had the radio tuned to classic rock and was pushing eighty on the Taconic. She just wanted to get home.

The blue lights of a police car lit up in her rearview mirror. She knew immediately that they were for her. "Fuck," she muttered to herself, and put on her blinker as she slowed and pulled onto the shoulder of the parkway.

She put out her cigarette in the car's ashtray and turned off the radio. The cop car, with the words HIGHWAY POLICE stamped on the hood, slowed and parked behind her. She checked her reflection quickly in the overhead mirror and pinched her cheeks and lips for a flush of color. As the officer walked toward her, he grew larger in the side-view mirror. Aviator sunglasses obscured his eyes. She rolled down her driver's-side window.

"Hello, Officer," she said. He pushed his sunglasses to the top of his head, and now she saw what she was working with. He was probably in his early twenties, with chubby cheeks and a hint of a moustache that looked like it was having trouble growing. She took a quick look at his name tag: OFFICER DANIEL MCGILL.

"Ma'am, are you aware of how fast you were driving?" Officer McGill asked, tentatively peering into Denise's car.

"Was I speeding?" Denise had at least fifteen years on him. "I had no idea."

"I clocked you going eighty-three in a fifty-five."

Denise gasped—which, as soon as she did it, felt ridiculous to her. But she did what she had to do. "I'm so sorry, Officer McGill," she said, bringing an equally ridiculous hand to her mouth.

He took a pad and a pen from the breast pocket of his uniform and wrote something down. "License and registration, please," he said.

Denise beamed up at him. She wasn't as young as she used to be, but she was still attractive. Only, he wasn't even looking at her.

"Do you have kids, Officer?" she asked.

He shook his head.

"I was visiting my daughter at camp," Denise said. "I still

have another six weeks without her, and she's so young." She saw this elicited no response from him. "She's all I've got," she tried.

"It sounds difficult, ma'am." His voice cracked into a higher register, and he cleared his throat. "But if you could just give me your license and registration, I can run your information, and this will be over in no time."

She imagined how freeing it might be to start the ignition and drive over the divider onto the other side of the Taconic and go back in the direction she came from, to scoop up Rachel and bring her home. Every summer, Denise would see how happy her daughter became when she got to camp. But then, during Denise's drive back to the city, her regrets would grow. Rachel didn't belong there. She was a city girl, like Denise: hard and street-smart and tough. Denise knew it took two people to make one kid, but she resented every hint of Mark she saw in her daughter. Every time Rachel asked for a designer bag or went to the suburbs to ride horses with Fiona, Denise's heart flinched. That kind of spoiled, materialistic behavior could only have been borne from him.

"Let me tell you," Denise said, trying to make herself emotional. "It's the biggest sacrifice of your life. Don't ever do it." She wiped a fake tear from her eye. "They need you, and they need you, and then, just like that"—she snapped her fingers—"they don't need you."

"Ma'am," Officer McGill said, "I'm sorry that you're upset, but if you're not going to cooperate, I'm going to have to ask you to step outside of the car."

"And you know why?" she said. "It's because you can't

give them what they need anymore. Imagine that. A mother, not being able to give her own daughter what she needs."

Denise opened her purse and took out her wallet. She opened it, and then remembered the unpaid tickets. For some time now she had been receiving the envelopes with the red block letters on the front of them, and she had ignored them, quietly hoping they would go away. Mark always paid for a rental car in the summer for Denise and Rachel, for camp. Somehow last summer she'd managed to get pulled over several times. She couldn't help the feelings of rage that fucking camp brought out in her.

Quickly, she closed the wallet.

"Officer, I completely forgot my license back in the city," she lied, rapidly thinking of ways to get out of this.

"Ma'am, if you don't have your license with you, I'm going to need your name and Social Security number."

"Does it really need to come to that?" she said. He didn't smile back at her. So she took her hand and reached outside the car window, toward his leg, and grazed his inner thigh with her fingers.

But she could make contact for only a moment before he slapped her hand away and pulled the gun from his holster, which, she then realized, in an instant of panic, was inches from the spot she'd touched.

He pointed the gun shakily at her. "Ma'am, keep your hands inside the car."

Denise shrieked and cowered with her arms over her head. She squeezed her eyes shut. She heard him speak into his portable radio and report his location. She wanted to say that this was all just a misunderstanding. She tried to explain herself, but nothing came out except a stream of tears—real this time—and short, labored breaths.

Someone radioed back. She peeked one eye open; the gun was still pointed toward her window. She made a squeaking noise when she saw it there so close to her face, and ducked farther down, squeezing her eyes tighter.

"Copy that," she heard the boy say into his radio. He let out a sigh.

She peeked again and now looked up at the boy. The gun was back in his holster. He was looking at her with an intensely worried expression on his face.

"Ma'am," he said, and she watched him with one squinted eye as he lowered his face to window level so that the worried expression was hidden away. "It's okay. I'm not going to shoot you."

Slowly she opened her eyes and lifted her head.

"You can't touch me again," he said. "Do you understand?"

She nodded emphatically. "I won't."

"It's a felony," he said.

"Okay," she said, wiping away a tear. "I didn't know."

He looked around. The other cops hadn't arrived yet.

"I'm sorry," he said, and exhaled. He put his face into his hands. He pressed his palms into his eye sockets and groaned.

When he removed his hands, his eyes were red from the pressure or maybe from tears. Denise couldn't tell.

"I'm sorry," he said. "I panicked."

"That's okay." Denise sat up straight. She wanted to touch him again, but in a comforting, maternal way.

"It's my first week on the job."

She nodded. He looked so uneasy. He was searching her eyes for reassurance. "You're doing great," she said.

The East Fishkill Police Station was a small gray brick building on a quiet country road. A stone pathway led to a modest garden up front, which a Hispanic man was happily tending. The building looked more like a tourist center in a nice country town than a police station.

"*Hola,* Oscar," said the older cop now accompanying her—Officer McGill's backup.

"*Hola, señor,*" Oscar said back to him.

But inside, the station looked like what Denise had only seen on TV: linoleum flooring, fluorescent lights, one open room with a few folding metal chairs at the front, an old woman at a reception desk, and, behind her, rows of desks facing one another, mostly unoccupied, with scattered papers on top of them all.

"Hiya, Doreen," the cop said to the woman at the desk, who wore her hair in a frizzy gray bun and sipped coffee from a mug that said I'M SILENTLY JUDGING YOU.

"Hey, Bud," she said, looking up from her clunky desktop computer. She made eye contact with Denise and tilted her head in surprise, as if this were the first time in years she was seeing a stranger.

"She needs to use the phone," Bud said, and Doreen skeptically pushed the tan rotary phone across the desk.

Denise dialed Mark's cell number, which she knew by memory, and waited for him to pick up.

"It's me," she said.

A pause. She could hear some cheerful domestic commotion: a teen boy's laugh, a dog barking, the wife's upbeat voice in the background: "Who is that, sweetie?"

"Hold on a second," he said into the phone. She heard something muffled, imagined him covering the receiver, telling his wife it was work. Then shuffling and a door shutting.

"What the hell are you doing?" His voice was hushed. "It's a Sunday."

"I know. I'm sorry. It's an emergency."

"What's going on?" he said with sudden urgency. "Is she okay?"

"She's fine. She's doing great."

Denise looked up at Bud, who was standing expectantly, watching her, listening to the conversation, his arms crossed. And then at Doreen staring stone-faced, holding her oversized mug in both of her wrinkled hands.

"I got pulled over," she whispered into the phone, as if the people at the police station didn't already know.

"So what?" Mark said.

"So my license is suspended."

When Bud had gotten to the highway and run Denise's info, he'd discovered those many envelopes that had been accumulating over the year, and that another envelope had come informing Denise of the license suspension.

"Jesus, Denise."

"They won't let me drive," she said sheepishly. She felt like she was a little girl again, confessing to her father right before he spanked her that yes, she had stolen five dollars from his drawer.

"How the fuck were you able to even take out a car?"

"I dunno." She'd just gone to the same shoddy Avis that she went to every year, the one with the Mexican guys behind the counter who always flirted with her.

A sharp, angry exhale. "Where are you?"

After she hung up, Denise waited in one of the metal chairs near Doreen's desk. A few cops were milling in and out of offices, drinking coffee. Some made phone calls from their desks in the open room. Doreen typed, periodically looked at Denise, sipped her coffee, typed again.

"You work here long?" Denise finally said to break the silence.

"Thirty-seven years," Doreen said.

"Wow," Denise said. "Impressive."

Doreen raised her eyebrows in a way that said *Yeah, I know.*

"I'm a secretary too," Denise said. "In the city."

"The city, huh."

"That's right."

"Never liked it."

Denise nodded. "It's not for everyone."

Doreen leaned forward, took another sip from her mug. "That was your husband before?"

Denise shook her head. "We were never married."

"But you wanted to be."

Denise considered this. "It's complicated."

"But you got a kid with him?"

"I do." She thought this might be her in with Doreen. "Rachel. She's thirteen."

"Never had kids," Doreen said. "We didn't want 'em."

Denise had met Mark on her first day at Kimmel, Johnson, and Murphy, LLC, spring of 1985. She wore her pencil skirt and her kitten heels, and she was so nervous. She had been the receptionist at her stepdad's tiny real estate office in Downtown Brooklyn for the previous five years, since she had graduated from high school, but then her mom had divorced her stepdad, and the job went too. This was her first time working in Manhattan. She'd answered an ad in the classifieds, and amazingly, they'd hired her. She had a lot of experience, and her new supervisor said she had "spunk."

The law firm was on the thirty-fourth floor of a sky-scraper on East Thirty-Ninth Street; the Chrysler Building was so close that Denise couldn't see to the top of it from the office. She was working for a short and fat attorney who sweated profusely, and she had been told in the interview that part of the job was constantly running to and from the dry cleaners to switch out his dirty shirts for clean ones. He went through at least two of them each day. Her desk was situated outside his office, and his phone did not stop ringing all morning. In fact, the whole office was men walking briskly between offices in their suits, and phones continually ringing on the desks outside the offices, and secretaries at the desks picking up the phones and speaking in their cheerful yet professional, capable voices: "So-and-so's office; and who may I ask is calling?" Denise, on the other hand, felt as if she bumbled every time she picked up the phone and had already disconnected the line twice when trying to transfer a call to her attorney. At one P.M. on her first day, she had not yet eaten or gone to the bathroom, and she wouldn't have minded taking a fifteen-minute break to do so.

She noticed the man walking toward her attorney's office, swaggering, really, with his head held erect and a calm, satisfied expression on his face. He seemed so comfortable, so at ease, so very capable. He was tall and he had wide shoulders, and though Denise knew nothing about expensive suits, she recognized that he was wearing one. He noticed her—she knew he did—and bashfully she looked down to scribble nonsense onto the pad of paper in front of her.

"Hi there," she heard the man say, and she looked up at him. His face was so clean-shaven that there wasn't a hint of stubble, and she had the urge to reach out and feel how smooth it might be. He had long eyelashes, like a girl's, which made his eyes seem deep and important.

He put a hand out when she didn't say anything back. "I'm Mark," he said.

"I'm Denise."

His hand gripped hers hard. "Is it your first day?" he asked, so kindly, so sweetly, that she wanted him to wrap her up in his arms just then. It was odd; this man must have been in his forties. He had some gray hairs on his head and lots of wrinkles around his eyes. She had a boyfriend in Brooklyn, a mechanic she met getting her car fixed, who was twenty-three like her.

She nodded. "Yes," she said.

"And how is it going?"

"It's fine," she said. "I really need to go to the bathroom."

He broke into a wide grin, showing his rich white teeth. "Do you want me to sit at your desk?" he asked.

"That would be so nice," she said with a grateful sigh.

When she came back, he was sitting in her chair, legs up on the desk, talking to someone on the phone with his fingers twirling around the cord.

"Oh yes, we've begun hiring male receptionists," he was saying into the phone. "Equal opportunity." He looked up at Denise and winked at her, as if he was crafting this private joke for just the two of them.

Mark appeared breathless at the front door to the police station an hour later. He was dressed in jeans, boat shoes, and a polo. Denise was used to seeing him in his suit jackets and loosened ties on weeknights. She wished that she wasn't still attracted to him—it would have made things so much easier—that his extra weight and increasingly high forehead repelled her, made her pity his age and his mortality, for she was twenty years younger than him and still wore the same dress size as she had when they met. But his aging made her feel a tenderness toward him. It was dignified, even, the way he was growing older; it made her feel, as she always felt about him, as if he knew more than she did, as if she was being taken care of. It was just a few months since they had last slept together.

"You made good time," Denise said to him. At camp, after seeing the other mothers in their conservative Bermuda shorts, she had wondered if her outfit was too provocative. But now she was glad for what she was wearing: denim shorts that showed off her legs, platform wedges, and a tight graphic T-shirt that she shared with Rachel.

Mark took one wordless look at Denise and then walked over to Bud.

"Mark Weinberg," he said, shaking the older cop's hand. "Is this going to cost me anything?"

Bud seemed alarmed by Mark's brusqueness. He glanced at Denise sitting with her hands in her lap. "Technically, no bail posted. But your, um—"

"My ex," Mark said.

"Yes." Bud cleared his throat. "She has overdue speeding tickets. That's why her license was suspended. Altogether she owes four hundred and eighty-five dollars."

Mark turned to Denise. "How do you have so many speeding tickets? You only drive once a year."

"Three times," she corrected. "To drop Rachel off, Visitors' Day, and to pick her up."

"And you get pulled over every time?"

"How would I know?"

Mark paid to get a tow truck to pick up the rental. Then, in his own car, he took Denise into the city.

They were mostly silent on the drive. Ray-Bans shaded his
eyes, even though the sun was beginning to set. He was
speeding.

Soon the parkway widened, and traffic slowed at a light
when the road turned local in Westchester. It was eight
o'clock; the sky had become an expanse of dark purples and
blues. As they merged onto the Saw Mill and got closer to
the city, traffic slowed more dramatically. Mark wasn't giving
in to the new pace. Each time the car in front of him deceler-
ated, he waited until the last possible moment to slam the
brakes, which would cause Denise's body to jerk forward,
then jolt back into the seat.

"Could you stop doing that?" she finally asked.

Just then his cellphone rang. He looked at it and cursed.
"Don't say anything," he told Denise, and then he turned the
radio all the way down.

He told his wife that no, he didn't hear the office phone
ring; it must be disconnected on weekends (a particularly
bad lie, Denise thought; he was getting lazy with the lies).
This case was such a shit show, he said. He would just be
another hour or two. It was a Sunday night, so who knew
how bad traffic would be? He said he was sorry again and
again.

Denise missed hearing him saying sorry like that to her,
plaintively, like he meant it. That was how it was at the beginning; he was always so sorry that he had to go back home
to his wife. So sorry that he had to cancel their dinner plans
again. When he got the apartment for Denise on the Upper
West Side, she thought the sorries were close to over. He told

his wife that having a place in the city just made sense for the nights he needed to work late. His lies were getting craftier, more complex, and the stakes were higher. Denise knew this was a good thing for her, that it meant there would be more sorries for the wife and fewer for her.

He never told Denise he'd leave his wife, but he made her feel soft and pliable; she let him do whatever he wanted to her. How she ached just watching him walk naked across their bedroom—*their* bedroom! He made her whole body feel bright and calm. She didn't have to do anything but bask in that feeling, like lying on the side of the bed where the sun shines right on you.

When they got into the city, Mark's cursing and road rage worsened. He flipped off cabbies and honked at pedestrians. "This is why I don't drive here," he said as he held down his horn when a bus cut him off.

"You *were* in the bus lane," Denise said jokingly.

"Out of all people, *you're* going to tell me how to drive right now?"

"I was just trying to make light of it."

He let out a chortle without an iota of humor in it. "Light? Make light? Okay, let's make light of this." He took one hand from the steering wheel and started counting off with his fingers. "You call me on a Sunday. You have me leave my family and come up to Upstate New York to get you. You have me pay five hundred dollars—"

"I didn't ask you to pay that!"

"You couldn't pay it, Denise! You're broke!"

"I am not. They just wouldn't let me leave."

"And then I have to take you all the way into the city and lie to my wife about it. Yet again."

"I could have taken the train."

"Well, you didn't present that option at the time, did you?"

She'd promised herself she would never cry in front of him. Her mother used to warn her about that, even when she was a girl: "Don't you *ever* cry in front of a man. They'll take your weakness and build themselves up with it." But she'd broken that oath a long time ago. He'd seen her cry so many times at this point that he now held her weaknesses in the palm of his hand.

He turned onto Amsterdam. He looked over at her.

"I'm sorry," he said when he saw that she was upset. "That was uncalled for."

Denise quickly wiped away a tear with the back of her hand.

He pulled onto her block and slowed the car in front of the apartment building.

"Why do you hate me?" she said.

He put the car into park.

She wanted to hear him say "I don't hate you." Instead he took a breath through his nose, like a bull preparing to fight.

"I heard on a talk show that the opposite of love isn't hate," she said, sniffling. "It's neutral."

"It's not the same as it was."

"But don't you remember what it felt like? It was the best feeling in the world. That kind of thing just doesn't go away."

"I remember," he admitted, and then used his fatherly

tone again. "But you knew the deal. It was your choice to . . ." He trailed off, not saying the unspoken thing that was always there. Rachel was a choice; Rachel was *her* choice. "You know I wouldn't give her up for the world now. It's just that this"—he gestured between the two of them—"this was never going to happen in a real, long-term way." He put one arm on her shoulder. "It *can't* happen." He always said this, and then they would always fall into things all over again.

When Rachel was a little girl, Denise had tried to make it work, being a mistress. She raised Rachel in the apartment that Mark paid for. They would get a babysitter and go out on weeknights, and though Denise initially thought having a child together would put a damper on the sex, she found it actually brought them closer, sharing this person together. It was a more profound bridge between them than she could have ever imagined. As Rachel got older, Mark had started to pull away from Denise, but they would still sleep together from time to time. Their sex became more secretive and urgent—no more dates, just late-night visits, him leaving early in the morning before Rachel awoke.

"If Rachel hadn't been born," Denise said now, "do you think—"

"I'm married, Denise," he said softly. "I have a family."

"You have two families."

She could see how sorry he was, the bags underneath his eyes lined with weariness. "I have two families. And I love both of my families. I love Rachel very much, and this isn't good for her," he said.

She could tell by how sad he looked, how hard it seemed for him to say this, that he was serious about it now. Like picking her up from this faraway police station had been his final straw. She had done this to herself.

"The on-again, off-again. Her knowing about my situation, us literally shoving it into her face every time I'm around. The sneaking behind her back, which she definitely knows about. I just think . . . I think a strictly platonic relationship between you and me is healthier for her."

She fought it; she cried; she pawed at him and said hurtful things about his wife, about who he was as a person. Uncharacteristically, he sat there and took the flak, which also meant that he meant it this time.

But she knew he was right. He loved their daughter. He loved her so much.

Denise got out and slammed the door without saying goodbye. She starting walking toward the glass door of her apartment building and then, instinctively, turned around. She could see that he already had his hand on the gearshift, but she tapped on the passenger-side window before he could drive away.

He rolled down the window and looked at her.

"I'll pay you back," she said adamantly.

He shook his head. "No you won't."

"That was the deal," she said. "Not a dollar for me."

"I'm not saying you shouldn't pay me back. I'm saying that you won't."

"But you don't—"

"You are an adult woman, Denise," he continued. "This is not a matter of being 'too busy' to pay speeding tickets. You have responsibilities that you do not take seriously."

He had always taken care of her, but there didn't used to be this hardness.

"Frankly," he continued in that patriarchal tone, "it's worrisome."

"I'm paying you back," she said again. "And don't fucking talk to me like that. I'm not your daughter."

Denise looked into his face. Rachel got those long eyelashes from him.

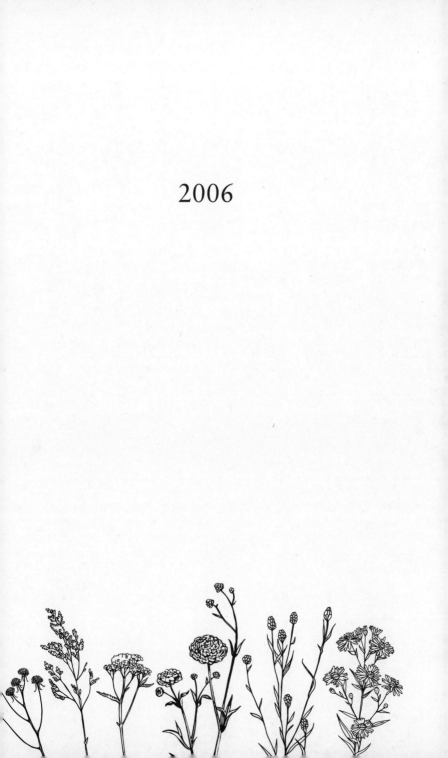

2006

3

Helen Larkin wasn't paying attention in biology. She was writing her name in bubble letters in the margins of her Five Star notebook. She figured a person paid attention to the things she wanted to pay attention to, and there was a reason for that.

It was March 1, 2006. As her creepy teacher, Mr. Browne, droned on, she counted the remaining days in the calendar at the back of her notebook. One hundred sixteen to go until camp. Her last summer at Camp Marigold, as it would turn out.

Perhaps it was better not to count.

There was a diagram of a human heart on the board, and Mr. Browne was using his long, skinny pointer stick to identify different parts. ("Of the four chambers, the left ventricle

contracts the most forcefully.") He had a perpetually glistening forehead and kept a dirty handkerchief in the pocket of
his crinkled khakis, always pulling it out, wiping his brow,
putting it back. When he got excited about something, he
crumpled it into his hand, squeezing it and shaking his fist
with the disgusting thing inside it.

Helen rarely heard the words he was saying. He spent the
end of the class talking about what can go wrong with the
heart: murmurs, irregularities, diseases present at birth. But
Helen wasn't paying attention.

She had forgotten to bring clothes to change into for gym
that day. She sat on the bleachers watching her classmates
chase after a plastic orange ball with their plastic hockey
sticks.

Marla Steinberg, who never changed for gym, was sitting
a few spaces away from her on the bleachers, keeping time
with the stopwatch the teacher had handed her. She had a
purple streak in her brown hair and safety pins pierced into
her infected-looking ears. Their teacher had put them in
charge of time and scorekeeping, and Helen turned over a
laminated number on the small flip chart in front of her each
time one of the teams scored.

Helen turned to Marla, who had large breasts—the largest of any girl in the seventh grade—that bounced promi-
nently with her slightest movement. "Do you know when
this period's over?" Helen asked.

Marla shook her head and made a *tsk* sound. "Fuck. I know. I once had that shit for three weeks."

"What?"

"How long's it been for you?" Marla leaned in. Her boobs bounced in her low-cut tank top. "Cramps? How bad?"

Helen shook her head. She hadn't gotten her first period yet. "I said, do you know when *this period* is over? Like, the game period."

Marla burst into a cackle. "Oh my God. You said *this* period!"

Helen waited for Marla to finish laughing.

Marla finally looked down at the stopwatch. "Two minutes and thirty-two seconds," she said. Then she considered Helen as if she hadn't thought to look at her before. "You're really pretty, you know."

"Thank you," Helen said, trying to strike the appropriate mix between humility and self-awareness. At twelve—almost thirteen—years old, she had already been called pretty enough times to know that one couldn't act too clueless or too conceited in response. She of course also knew that she was, indeed, pretty.

"What are you doing after school today?" Marla asked.

Usually Helen walked home with her neighborhood friends, Kayla and Kelly and Kim. They had been her friends since nursery school, friends that always seemed to be ready to spend time with her.

"Nothing," Helen said.

After ninth period, Kayla waited for Helen at her locker.

"You wanna come over and do homework?" Kayla asked. "My mom made blondies."

"I have plans," Helen said, and left to meet Marla Steinberg and her friends in the woods behind the gym.

They were all pierced and dyed—a nose ring here, a streak of pink there. They lived in Mamaroneck, the town over from Larchmont. ("The other side of the tracks," Helen's dad called it. Helen had protested that no train ran between the towns. "It's a matter of speech, Helen," he'd sighed.) They were smoking a joint, which Helen had seen only once before, at a party at Matt White's house. The party was awkward, because although only Helen and Kelly had actually been invited (Kelly was sort of boring but very pretty), Kayla and Kim tagged along, and Helen felt like they expected to be taken care of the whole time. She was interested in having more friends like Marla—girls who could take care of themselves.

Marla passed Helen the joint. At Matt White's, Helen hadn't tried it. Now she took the flimsy, damp thing from Marla and pinched it between her thumb and pointer finger as she'd observed Marla and her friends doing.

There was pink lip gloss around the tip of the joint. Helen put her lips over it and inhaled. All she could taste was strawberry pink lip gloss.

"You have to pull harder," one of the girls said, her eyes already bloodshot.

Helen nodded and sucked in the smoke as she'd been instructed. She felt it fill her lungs and an astonishingly fast rush to her brain, and she coughed, her eyes watering as a bitter taste came up through her throat.

Marla laughed. "Atta girl."

They leaned against the base of a large oak tree. The girls discussed how pathetic the boys at school were, their terrible parents, their plans to run away to California. The weed seemed to make them animated, energized. But Helen felt like she was thinking twice as slowly as they were; every time she was ready to add something to the conversation, they had already moved on to another topic. She would laugh whenever the other girls laughed at something, trying to disguise herself as a member of their group, but once she heard herself laugh right after they had finished, and they looked over at her, entertained. Then they went back into their conversation. She was grateful for that, their not calling attention to her inexperience.

Being outside with the girls as it started to grow dark reminded her of camp, when rain pounded on the canvas of the platform tent at night, and wind pulled at the bottom sails and sent a cool August breeze through the tent, and she felt the need to melt farther into her flannel sleeping bag. It was a feeling of deep contentment and safety—it was something that could not be reproduced anywhere else. She loved being so close to the elements that she could almost taste them, flirting so much with being in the rain that she could see the canvas covering of the tent swaying slightly in the storm. Being safe and inside but just barely. She couldn't feel like that in a house with a roof and walls.

"Living outside changes everything," she said then.

"The girl's a fucking poet," said Marla.

Leaving the girls on the mossy ground, Helen used the lowest branch of the oak tree as a ledge and propelled herself up two more levels of branches until she landed on the perfect one, long and wide enough to lay her whole body on. If Kayla and Kelly and Kim were here, they would have yelled, "Get down, Helen!" But Marla and her friends watched with amusement from below and lit a second joint. Helen, high enough already, let a gust of cold almost-spring breeze run over her and closed her eyes.

"You'd be amazed at the amount of activities people did just to get in," Fiona told Helen at dinner a few weeks later. "One kid I know has his own patent for some glue he invented. It dries extra fast."

"Cool, Fiona."

"Whatever. It's not my problem if you don't get into college."

"You're right. It's not."

"She's in seventh grade, Fee," said Liam.

Fiona was a freshman at a small college in Pennsylvania; she had always played the role of uppity older sister to Helen. Liam was a junior at Yale: smart, quietly confident. Fiona's work ethic had enabled her to graduate in the top 10 percent at Mamaroneck High School, but she would never, despite her most laborious efforts, have anything close to Liam's sharp wit or near-photographic memory.

Fiona looked around the table for support, her face considerably more swollen than it had been six months ago. She had definitely gained the Freshman 15. Their father was working late, closing an important case that had to do with the stuff inside diapers and whether or not it was flammable.

"Helen, you do have a lot of free time these days," their mother said, getting up from the table and walking into the kitchen to refill her glass from the magnum bottle of Barefoot Chardonnay in the fridge.

"I do not!" Helen called from the dining room table. "Seventh grade is really hard."

"Maybe you would have more time for homework if you spent less time with Marla Steinberg and all of those girls," Fiona said.

"She's a really good person," said Helen.

"She's a slut," Fiona hissed quietly, so their mother wouldn't hear.

"Just because you're a prude doesn't make everyone else a slut," Helen hissed back.

Fiona tried to burn Helen with her eyes but didn't have anything to say in return.

"Too far, Helen," Liam said.

Their mother returned to the table. "What about lacrosse?"

"I hate lacrosse," Helen said. Liam and Fiona played lacrosse. And Helen did not do anything she didn't want to—that had been clear since she was an infant, when she would let only Liam hold her, unless she was nursing. Passed to Fiona, to any other relative, or even to her own father, Helen would scream her throat sore until she was returned to the only person who could calm her. That was eight-year-old Liam's role in 1993—caretaker for his youngest sister, his thin arms tentatively cradling her into the night.

After Helen was born, their mother got her tubes tied. At the time, the kids had pictured plastic cylinders inside her body that babies traveled through, like the suction tubes in the ball pits at the Discovery Zone.

Without Camp Marigold, Helen and her siblings wouldn't exist. Their parents had met there when they were nine, a fact that was unfathomable to Helen. It seemed utterly impossible that she could have already met someone—four years ago—that she was going to spend the rest of her life with.

Liam hadn't gone to Marigold since he was eleven, when he replaced it with lacrosse camp. This upcoming summer, Fiona would be a counselor at Marigold with her own tent of campers.

"I think it's terrifying that you're going to be in charge of a whole tent of nine-year-old girls," Helen told her sister later at dinner.

"They wouldn't have hired me if they didn't think I was ready," Fiona said defensively, as if she too was slightly terrified by the prospect.

When Helen told Marla about how her parents met, Marla said, "I didn't think anyone actually met people they *married* at camp."

Marla thought the idea of summer camp was a riot, and yet she seemed intrigued by it. She'd never been friends with anyone who had gone, the kids from Mamaroneck tending to hang out only with one another and the same for the kids from Larchmont, and hardly anyone from Mamaroneck went to camp.

"So you *pay* to live outside? Shouldn't that just be free?" Marla gestured to the woods around them. They were in their usual spot on an afternoon in April—just the two of them that day—leaning and smoking against that same oak tree.

"Well, you pay for the activities and stuff."

"What kinds of activities?"

"Everything," Helen said. "Swimming, boating, theater, sports, arts and crafts. There's even a radio station."

"Boating?" Marla said. "Where do you do that?"

"There's a lake."

"A lake?" She considered this. "That's cool."

They could hear the sports teams practicing on the other side of the gym. Mr. Browne, who was also the girls' lacrosse coach, was yelling.

"What the hell are you doing, Kayla? You look like a chicken with your head cut off."

Marla laughed, and Helen imagined her childhood friend, fast but uncoordinated, blushing uncontrollably in front of her teammates.

They continued smoking as Helen and Marla imitated all Mr. Browne's sports-isms: "Good idea, Kayla. Bad execution." " 'Can't' is a four-letter word, Kayla. Watch your mouth."

"God dammit, girls," they then heard. "I am so sick and tired of this crap. Five laps of Indian drills around the gym. Go."

There was a collective groan from the team.

"Ten? You want ten?"

Marla and Helen took a beat and then, realizing they could easily be seen from the side of the gym closest to them, put out the joint, fanned the cloud of smoke that had emerged around them, and began to run deeper into the woods.

It was all thick and undeveloped back there, and Helen concentrated on the ground below her, avoiding upturned roots and fallen branches. Ahead, Marla was laughing; she knew they wouldn't get caught. But as Helen looked down, she felt a dizziness begin to overtake her—white and purple spots appeared over everything, coloring the wooded ground into a misty pointillist vortex.

"Helen?" she heard. "You okay?"

The woods swirled and twirled and tipped onto their side, as if Helen had entered some carnival funhouse where everything was tilted and distorted. Her sneakers began to lose their traction, and the mossy ground slipped from under her. She felt a lurching in her stomach propel her forward. She accepted it with a sort of grace. Nowhere to go but down.

When she came to, Marla was standing over her, waving her hands in front of Helen's face.

"Blink twice if you can hear me!" Marla said.

Marla walked Helen all the way home, even though it was out of her way, with her arm draped over her friend's shoulder. She bought Helen a Gatorade from the gas station. Helen had experienced a fall like this before, during gym class when she was in fifth grade; the school nurse had given her a juice box and told her she needed to eat more frequently. She wasn't sure if she'd fallen this time for the same reason or because she'd been too high.

"Are you sure you're okay?" Marla asked when they got to Helen's front door.

Helen nodded. "Don't tell anyone about this, okay?" She was embarrassed.

"Of course not," Marla said, and they linked pinkies and shook them.

Inside, Helen told her parents the fall had happened in gym class again; she was sprinting after a soccer ball, she said, when she passed out and fell face-first onto the field. A lump the shape of a goose egg, throbbing on her forehead, had turned a deep purple, the color of an eggplant. She would have to steal her mom's makeup to cover it for school the next day.

"Why didn't the nurse call us?" Helen's mother asked.

"She said it was nothing to worry about," Helen said.

"She's right," her dad said. "Low blood sugar runs in the family." He pulled affectionately on Helen's ponytail. He made her a strawberry-banana smoothie to drink with her dinner, which she finished in a few greedy gulps.

———

A few days later, Helen and her family went to visit her grandparents in Florida during spring break. She spent her days in the pool at their retirement complex, lying on a float and thinking about Marla. Helen had a best friend from camp, Sarah, but that almost felt like it couldn't count, because she lived two hours away and so was only really Helen's best friend two months out of the year. School was where *real* life was supposed to be, Helen suspected, even though she always felt like a more real version of herself in the summer.

But with Marla, it felt like there was hope for a real-life friendship. Marla was so blunt and a little bit bad, but she also seemed to care about Helen in a deep, unprejudiced way. Helen trusted, without question, that Marla wouldn't tell anyone about her fainting. The girls she grew up with in Larchmont were sweet, but they were so *good*. If they'd been with Helen when she'd fallen, they would have immediately called her parents or maybe 911. Helen knew that Marla had a single mother who bagged groceries at the Stop & Shop and an older brother who was on the verge of failing out of high school and that once Marla turned fourteen her mom was going to make her get a part-time job to help with the bills. Her life was not easy; in fact, it seemed pretty hard. But she was a good friend; she laughed with Helen, she took care of her when she was hurt, and, moreover, she seemed *happy*. There was something to this, maybe: Being sheltered from the bad things didn't really bring you any more joy. It just made you dull.

Helen felt hands pushing into the bottom of the plastic float she was lying on. The float tilted, and she fell into the water, her whole body going under.

"Liam!" she shrieked when she came up for air, splashing her older brother.

He laughed, then picked her up and threw her several feet across the swimming pool into the deep end. Her tiny body floated through the air and landed with a graceful *plop*.

"Come in, Fee!" she yelled to her sister.

"I'm good," said Fiona, who was sitting in the shade. She was still wearing her cover-up; she hadn't swum this entire trip. All she did was read. Sometimes Helen felt like she was missing out on having an older sister: the kind who was supposed to teach you how to paint your nails with your left hand, or how to kiss a boy, or how to shave your legs so you didn't cut yourself. The kind you were supposed to be able to steal clothes from: You would fight about it, but the fights wouldn't mean anything, because you lived in the same house and you knew where to find your sweater; it was just in the closet in the room next to yours.

When they were kids, it was different. Fiona used to play. But in the past few years, she'd seemed to stop caring about Helen because she was so preoccupied with her own stuff, always studying and doing as many extracurricular activities as she possibly could. Helen knew that Fiona thought she could become a different person in college, because once she'd said something like "Do you think I should go by my middle name when I get to school?"

"Why would you do that?" Helen had asked.

"I don't know," Fiona said. "Just for an experiment. College is all about experimenting, you know? And for finding out who you really are."

But what if she was *really* just someone mopey and boring? That's what college seemed to turn her into, anyway.

When Helen got back to school the next week, Marla had disappeared. The rumor was that her family had picked up and moved to Texas. Helen had no reason to believe this was true, but she also didn't have any reason to believe it wasn't. She tried calling Marla's cellphone several times, but it was always off.

April 30 was Helen's thirteenth birthday. There were fifty-six days until camp and no birthday wishes from Marla. Helen now had no interest in spending time in the woods with the other Mamaroneck girls; Marla was the common thread between them all, and without Marla there, Helen found little to say to them.

For Helen's thirteenth birthday, she saw a movie at the mall with Kayla, Kelly, and Kim while their moms got frozen margaritas at Chili's. After the movie, they met their moms at Chili's for dinner and cake. The cake came, they sang "Happy Birthday," and Helen cut herself a generous piece.

"God, to have that metabolism again," Kelly's mom said.

"I know," said Helen's mom. "I can't feed her enough, and she's still a beanpole."

Every other girl at the table, Helen knew, had gotten her

period. It didn't bother Helen; in fact, she dreaded the day she'd have to start wearing an underwire bra. Life was so much easier without curves.

Helen finished her piece and asked for another, just to spite them.

When Helen got home, she tried calling Marla again. Once more, it went straight to voicemail. She decided to leave a message this time.

"Hey, Mar," Helen said. "I hope things are good, wherever you are." She paused. "It was my birthday today. I wish you could have been here. I'm officially a teenager now. Still no period, though." She was talking into a void. "I miss you. I wish you said goodbye." She cleared her throat. "Call me if you get this."

She hung up and cried for just a few minutes, just enough to get it out of her system. She hadn't realized how angry she was with Marla for dangling the promise of a friendship in front of her face and pulling it so abruptly away.

Maybe her real life wasn't meant to be at school after all.

❋

"John, where are you going?" Helen's mother asked from the front seat.

"I'm taking 684," Helen's father said.

"We never take 684. We take the Taconic."

"Yes we do. We always take 684 to 22."

"Are you serious? We've been taking the Taconic to Marigold for as long as I can remember."

"Hon, that might have been true when Fee was little, but I can tell you, for the past five years, I have never once taken the Taconic."

"Helen," Mrs. Larkin said, turning to look at her daughter in the backseat, "your father has lost it."

Helen was looking out the window, marveling at the speed at which the scenery was moving by. Recently, she had been feeling a certain fear about being in a car, especially on a highway, where her dad's speedometer regularly inched past eighty miles per hour. How did all the cars trust the other cars not to crash into one another? They were full of strangers entering into a life-or-death pact every time they got on the road. But there was something about the way that her parents bickered that made her feel a special kind of ease; as they did so, she could disappear into her own thoughts, and that in itself was a relief. More often than not, as someone six years younger than anyone else in the family, she felt like the attention was always on her.

The ride to camp always felt longer than it actually was. Helen was jittery. She wasn't hungry; she couldn't nap; she didn't want to talk to her parents even if they weren't bickering, because she had too many thoughts. But none of them could be formed into words because what Helen felt was unnamable—a vague sense of waking up to the wild possibilities of that summer and an innate knowledge that camp's magic, at its core, was unexplainable.

They arrived at camp around ten in the morning, and

they parked their SUV on the grassy lot among all the other SUVs. Camp smelled exactly the same, like wet grass and damp soil that was perpetually drying off from the morning dew. She saw some new faces and some old. Then she spotted Fiona in her navy Camp Marigold staff polo, over with the youngest girls, holding their hands and chatting with their parents. She had come separately, driving up with her friend Rachel a week earlier for staff training. Helen's mom seemed to spot Fiona at the same time, and she lifted her hand to begin to wave to her older daughter, but Helen's father said to her mother, "I don't think she'll want to acknowledge us."

"Why not?" Helen's mom asked. "I'm just saying hi."

Helen caught Fiona's eye, and Fiona quickly looked down at the girl whose hand she was holding.

"She's working," Helen's father said. "Let her feel independent. It's good for her."

"I don't see how the two things are mutually exclusive," Helen's mother said, but she dropped her hand.

When Helen finished checking in, her parents drove her up to the girls' Hemlock section. She was in tent three; she already knew that Sarah would be in her tent, because they had requested each other, and that Rachel, Fiona's best friend, would be their counselor. Sarah lived in Simsbury, Connecticut, and the last time the girls had seen each other was over Christmas break. But they were the kind of friends who could pick up exactly where they'd left off.

Helen and her parents entered the tent. The bunks were still about half-empty, and Rachel was helping a new girl and a man Helen presumed to be the girl's father put up a mosquito net.

"Hi, Rach," Helen said, grinning. Helen loved Rachel, and she didn't understand why Rachel was still best friends with Fiona. Maybe when they were younger their personalities had been more alike, but her sister was so negative these days, and Rachel continued to be such an upbeat, confident person. When she was in a group, all the attention was on her, and it wasn't even like she was asking for it. Fiona just brought that energy down.

"Helen!" Rachel finished fastening a corner of the new girl's mosquito net to the canvas siding and approached Helen with a wide smile and open arms. "So good to see you!" She gave Helen a tight squeeze. "I was so happy when Fiona told me you'd be in my tent."

"Me too," Helen said.

"Hi, Mr. and Mrs. Larkin," Rachel said, climbing over trunks to give both of Helen's parents equally warm hugs. They responded in kind.

"How are you, sweetheart?" Helen's mother asked.

"Yes, how's Michigan?" her father said. Helen found it funny that her father, who was so bad at remembering details about people, remembered this.

"It's great," Rachel said. "I'm super overextended between classes and activities, but I guess that's what I'm there for."

"Big party school, from what I've heard," Helen's father said.

"John," her mother said by way of warning, as if Helen had never heard the word "party."

Rachel grinned knowingly. "It has its moments."

Helen looked over at the man and the girl by the back of the tent, who were still waiting politely for Rachel to help them finish the job; the mosquito net was only half-fastened with safety pins, the whole front of it flopping over the bunk.

Rachel followed Helen's gaze to the pair, remembering she still had work to do. She hurried over and finished fastening the mosquito net like she'd done it a thousand times before. "Helen, this is Sheera. She's new to camp this year. She's from the city, like me."

The two younger girls waved shyly at each other. Sheera was tall and developed; she was wearing a pink T-shirt and oddly fitting khaki shorts, too tight around her waist and hips but then looser at the legs, reaching all the way down to the tops of her knees. She had light brown skin, and her black hair was arranged in tight braids across her scalp, which were fastened at the ends by elastics with baby pink baubles.

"Arthur Jones," her father said, a man so tall that Helen was sure if he lay down on one of the bunks, his legs would dangle over the edge. He lumbered across the tent and shook the hands of both Mr. and Mrs. Larkin.

"John Larkin," Helen's father said in the deep voice he put on when he was talking to other men. "And my wife, Amy."

Mrs. Larkin looked as if she was about to say something,

and Helen knew that she was wondering what Helen herself also was—where was Mrs. Jones? But Helen was glad for the interruption that ensued: Sarah bouncing into the tent and squealing as she engulfed Helen in a hug.

Sarah and Helen had met on the first day of their first summer at camp, when they were nine years old. They were in the Maple section then, the youngest group of campers. Helen didn't want to be there; she was homesick. Her parents had insisted that she go away to Camp Marigold that summer because Fiona was also nine when she first went. Fiona "could not have been happier that summer," her mother had explained—so surely for Helen it would be the same. She had tried to fight it at first, but her mother was so sure that Helen—sweet, lighthearted Helen—would have no trouble adjusting. But when her mother gave her one last hug before driving away, Helen whispered, "Don't go," which made the both of them tear up with regret.

All day long Helen didn't talk to anyone in her section. She saw Fiona at the dining hall at dinner, and they ignored each other, Fiona too busy chasing behind Rachel to notice her sister's sadness. Some counselor got up in front of all of girls' camp and made a speech about marigolds. They were annual flowers: They grew only throughout the course of one summer, and the following year, they had to be replanted in order to bloom again. The counselor welcomed all the newcomers: all the little seed girls who would soon grow into beautiful marigolds.

After dinner, the counselors organized an icebreaker activity in the Maple section. The thirty girls were arranged in two circles—an inside circle and an outside circle—and one of the counselors posed questions to the group. ("What's the most embarrassing thing that's ever happened to you?" "Who's your favorite Disney princess?") The girls facing each other introduced themselves and discussed their answers. Then the outside circle rotated one person to the right, another question was posed, and this kept going until everyone in each circle met everyone in the other.

The first two girls Helen talked to were shy and quiet like her. They answered the questions quickly and then stared at each other waiting for the next turn. Already Helen was dreading bedtime; she felt there was no doubt that she would cry herself to sleep. What if she wet the bed? She'd done that once, at her first sleepover, earlier in the year.

But the third girl stepped in front of Helen smiling widely, revealing a gap between her two front teeth. They protruded slightly out of her mouth in a *V* shape. She had a pale face and thick, dark hair parted straight down the middle.

"I'm Sarah," she said, still smiling wide.

Their section leader said, "What's your favorite ice cream flavor?"

"You wanna go first?" Sarah said, eager.

"Um," Helen said. "I don't know. I guess I don't have a favorite."

"Really? I have so many favorites that I'm not sure which to pick!" She had a slight lisp, so that she slurred the *s* in "so."

"I guess I like cookies and cream."

"I *love* cookies and cream. I also really like chocolate chip cookie dough, and I like strawberry but more in a milkshake. The problem with chocolate chip cookie dough or really anything with chunks like that is they get stuck in my palate expander." She opened her mouth wide and tipped her head back, pointing to the roof of her mouth and revealing an industrial-looking metal contraption lodged behind her teeth.

Helen giggled a bit, though she hadn't meant to.

"I know!" Sarah said. "Weird, right?"

"Yeah," Helen said. "What's it for?"

"I used to suck my thumb too much," Sarah said. "Actually, up until last year. *Late*. It screwed up my teeth."

"Does it hurt?"

"Only when I have to turn the key."

"There's a key?"

"Yeah." She grinned. "I can show you later, if you want."

"Okay," Helen said. Then there was an immediate feeling of ease, a feeling that she wouldn't be alone there.

Helen was shocked now by how much Sarah had developed in the six months since they saw each other over Christmas. Her breasts, which used to be like two golf balls in a bra, had swelled and were straining against the text on a T-shirt that read GIRL POWER in purple bubble letters. Her belly button peeked out from under the shirt's hem. It seemed as if Sarah's perceptions of herself hadn't quite caught up with the realities of her body.

Helen was mortified to notice both of her parents' glances lingering a beat too long on her friend's body.

"Hi, Sarah dear," Mrs. Larkin said, giving the girl a chaste hug and kiss on the cheek. "Are your parents here? We'd love to say hi."

"No, they left already," Sarah said. "It was Davey's first day too."

"Oh, too bad," Mrs. Larkin said.

"I saved you a spot," Sarah said to Helen, patting the top bunk next to her own.

When Helen awoke the following morning, the first thing she noticed was the distinct smell of urine.

"Who pissed themselves?" said Jessi, a tomboy who'd been going to Marigold as long as Helen had.

"Not me," Sarah said.

"Me neither," said Helen.

Helen noticed Rachel's face pucker and sour for a brief moment, but then turn quickly toward neutral.

"I don't smell anything," Rachel said. "Girls, go take your showers."

"Must have been the new girl," Helen heard Jessi mutter to Sarah and the other girls as they all grabbed their towels from their hooks and their shower caddies from their cubbies and made their way out of the tent.

Only Helen, Rachel, and Sheera, the new girl, were left in the tent now. Sheera was pulling herself out of her bunk slowly, but once her entire body was exposed, Helen noticed a distinct wet spot in between the girl's legs. Then Sheera hurried toward the back of the tent, where her towel hung.

She reemerged a few moments later from behind the

cubby with only a towel around herself and her pajamas heaped into a ball in her arms. She approached her bunk again and zipped up the sleeping bag, straightening it neatly over the mattress. She turned and noticed that both Helen and Rachel were looking at her.

Rachel approached Sheera. "It's okay, sweetie," Rachel said in a quiet voice, as if Helen couldn't hear her.

Sheera neither nodded nor said anything to confirm or deny Rachel's presumption. Instead, she looked away from her counselor and walked straight out of the tent, being careful not to make eye contact with Helen.

Once Sheera had left the tent, Rachel said to Helen, "Please don't tell the girls about that. She's probably pretty embarrassed."

"I won't," Helen said.

But later she did find herself telling Sarah during free period. She couldn't help it. The thing was, friendships were so much sweeter when there were secrets to be kept.

4

Their first night off: a Monday evening in Torrington, Connecticut, a place that felt so void of personality or style that Fiona was embarrassed by it with non-Americans in her presence. Her Jeep was parked in the lot of a strip mall on Route 4. The boys—Chad, who was English, and Yonatan, who was Israeli—were both twenty-one and went into the liquor store while the girls waited in the car.

Steph, whom Fiona knew the least, lit a cigarette from the backseat.

"Could you smoke that outside?" Fiona asked. "I have asthma."

Steph apologized, got out of the car, and leaned against the parked Jeep while she smoked.

"Liar," Rachel said in the front seat.

"I don't want my car smelling like an ashtray."

Rachel was sitting Indian style, her legs folded into each other. After their first year away at college, Rachel looked the same as she always had: olive skinned, thin limbed, brown hair worn over one shoulder. Fiona did not. She had never been tall or petite; her skin was not terrible but not great; and her face was quite squashed, as if all the features had gathered together too close in the center of it. And now she was twenty pounds heavier. The best she would ever look was average, and this summer she was flirting with ugliness.

"You know," Rachel said to Fiona, looking over at Steph smoking, "she tells everyone she's from L.A., but she's really from Sacramento."

Fiona and Rachel were the only counselors on this outing who had spent their childhood summers at Marigold. All the others were new. Still, the girls had been fifteen the last time they were there. The summers in between, they had been too old to be campers and too young to be counselors.

Chad and Yonatan now appeared in the rearview mirror carrying two handles of vodka, a jug of cranberry juice, and a case of Coors Light. Chad grunted as he dropped the case onto the ground and knocked twice on the Jeep's door.

"A little help would have been nice," he said when they got into the Jeep.

"We're dainty," Rachel said.

"Dainty American girls," Chad said. "There's an oxymoron."

Fiona drove a few miles up the main drag toward the Super 8, where they would stay that night and party, the five of them. Lakeville, where Camp Marigold was located—

about twenty-five miles up Route 63—was a pretty, rural town. There wasn't much to do, but at least it had all the idyllic country attributes: farms with grazing cows, charming milk silos, unmanicured fields full of dandelions. Torrington also felt like the country but a less charming version of it. Everything was paved, and the only open spaces were parking lots between the Grand Union grocery store and the KFC and the Applebee's.

Fiona pulled into the mostly empty parking lot of the motel. The only person in sight was a shirtless fat man smoking outside the front entrance.

"We're not in Kansas anymore," Yonatan said.

Chad stayed in the backseat while the rest of them got out of the Jeep.

"You're not coming in?" Fiona asked.

Rachel and Chad looked at each other. "Only four of us are allowed to stay in a room," Rachel said to Fiona. "We talked about this."

Fiona was sure they hadn't talked about this and that Rachel had withheld this information because she knew that Fiona would not be okay with it. Chad said he would wait in the car and would come to their room—with the alcohol—once they were inside.

Rachel linked her arm in Fiona's as they walked. "It's gonna be fine. Just act normal." She let her gaze linger on the fat man and then turned to Fiona with a disgusted look on her face. Fiona forced a laugh.

As eleven-year-olds, they had become friends riding horses together. They were the best riders at camp. Then they began to tell each other things they'd never told anyone else. Rachel told Fiona that she was the result of an affair; her mom had been a mistress, and her father kept Rachel a secret from his wife of twenty-something years. Fiona told Rachel that she wished her sister, Helen, had never been born.

An overweight twentysomething woman at the front desk typed on a PC with a deadpan look on her acne-scarred face. She was wearing a yellow Super 8 polo that was too small on her, the sleeves cutting into her arm fat. She did not look up at the four of them standing there.

Rachel leaned across the desk and peered at the woman's name tag. "Hi, Mary Ann," she said.

Mary Ann looked at Rachel sternly, as if to warn her about crossing too far into her territory. "Can I help you?"

Rachel smiled and told her they needed a room for four.

"How old are you all?" she asked suspiciously.

Yonatan slid his passport across the desk. "We're twenty-one," he said.

Mary Ann took the passport and opened it. "*You're* twenty-one."

The girls, all under twenty-one, did not have fake IDs.

"You all from the camp?" Mary Ann asked. "I can't have any funny business again. Not like last summer."

"We're just here to get away for a night," Rachel said in the voice she put on when she wanted to sound older. "You know how tiring kids can be."

Rachel was a charming girl, but Mary Ann had yet to be

charmed. "Rooms are nonsmoking. I see beer, you're out. No refund."

Rachel gave Mary Ann a wink and a thumbs-up.

Mary Ann sighed. She typed into her PC. "I need a credit card on file in case there's any damage to the room."

Rachel turned, without hesitation, to her best friend. "Fiona, would you mind?" She knew that Fiona had a family credit card in case of emergencies.

"There won't be any damage," Rachel said in response to Fiona's hesitation. "And we'll give you cash for the room."

Rachel had this way of making Fiona feel like certain things were just part of her job as the "responsible" friend: driving the car, putting the credit card down. In a way, Fiona liked it. It made her feel like she had agency, like she was more than just Rachel's sidekick. Surely Rachel sensed this—that each time she asked Fiona to do something, she was handing over a bit of her own power to Fiona, saying, "Here, hold this. Doesn't that feel nice?"

Fiona slid her American Express across the table. Rachel took Fiona's arm again.

"God, what a sad case she was," Rachel said quietly to Fiona when they had stepped away from the desk, and they took the elevator up to room 304.

They could see Chad in the parking lot from their window, and he walked fast with the case of beer. He entered the Super 8 with ease through a side entrance.

The sleeping arrangements were set: Fiona and Steph in one bed, Rachel and Chad in the other (they were "just good friends," she answered when Fiona had asked about the status of their relationship), and Yonatan on the floor. There were cards, and someone suggested strip poker. It was seven P.M.; Fiona had assumed that, at some point, they'd go out for dinner. She was hungry. But since gaining the weight, she felt as if she could never be the one to bring up the topic of food. It felt like there would be something desperate in that, transparent and obvious. She poured herself a cranberry and vodka and sat down on the edge of the bed.

"You're not playing?" Yonatan asked.

She shook her head. "I hate cards."

Rachel made eye contact with Fiona. Fiona usually loved when they shared glances across rooms. This one was disapproving. It said, "You're drawing more attention to yourself by not playing, you know." Or at least, that's what Fiona imagined it said. Fiona shook her head again. Rachel shrugged in response.

No one had ever taught Fiona how to play poker, and she didn't try to follow the game. Everyone was wearing T-shirts and shorts, no shoes, so the clothing would come off quickly. And what did Rachel or Steph have to hide? To think, Fiona used to be that skinny! Fiona's high school self wouldn't have played strip poker either, but what a waste. She'd disliked her body then too: those large breasts, which sexualized her without her permission; those thick thighs that rubbed together in the heat. Now her breasts spilled out of the bras that used to fit. Now she pulled at the crotch of her shorts when she walked. What she would have given to get back the body she'd once hated.

Rachel was cheering; she pointed to Chad. "Off."

He rolled his eyes and took off his shirt. They'd all seen him shirtless anyway, freckled and hairless as he walked along the lakeshore getting kids in and out of canoes.

Fiona poured herself a second cranberry and vodka. Yonatan won a round and told Steph to strip. She pulled her shirt over her head in one smooth motion, the way someone would in a movie. The more Fiona drank, the hungrier she got, and she dug out a bag of SunChips she'd had her eye on from the bottom of a shopping bag. Soon Rachel and Steph were in their bras and underwear, the boys in just their boxers. The game dissolved, but clothes stayed off; Fiona alternated: vodka, chip. She was sitting at the foot of the bed, and her feet did not touch the ground. Yonatan lay next to her and stuck his hand into the bag of chips.

Fiona had noticed Yonatan immediately during staff training. She had been sitting on the bench of a picnic table near the soccer fields; Rachel had been sitting on top of the table, braiding Fiona's hair. They were chatting with some of the new girls while the guys played a pickup soccer game. Yonatan was the fastest one on the field, darting continually from one goal to the other, seemingly tireless. He had tan skin and muscular calves and curly brown hair, which he wore longer than the boys in America did. His curls kept falling into his face as he ran, and he kept pushing them back. She wondered if it bothered him.

"So you two know each other from a while back?" asked

Nell, the pretty redheaded girl at the picnic table. She'd been quiet until then.

"Since last century!" Rachel said, fluffing Fiona's hair affectionately.

Nell looked at both girls blankly. Rachel looked back.

"You know, 'cause last century was, like, seven years ago," Fiona explained. She always did this, felt the need to make moments like this one less uncomfortable by filling in the blank spaces.

Nell nodded. "I got it."

Rachel gave one of Fiona's braids a tiny pull, the clandestine equivalent of an eye roll. Once Rachel decided she didn't like someone, that was that.

The boys took a break and came over to the table for their water bottles. Yonatan poured his on top of his head and shook his hair dry the way a wet dog would. A couple of droplets landed on Fiona's thighs, and she wiped them off, hoping he wouldn't notice.

"Sorry," he said, flashing a smile and then jogging back to the game.

Rachel drummed the fingers of one of her hands on Fiona's shoulder. "Cu-ute," she sang quietly.

Now Yonatan was lying on the bed next to Fiona, shirtless, but she didn't know what to do in situations like these. Some girls, such as Rachel or Steph or even Fiona's sister, Helen, seemed to be blessed with the flirting gene, but somehow she was missing it. She'd assumed that her college would be filled with girls like her, girls who had been prudish and awkward in high school but were on the path to coming into their own. She soon learned this was not the case. The girls were experienced and confident and self-proclaimed feminists who had sex for sex's sake. They came from Manhattan; from L.A.; from international high schools in Tokyo, in Brussels. They called themselves "bi-curious."

Fiona felt like she'd spent most of the year trying to get out of her own skin in the only ways that seemed available to her: smoking weed and ordering Domino's with the stoner girls on her hall or downing sugary red drinks in a sticky dark basement where Top 40 hip hop blasted and she practiced her nonflirting on some pimply theater major. The drinks, the unlimited d-hall, the late-night munchies—they were all just ways to make it through the discomfort of being herself, which of course resulted in the inverse: Now there was just more of herself to hate.

She knew it was so typical, the Freshman 15 (or, in her case, the Freshman 20). But the commonness of it didn't make her feel any less uncomfortable about the way she looked. Inside she was uneasy all the time, squirming within herself. She wanted to yell out to every person that met her at her heaviest "This isn't me! I'm not this person!" But of course, she *was* that person, inhabiting and maintaining that awful body.

She ended up losing her virginity to a boy named George, who, by second semester, was the only remaining single, straight guy on her freshman hall. He was tall and lanky and nice, and they were drunk, and it was awkward and painful, but she just wanted to get it over with so she didn't have to carry around the shame of being a virgin anymore. Now that it was done, she could have sex for real, and one might say that the logical person to have it with would be the shirtless guy lying on the bed next to her. But how did one make something like that happen? How did you let the boy know you were interested? And how, most of all, did you do it without making a fool of yourself?

He'd had his hand in the chip bag for longer than the normal amount of time, Fiona thought, and he briefly grazed her fingers with his own. He looked at her and smirked. For a moment, she felt like this was when you did it: When they gave you a bit of something, you took the bait.

Then he took his hand out and crunched a handful of the chips into his mouth. "Arghhhh," he said with his mouth full, sounding like a pirate or a wild animal. He was just drunk was all. She reminded herself what she looked like, the implausibility of his interest in a person like her. Crumbs fell onto his bare chest. Fiona brushed them off, like a caregiver.

She kept drinking. The radio played; the window opened and shut, opened and shut; and Chad and Steph leaned out to smoke, tapping ash along the side of the building, putting out their cigarettes on the Super 8's cement exterior. Fiona's head fell back on the bed, and she looked up at the yellowing ceiling. Rachel's head met hers. Rachel took Fiona's face in her hands, kissed her briefly on the mouth. "Love you forever, Fee-Bee," she said. *Why?* Fiona thought. *Why do you love me?*

Yonatan and Chad sang loudly, practicing the camp songs: "Here's to sister Rachel, sister Rachel, sister Rachel!" Steph went to pour herself another drink. "Ice! We need ice!" she said. She put on Yonatan's shirt, which came down to just above her knees. She swung the door open, and it stayed that way. "Here's to sister Rachel, the best of them all." Fiona felt alarmed about the door being open like that. In her increasingly drunken state, her caution had dissolved, but now it was coming back up, more bitter than before. "She's happy, she's jolly, she's"—and they changed it here—"*fucked up,* by golly!"

Fiona stood and rushed to the door, slamming it louder than she'd intended. Yonatan and Chad stopped singing.

"What?" Chad said.

"You guys are being so loud," Fiona said. "We can't just leave the door open like that."

A loud rap on the door. Fiona started before remembering Steph.

"Lock me out, why don't you?" Steph walked past her into the room and added ice to her drink before lighting another cigarette.

The others were all sitting near the window, Chad and Steph on the inside ledge and Yonatan and Rachel on the edge of the bed facing them, forming a neat square. Fiona took a seat next to Rachel, upsetting the symmetry. They gossiped about their campers and their fellow counselors, but there was a hush, a shift in the atmosphere, like they all had to watch themselves around Fiona now.

"I have to pee," Fiona said. Instead of walking through the square, she rolled awkwardly over to the other side of the bed to get to the bathroom.

She turned on the fluorescent overhead light and closed the bathroom door. She looked at herself in the mirror—her frizzy, unruly hair in a messy bun on top of her head; the skin around her eyes black from mascara that had smeared throughout the course of the night; a greasy face and a few new pimples: one there between her eyebrows, another at the tip of her nose. There was something about the water in Lakeville, or maybe it was summer humidity: She couldn't keep her skin or her hair under control. Or, maybe, she had just stopped trying. She swayed as she stared at her disappointing reflection; she was drunker than she'd realized. She lifted her shirt and inspected how the night's vodka and SunChips made her stomach protrude. Her breasts strained against her now-too-small bra, and below the bra's underwire, her thick stomach stretched away from her body as if it had an agenda of its own.

She sat down to pee, and as she did so, she could no longer hear the conversation in the room clearly. The voices sounded deliberately lowered. When she finished peeing, she stood up from the toilet and put her ear to the door.

". . . such a narc," she heard from Chad.

There was some mumbling, the female voices. Rachel's so quiet.

"True," Chad said as Fiona strained to hear. "There's always the car."

A few more mumbles; then their voices were normal again.

"I'm starving!" Rachel announced.

Fiona flushed the toilet, washed her hands, and looked at her puffy face once more.

As soon as she emerged, there was another knock on the door.

"Front desk," came the voice from the other side.

Chad stubbed out his new cigarette and threw it out the window, stupidly using his hands to try to push the smoke outside. Steph gave Yonatan his shirt and put on her own. They were all scrambling to hide the vodka under the bed, and the beers, but there were so many cans now, and rings of condensation on the tables, and probably even the smell; there had to be a smell by now. Chad went into the bathroom and quietly closed the door.

Another knock.

"Coming!" Rachel said, her voice high and cheery as she pulled an arm into her T-shirt.

"Get into bed," she said to the others in a low voice, and they did as they were told, Steph and Fiona in one bed and Yonatan in the other. Rachel glanced around the room one last time, then opened the door.

It was Mary Ann. She was frowning, and her round face was glistening. "Do you know what time it is?"

"We were just climbing into bed," Rachel said innocently. "Were we being too loud?"

"We got a noise complaint from the next room."

"Really?" She cocked her head to the side. "We just finished a movie."

"The TV was probably too loud," Yonatan said from the

bed. He was sitting up against a pillow, his arms folded over the comforter. "It was an action movie."

"Someone said they heard singing," said Mary Ann.

"Weird," Rachel said.

Mary Ann peeked her head through the doorway. Fiona thought she saw her sniff the air. Her face was red and contorting in an ugly way.

"Unbelievable," she said. "You camp people are unbelievable."

"Ma'am?" Rachel said.

"This room reeks."

"I don't understand."

"Is it really that hard to follow rules for one night?" Mary Ann seemed jumpy, almost excited, and then turned to point into the hall. "Get out."

Rachel's shoulders slumped, and she pursed her lips into a pout. "But it's two in the morning," she whined.

"That's not my problem."

Then Rachel stood straighter and folded her arms in front of herself. "You can't make us leave," she said. "We're paying customers."

The others said nothing.

"Yes I can. I can make you leave for"—Mary Ann counted the reasons off on her fingers now—"disorderly conduct. Smoking in a nonsmoking motel. Underage drinking. Sneaking in a nonpaying guest." She gestured to the closed bathroom door. "And I can call the cops if you don't go."

"No one signed a contract," Rachel said.

"Sure you did. That girl"—she pointed to Fiona—"signed something when she gave us her credit card." This was Mary Ann's moment, reminding the kids that she was the adult here. She was the one with the power. "Which I'm charging for damage, by the way."

Rachel, Yonatan, and Steph all turned to look at Fiona—searing, blameful looks. She wanted to hide herself under the overstarched comforter of the motel bed and fall unconscious beneath its dark weight.

Out in the parking lot, they fought over who would drive the car back to camp.

"What the fuck are we supposed to do, Fiona?" Steph was saying. "You won't drive, but you won't let anyone else drive either?"

"Someone could come pick us up," Fiona suggested, half-knowing she'd be shut down.

"We can't call the camp," Rachel said. "I can drive. I'm honestly not that drunk."

"I don't believe you," said Fiona.

"Test me," said Rachel. She put her arms out and walked in a straight line.

"Look at that!" Chad said. "She's perfect."

"Fiona," Yonatan said. "The camp can't find out about this. Chad and I will lose our visas." How reasonable it seemed when he explained it.

"It's only a half-hour drive," Rachel said, "in the middle

of nowhere, in the middle of the night. There's no one on the road. I'll drive ten miles under the speed limit." She put her pinkie out and waited for Fiona to take it.

How did Fiona go from being the one in control—the one who drove them here in the first place, who put her emergencies-only credit card down—to the one being blamed? And how would she explain to her father why there was a charge for almost $350 for one night at a Super 8 in Torrington, Connecticut? This was the underbelly of responsibility: When things went wrong, the fingers turned back at you. Fiona had gotten them to the motel and gotten them the room, but it was a given that she would do that for them: because she had the car; she had the money; she was the reliable one. Now she started to see that reliable people were just the type that more self-respecting people could walk all over.

In the Jeep, Fiona sat in the front seat. She felt totally sober now, and large, and useless. She looked over at Rachel. She told Fiona she loved her in one moment and then turned around and talked shit about her the next. That was just something else that Rachel could do that Fiona couldn't: be so many steps ahead of the situation that she could remain in control of it. Rachel would not allow herself to be aligned with a narc, even if it meant throwing her best friend under the bus. Sometimes Fiona hated herself for allowing Rachel to do that to her again and again. But in fact, she understood it; she too would have been embarrassed by herself that night.

As they drove, Fiona felt a sort of wounded jealousy of

her best friend—if she could be more like Rachel, look more like Rachel, then maybe this wouldn't hurt so bad. Rachel seemed to know how to do everything that Fiona didn't: how to flirt; how to gossip in a way you could defend later; how to stay thin; how to drive drunk. She was in awe of the way Rachel could manipulate any situation so that it would end up working out in her favor. Fiona was so envious of Rachel's compact body that she wanted to dissolve her own and inhabit that one, to be the owner of the thin wrists that capably steered them back to camp.

They got into camp and parted ways as they walked back to their respective sections. Fiona lay down in her bunk but couldn't sleep. She got up after a few minutes, bringing her toiletries with her, and made her way to the Maple girls' bathroom, walking through the circle of platform tents, every little girl asleep. In the bathroom, she looked at herself in the mirror above the row of sinks. She looked exactly the same as she had hours ago in the motel: puffy and greasy and ugly. She did not know why she imagined she'd look any different. Mirrors these days were a perpetual and profound disappointment.

She thought about Yonatan, probably asleep by now. What she saw in the mirror was also what he saw, and the reality of that made her cringe and hate herself more.

She ran the water warm and washed her hands. Without thinking about why, she began to turn the cold water valve to the right—turn, turn, turn—until it was all the way off and the water was steaming from the sink, her hands scalding. She closed her eyes and breathed sharply through her nose through the pain. If someone had walked in, she wouldn't have been able to explain it. It just felt numbing, even good inside the pain, like she was washing away the detestable parts of herself, burning away her mediocrity and powerlessness, her ugliness. She opened her eyes and looked up into the mirror again and was surprised to see herself grimacing.

When she was finished, she pulled paper towels from the dispenser and dried her wrinkled, red hands. She let out a long breath, as if she'd just completed a difficult but worthwhile task. She returned to her tent and fell instantly into a dreamless sleep.

5

It was Sheera Jones's first summer at Camp Marigold. The lake was, so far, her favorite place on the camp grounds, and she signed up for as many activities there as she could. In the South Bronx, there were plenty of trees, a couple of public pools, the Harlem and East Rivers, but no clear, open water—nothing where, if you were standing in the exact right place on the shoreline at the exact right time, you couldn't see a single person.

During the first week, Sheera had discovered that that exact right time to gain some solitude at the lake was just before the day's activities started or right after they ended. So on the Monday morning of the second week of camp, She left breakfast the minute the girls were dismissed to get to the beach before anyone else. There were two ways to get there: by road, down a wide gravel drive that rounded the circumference of the hilly camp, or by trail, the more direct but steeper, narrower, and more treacherous of the routes. Sheera always chose the trail. She walked down it enough times that the route became familiar: Here was the fallen log you had to climb over; here was the muddy patch you had to tiptoe around, for it often rained at night; here was where the trail broke for a moment and you walked down twenty man-made steps before you hiked the rest of the way. And here the trail cleared and opened right onto the beach: only a few steps on grass before your toes were in the sand. The lake, she'd learned at the nature lodge, was three miles long—the length of sixty city blocks. The camp used only half of it, mostly for safety reasons. You could see across the width of the lake to the other shore, which was covered in bushy trees, seemingly with not an inch of open space in which to wander; in the distance were the gray-blue outlines of the Berkshire Mountains. But lengthwise, even if you stood at the edge of the beach and craned your neck to the right as far as it could go, you still couldn't see where the water ended and became land again. Canoes or swimmers could get lost over there.

That morning Sheera was able to get only one or two minutes alone with her toes in the water before she heard steps crunching down the gravel road and then padding in the grass behind her. She turned to see Chad, the boating counselor, pulling canoes from their parking spots on the grass and lining them up in a row along the shoreline, their noses dipping into the shallow water. Chad had a British accent, and he often walked around shirtless, showing off his perpetually sunburned chest. He was unfriendly and played favorites, and Sheera wasn't one of them.

Chad didn't say hello to Sheera, nor she to him, but soon after he had lined up the canoes, she heard the quickened footsteps and easy laughter of kids coming down the same gravel road. She turned and walked away from the lakeshore, toward the oar house, to pick out a life vest and a paddle. She tried to blend into the pack of just-arrived kids scrambling for the newer-looking life vests rather than appear as if she'd already been there by herself. This was something she was still trying to balance: not coming off as a loner while still getting the solitude she so desperately craved.

After everyone had their life vests and their paddles, Chad told the campers to get into pairs and pick their canoes; they all appeared to have their partners instantaneously and, in a matter of moments, were walking down to the shore two by two. Sheera had hardly had time to scan the crowd. Something else she was learning about this camp life was that, while she signed up for activities alone, most of the other kids did so with friends. It felt like Sheera's reason for coming to camp—namely, the opportunity to get out of suffocating, grimy city life, which included, by extension, a certain amount of space between herself and others—was in direct opposition to the reasons of the other campers. They never wanted to do anything alone. It wasn't that Sheera didn't want to make new friends—she did, very much. It was more that she thought there would be a greater emphasis on being outside in a more quiet, more peaceful way. Learning about nature, being active in the outdoors: These were things she always wanted more of, and she'd assumed everyone else did too.

"Hey, girlie," Chad said to Sheera. She'd been at the lake every day the previous week, and he still had not managed to remember her name. "You wanna pick a group to tag onto?"

Sheera didn't recognize any of the kids except for two girls who lived in her section. She began walking toward them, the load of the paddle weighing her down. How was she supposed to walk with this? Carry it above her head? Beside her like a walking stick? It was oppressively heavy.

When she got to the water's edge, and the two girls from her section were loading themselves into their boat without acknowledging her, she heard Chad whistle.

"Girlie!" he shouted.

She could see Mikey Bombowski next to Chad, arms crossed over his chest, his eyes hidden behind aviator sunglasses. The girls in Sheera's tent had talked about Mikey before; Helen in particular thought he was cute. But Sheera found nothing attractive about his skinny body and his gel-spiked hair. Though Sheera had gotten her first period two years earlier and now had what her grandma called "a body that could get her in trouble," she found herself mostly uninterested in the opposite sex. At camp, especially, she regarded the boys no differently than the girls: carefully, attempting to discriminate who had the potential to be her friend. She had three older brothers, and she understood through them what boys were like: fun, yes, and playful, but also crass, and dirty, and dangerous, the kind of danger her grandma warned her about. The way the girls in her tent talked about boys, it

sounded like they were imagining an entirely different species, one that was affectionate and romantic and talked about
its feelings. Sheera had begun to wonder if rich white boys
really were like that, if they were really another species from
the boys with whom she'd grown up.

Chad said something to Mikey out of the corner of his
mouth, handed the boy a life vest, and nudged him with his
elbow. Mikey walked slowly to the empty canoe next to
Sheera. The two girls from Sheera's section stopped paddling
for a moment and looked over at her and Mikey curiously.

Sheera directed her gaze toward the lake to avoid Mikey's,
watching the canoes gliding slowly from the shore and the
paddles chopping the water. She heard splashes, giggles, was
amazed at how the sound traveled over the distance. It had
something to do with still bodies of water and echoes; she'd
learned this in school once.

"You wanna get in?" Mikey asked. "I'll push."

She settled onto the wooden seat that had been indented
by hundreds of bodies of campers before her. A puddle of
cold lake water sloshed around her feet, and she rested the
overbearing paddle on her thighs, which had promptly
spread and stuck to each other. Facing the open lake—a motorboat pulling a water-skier, the roped-off swimming hole
to their right—she wondered, as she often did, what lay
across the way in that densely green and wild forest beneath
the Berkshires. She felt the canoe scrape the soft bottom
of the lake and turned to see Mikey wading knee-deep
through the water, getting their boat out of the muck. He
hopped in.

"No paddling past the buoys!" Chad yelled from the shore.

They didn't discuss steering or a plan of where to go. They paddled out into the center of the lake, and when Mikey stopped, so did Sheera. He exhaled, looking around in wonder at the lake and back at the camp in the distance, like he was seeing them anew. The girls from Sheera's section paddled beside her and Mikey's boat, trying to catch Mikey's attention by splashing each other, looking over, hoping he'd laugh or even look in their direction. He didn't.

Chad had gotten into a boat with two younger boys and was helping them paddle just past the dock, not paying attention to any of the other campers.

"It's your first summer here, right?" Mikey asked.

Sheera nodded. Growing up, she had gone to some day camps in the city, and they'd taken field trips into the country, but this was her first summer at a sleepaway camp. She didn't know any kids from home that went away to camp, but she'd watched a reality show on Nickelodeon about a camp in the Berkshires, and a bunch of the kids on the show were from the city and looked and talked like her. They climbed rope courses and rode horses and hung out with one another *and* with the white kids—which she wasn't used to seeing, all the groups mingling like that. Most of her friends at school were black or Hispanic—because most of her school was black and Hispanic—but something about the appearance of seamless diversity intrigued her, as if nature itself was some kind of great equalizer.

So she looked up "Berkshires summer camp" on the Internet, and she found Camp Marigold, which had a website with happy diverse kids too. Her dad refused to let her go until she did enough research to find out there was scholarship money. And once they got a bunch of it, he was okay with the idea. It would be one less kid he'd have to worry about that summer.

But when she got to Camp Marigold, very few of the kids did look like her. She'd never been in a place so predominantly white, and she was sure her father hadn't either. "Watch out for yourself," he had said to her quietly the day he dropped her off, right before he got into his car to drive back to the Bronx. The girls in her section were nice enough, but they didn't seem to care to make any new friends; most of them knew one another already. Sheera didn't know until she got to Marigold that thirteen was considered old for one's first summer at sleepaway camp.

Mikey turned around now, checking for Chad. They sliced their paddles into the water. "Paddle forward," Mikey kept saying. As he paddled faster, so, in imitation, did Sheera. Closer ahead now were bushy-leaved trees with wide, imposing bases and a shoreline surrounded by elephantine gray rocks. As they inched forward, Sheera didn't say, "We're not allowed to be here," but she turned around to look at Mikey in a way she hoped conveyed it. If they were to get in trouble, she didn't want anyone to think it was her idea.

"It's fine," he said, and his tone of voice made her believe him.

After they steered toward a narrow space between two rocks, he unbuckled his life vest and threw it onto the bench of the canoe, climbed onto one of rocks, and, once he'd steadied himself on it, told Sheera to throw him the rope from within the canoe. He stood tall on the rock, pulling the canoe in while keeping his balance.

With the weight now upset in the boat, Sheera tipped forward slightly as Mikey bent to tether the rope to the thick branch of a tree. He held his hand out to her. She climbed over the rocks and landed on the soil on her hands and knees. She stood quickly, collecting herself, wiping dirt on her thighs.

"Whose property is this?" she asked, looking around and feeling small. The impressions she'd had of the place from afar were confirmed: The land was dense and overgrown, and there seemed to be no discernible trail.

"It belongs to the state, I think."

Camp Marigold lay directly across from them now. A few remaining red canoes sat docked at the lakeshore. To the left, in the swimming hole, heads bobbed like beach balls on the surface. Sheera saw the beginnings of the hiking and biking trails—worn-out, rocky paths blazed between the trees—but they disappeared into the hills that held everything else.

Mikey turned away from the lake and led Sheera to a trail she wouldn't have noticed herself; it was not cleared out like the trails at camp, and was so narrow that the two of them had to walk single file.

"Where are you from, anyway?" Sheera asked, following Mikey through the woods. There were pesky roots and loose stones and untamed branches that scratched her arms as she passed. She wished she weren't wearing flip-flops.

"I'm an army brat," he said. "You know what that means?"

She shook her head.

"It means I ain't from nowhere." He laughed. "In Alabama, they said 'ain't' and 'y'all' a lot. It's actually pretty useful."

"But where do you live now?"

"Near Chicago. My dad works at a military school there," he said. "I guess I could say I'm from there now."

"You come here all the way from Chicago?"

He shrugged.

They were walking on a steady incline. She was breathing heavily but trying to conceal it because Mikey wasn't.

"Where are *you* from?" he asked.

"The Bronx."

"No, I mean . . . where are you *from*?"

"The Bronx," she said louder, thinking he hadn't heard her.

"But, like . . . where are your parents from?"

"My dad is from the Bronx too," she said. "My mom was from the Dominican Republic, but she died." She forgot until she saw Mikey flinch that this was shocking news every time she told it. "I don't remember her," she lied, by way of apology.

"Oh," he said. "Do you speak Dominican?"

"Spanish?"

"Yeah, that's what I meant."

"Not really," she said, picking up a stick from the ground as she walked. "I understand it sometimes when my grandma comes over 'cause that's all she speaks, but she doesn't come over a lot." That was her other grandma, her *abuela*. Once Sheera had asked her father why her *abuela* came over less and less as Sheera got older, and he'd said it was because it was too sad for her to come to the apartment without Sheera's mom there.

They kept going until the lake was completely out of sight and walked for what felt like a long time. All the elements were starting to beat up Sheera's body—the mosquitoes that seemed to love to bite her, the prickly tree branches that stuck out too far, the loose rocks she kept tripping over in her flip-flops. She looked at her watch; it was ten-thirty. The activity period ended at ten-fifty.

"Don't you think we should get back?" she said.

"We're almost there," he said, pressing on.

They came upon a steep, rocky incline almost entirely covered in moss. Mikey slowed his walking as they approached it. He cupped a hand dramatically around an ear. "You hear that?" he whispered. When Sheera stopped, and the leaves stopped crunching beneath their feet, she did hear something different: a whirring maybe, like the sound the wind made over the platform tents at night.

Mikey began to climb the hill, and he directed Sheera on how to climb it too as he did so. "Hold on there," he would say, looking behind himself as he climbed, pointing to a root, a rock, or a trunk as the whirring noise grew and grew. He kept holding a hand out for her, but she didn't take it; she focused on finding the outcrops in the hill to propel herself up. Mikey stood at the top now, hands on his hips, watching her.

When she got there, he pointed down the other, mossy side of the hill where a waterfall rushed down the rocks and fell into a stream that meandered out of sight. She was surprised that something so small could make so much noise.

"It's called the Fall of Three Indians," he said. His pride in leading them there was palpable, and Sheera could almost catch some of it for herself.

They sat down and dangled their feet over the edge.

"Have you ever seen a waterfall before?" he asked.

"Obviously," she lied.

She kicked a stone and watched it arc and fall into the water below.

"Do you have brothers and sisters?" he asked her.

"Three brothers."

"Lucky."

"I'm the youngest. It's not that lucky."

"It's better than nothin'." He pointed to himself. "I got nothin'."

Her brothers beat up on her a lot. It was because it would make her tough, they said, because they loved her.

"I've seen you playing four square," he continued when she didn't say anything. "You're really good. And you're really nice to everyone even when you beat them. And you don't brag about being good or being nice."

She was surprised that he had noticed her. She didn't think that anyone at camp had noticed her.

A little bird, a sparrow or something, flew down and began to peck at the moss between the two of them. Sheera looked down at it. Birds this small, how could you tell the difference between the mother and child? Mikey hovered one finger over the bird as if he was about to pet it. Surprisingly, it didn't move.

"Aren't those things dirty?" Sheera asked.

"No. I don't think so," he said. Then Sheera too went to tentatively place her pointer finger on the animal, but it flew away before either of them could touch it.

The bird flapped up to the treetops that shadowed the stream and then deeper into the woods until it was out of sight.

Sheera looked at her watch, which read 10:55. "We have to go!" She stood suddenly and brushed the bits of dirt and grass off her shorts.

"It's fine," he said, waving a hand dismissively. "Chad's a softy."

"I don't wanna get in trouble." Without knowing whether Mikey was following, she began to take long, fast strides down the slope of the hill. About halfway through her descent, her right flip-flop lost its grip on the earth, and her foot was propelled forward while the back of her right thigh scratched itself on the face of a rock. Her sandal tumbled down the hill. Ignoring the stinging pain, she stood, righting herself on the uneven ground fast enough that Mikey wouldn't get a chance to see that she'd fallen.

"Are you okay?" she heard him say from behind her. "You're bleeding!"

"I'm fine." She took off her other flip-flop and hobbled down barefoot to where they first had landed. "Let's just go."

He ran down the hill to her, making it look so easy, and took off his shirt and wrapped it around her leg to stop the bleeding. It was just a scratch, she told him, grimacing as she felt the cloth now sticking to her raw skin. He had such a skinny torso, like he didn't eat at all. It looked a lot like Helen's, flat in every which way. Not like her own chest, which didn't want to stop growing, and her waist, which kept widening. When she stood up after sitting for even a few minutes these days, there were red lines on her stomach from where the skin folded over.

Mikey led the way back to the shore, and she followed, struggling to keep up and hiding a limp. When they got to the canoe, Sheera hoped he didn't see her grimacing as she sat down on the hard bench.

On the lake, she paddled furiously, wordlessly, her face hot with shame. She could see that across the lake at camp the kids were gone: There were no other boats in the water now, no heads bobbing in the swimming hole. There was only Chad at the shoreline, waving with his arms over his head. Her leg throbbed.

"Where the hell have you two been?" Chad spat as they got closer. He waded thigh deep into the water, his face red. "Paddles up, *now*." He pulled their canoe in hard.

"What is that?" Chad said, approaching Sheera as she stepped out of the boat. "Is that blood?" She looked down and saw that a few red spots had stained the shirt around her thigh.

"It's just a scratch," Mikey said, shrugging.

Chad closed his eyes and massaged the bridge of his nose. He took a deep breath, then looked at Sheera. "Are you okay?"

Sheera nodded, holding in her tears. She could not let them see her cry. It wasn't just that her leg hurt so bad—and it did hurt; it was a gash, not a scratch. It was that it felt like that one fall exposed her. She'd been getting along just fine until this point. Now Mikey, or Chad, or anyone else who learned what had happened could know that she might not be cut out for this place.

"All right, let's go to the nurse." He looked over at Mikey. "Walk with us. Explain what happened."

"We got stuck, dude," Mikey explained as they walked up the gravel road. "Wedged between two rocks. Sheera jumped out to try to get us unstuck, and that's when she scratched her leg." He glanced almost imperceptibly at Sheera. "I know we went past the buoys," he continued. "We fucked up. But we're here, right? And I promise it was all my idea."

"Watch your mouth," Chad said. He looked at Sheera. "Is that true?" he asked. "Was it all Mikey's idea?"

Mikey and Sheera held eyes for a moment. He was either challenging her to tell the truth or to go along with his story. She thought about her father telling her to be careful. She thought about what she knew about boys: that they were fun but trouble.

Sheera shook her head. "He's lying," she said. She understood, instinctually, that Mikey could get away with things that she could not. "We went to the other shore."

"Jesus." Chad stopped walking. "Do you have any idea what kind of trouble you two could get me in?"

"But you were supposed to be watching us," Sheera said.

Mikey looked at her in disbelief.

"Excuse me?" Chad said.

"I said—" Sheera began.

"I heard what you said." He locked eyes with Sheera for a minute: wide, wild eyes. He was scaring her, but she would not let him know it. She willed herself not to be the first to break the eye contact, and in doing so, she felt brave, almost impenetrable. She could feel Mikey's presence, could feel him looking between her and Chad, suddenly aware that this no longer involved him in a way he could articulate.

Then Chad turned around and walked ahead of them, muttering under his breath. He led them to the nurse's office.

It was a cabin near the dining hall; Sheera had not yet been inside it. The three of them walked in together. There was a waiting room with a worn fabric couch, a boy sitting on it with an ice pack pressed to his elbow, and chairs in equal disrepair. A TV high up on the wall played a talk show on mute, in which five women—some black, some white—were sitting at a long table, looking like they were making important points. The air conditioner in one of the windows was blowing cold air into the room.

"What happened to you?" Mikey asked the kid sitting on the couch.

"Beesting," he said, lifting the ice pack briefly to show the red mark.

Mikey shrugged. "That's no big deal."

"Whatever," the kid scoffed. "Where's your shirt?"

Mikey pointed to Sheera, who still had it wrapped around her leg.

Chad approached the nurse, a nice-looking older lady, and waved for Sheera and Mikey to follow.

"What do we have here?" the nurse asked Sheera with a sweet tone in her voice.

"I scratched my leg," Sheera said.

"Sweet of you to give her your shirt," the nurse said to Mikey. Then she looked up at Chad. "I can take her from here."

Chad seemed almost disappointed that the nurse hadn't asked him any questions. He gave Sheera one nod as a good-bye, still with that hard, scary expression on his face. Mikey looked disappointed to be leaving too, but Sheera didn't know if he was disappointed to be leaving *her* or just the air-conditioning and the TV. She had to admit, it felt nice to be in a real indoor room, even if it was only for a few minutes.

"Have a seat," the nurse said to Sheera after the boys left, gesturing to one of the folding chairs next to the desk. When Sheera sat down at first, it hurt her leg, so she moved her butt all the way to the edge of the seat. The nurse reached forward and slowly, gently untied the shirt from around Sheera's upper thigh.

"Yowza," the nurse said, looking first at the blood that had soaked through Mikey's shirt and then at the gash on the back of Sheera's leg. "You took quite the spill."

Sheera nodded wordlessly, afraid that if she said anything

she would start crying. Her leg stung intensely, and she real-ized, for the first time, that she missed home. Something about the muted TV and the air-conditioning and the ugly couch: It felt a lot like her apartment on a summer after-noon.

"How did you do this? You were in boating class?"

"I, um . . . I scratched it on a rock."

"Okay," the nurse said.

"It's a long story."

"I'll take your word for it," the nurse said.

Sheera was grateful she didn't have to explain anything further. How tiring it would have been to have to decide all over again if she would tell the truth or not.

"Let's go into one of the rooms, okay? So I can bandage you up properly." The nurse stood up from her desk. "You can go to your next activity now, Bobby," she said to the boy with the beesting, who frowned and slowly got up.

The nurse led Sheera into an examination room, where there was a desk with supplies and a padded table with a clean piece of wax paper over it. The nurse patted it. "Lie down for me, tummy first."

Sheera got onto the table using a step stool and did as she was told. She watched the nurse pull two plastic gloves from a box on the desk and put them on. Then she took a couple of creams and a large square bandage from a drawer.

The nurse took one of the creams and squeezed some onto her pointer finger.

"Is it gonna hurt?" Sheera asked, surprised by the weak tone of her own voice.

"No, sweetie," the nurse said, looking Sheera in the eyes. "It'll feel nice."

Sheera closed her eyes and let the nurse put the ointment on her. It did feel nice, cooling. The nurse stuck the bandage onto the back of Sheera's thigh and gave her a note saying she couldn't swim for a week.

"A week?" The thought of having to sit out at the pool or the lake and everyone looking at her made her want to cry again.

"It's a big gash, sweetheart. You don't want it to get infected. And trust me, it wouldn't feel good. Especially not the chlorine."

Sheera nodded, holding her tears in. But when the nurse placed her hand maternally on Sheera's shoulder, she couldn't help but let all the tears go.

"Oh, sweetheart," the nurse said. She sat down on the table next to Sheera and put an arm around her. She stroked the top of Sheera's head and kept saying things like "Shh, that's it" and "Let it out."

When Sheera was done crying, she looked up at the nurse.

"Can I stay here?" Sheera managed. "Just for a little longer?"

"You stay as long as you need," the nurse said. "Do you want to watch TV?"

Sheera nodded. They went back into the waiting room, and Sheera settled on the couch, which was torn up but comfortable, and watched the ladies making important points on the TV, occasionally hiccuping from a leftover sob.

6

"I'll go first," Rachel said in the tent that night. She was sitting on one of the girls' hard-topped trunks, an electric lantern upright in the space between her crossed legs. They were doing roses and thorns, one of her favorite bedtime activities from her own time as a camper.

"My thorn today," she said, "was hot dogs for dinner."

"They were, like, *raw*," Helen confirmed from her bunk.

"And my rose?" Rachel clapped the heel of her flip-flop against the platform tent's wooden floorboards, thinking. "Oh, duh. My rose was sticking a reverse off the high dive."

"She did," Helen said. Her hay-colored curls bobbed up and down, and the gigantic shadow of her head on the canvas wall behind her moved in tandem. "I saw it."

"Helen," Rachel said, "your turn."

Sheera turned her flashlight toward Helen, whose top

bunk was across the tent from hers. There were eight bunks in the tent with a square platform made of cedar planks below them and wooden posts on all four sides to hold up the canvas roof and walls.

Helen threw a freckled forearm over her eyes. "Sheera!"

Sheera tried to figure out where to cast the light, and the white-yellow circle darted around the tent like an unruly moth.

"Chill out," Sheera said, settling the flashlight on a spot toward the peak of the tent.

"Anyway." Helen cleared her throat and sat up in her bunk. "My thorn was swimming in the lake. I jumped in from the dock and touched the bottom of the deep end, and it felt like diarrhea."

The girls shrieked and giggled at this admission. Rachel saw a glimmer of her own younger self in Helen, who had a matter-of-fact way about her that most girls her age did not and a natural interest in pushing buttons.

"And my *rose*." Helen put a finger to her mouth. "My rose was getting to play four square with Mikey Bombowski." Her voice went up on *Bombowski* like it was a question.

"Oh, Helen," Rachel said. "He's cute." Mikey Bombowski wore long basketball shorts with his boxers showing. He was the sort of boy that Rachel herself would have gone for at that age, only Rachel would not have been excited by something like playing four square with him. She would have known even then not to relish such inanities.

"So cute," said Sarah. Rachel felt sort of sorry for Helen—still a very young-seeming girl stuck in a woman's body.

There were whispers now about Mikey and the other Hemlock-section boys: Johnny, Joey, Danny, and Sam. It was a Sunday night in early July; the coed dance was six days away, and Rachel had told the girls in her tent that a boy had up to exactly three days beforehand to ask a girl on a date. After that, she could, and should, make other plans.

Rachel checked her watch: ten P.M. She stood and switched off the lantern. "Time for you girls to sleep. Flashlights off."

Then she waited at the tent's entrance until the girls appeared to be swallowed by total darkness.

Post-lights-out was usually a good time to check email in the computer lab; most people were already drinking in the staff lodge by then, or sitting around a bonfire, or taking a late-night swim down by the lake, so the computers were unoccupied, and the Internet was relatively fast.

Rachel sat down at one of the desktops, opened the browser, and signed into her email to find some junk—a sale on the Gap's website, a Facebook invite to a house party in Brooklyn—and a note from her mother with the subject "call me when you get this." She opened the email; there was no message in the body.

She worried it might be about her grandma. Or maybe Pickles, their aging cat. She picked up the landline phone on the desk and dialed home.

Denise sounded breathless and tired when she answered, as if she had just come home from a long, hard day.

"Mom, it's me."

"Hi, hon. How's it going out there?"

"It's good. I just saw your email."

Denise let out a heavy sigh on the other end of the line.

"Is it Grandma?" Rachel asked.

"Grandma's fine," Denise said.

"Okay," Rachel said. "What is it?"

"I'm sorry, sweetheart," Denise said, her voice softening. "It's your father."

For a moment, neither woman spoke. The line between them was now weighted with meaning and consequence, and each one recomposed herself as she figured out the correct attitude with which to proceed.

"He had a heart attack, sweetie."

"What?" Rachel said. "Are you crying?"

"It's not an easy thing, Rachel."

"I thought heart attacks were no big deal."

"His heart just isn't working right anymore. It's all of the smoking," Denise said. "Sweetheart, it's not looking good. He's on life support."

At the words "life support," Rachel let out a slight and, she hoped, inaudible gasp. "How do you know all of this?" She was trying to speak as little as possible for fear her voice might betray her.

"She called me today. She knows you're at camp this summer."

"*She* called you?"

"It's really big of her," Denise said, "that she would even keep us in the loop."

"Gee," Rachel said. "How generous."

Denise was once a secretary at Rachel's father's law firm. Her mother was twenty-four when the relationship began; her father was forty-four. He was married—always had been, always would be, though Rachel was a young teenager when she finally understood this in a definitive way.

He had two children just a few years older than Rachel. Growing up, Rachel had been kept a secret from her father's family. She had understood this unspoken truth as if it were part of the weather: because he wore a wedding ring, because the money always came in cash, because he took his phone calls outside, because their time together was always limited. They might have a nice weeknight dinner in the city, see a Broadway musical, take a day trip to the beach, but it was always just the two of them and never a week or a weekend, never an overnight. It worked for a while in its way, how he paid for the apartment and camp and gave Rachel whatever designer bag she asked for for her birthday. For an illegitimate father, he could have been worse.

It worked, until he thoughtlessly left her unmailed, unsealed sixteenth birthday card on his desk, in his family's house in the suburbs, with the five hundred dollars cash inside.

The wife gave him an ultimatum: us or them. The kids, a boy and a girl, were away at college. Rachel imagined the wife—whom she'd never seen, whose name was never spoken—as a tiny, shrill lady, worn by her years of suspicions, becoming both scandalized and smug about having been proved right by the evidence at hand. Rachel imagined her standing in front of his home office, the money in her hand: "You can't just keep bankrolling them when we have two Ivy tuitions to finish paying. What about our retirement? The home in Florida we've always wanted? How long could we have had that home by now?"

He gave Rachel and her mother one last wad of cash—a settlement of sorts—and went on his way.

Rachel's secrecy had been so much a part of the deal that only when it was revealed as dirty, his presence revoked as a result of it, could she fully comprehend its power. How strange it was that she could threaten to ruin someone's life—or several someones' lives—by her mere existence.

The ultimatum happened just a week after Rachel had turned sixteen. Denise had only a high school diploma, but for Rachel, who went to a competitive New York City public school, college was around the corner. There was enough money for only one year's tuition—maybe two, if she got a scholarship.

In a panic, Denise took a second job waitressing at an overpriced French restaurant on Columbus Avenue. The elderly Upper West Side couples were grumpy, but she made good money, especially on weekends.

One Sunday night about a month after her sixteenth birthday, Rachel was studying for her calculus midterm at the kitchen table when Denise came through the front door, slamming it behind her. Rachel looked up: Her mother's white button-down was splattered with red sauce stains, and she was still wearing her apron around her waist. Denise dropped her purse loudly onto the kitchen counter and let out a frustrated groan.

When Rachel didn't ask what was the matter, Denise took her jacket off and threw it on the floor. She untied her apron dramatically and threw that on the floor too.

"These fucking people," she finally said, taking a wine-glass from the cabinet above her head. "I wasn't even sup-posed to work today. I cover for Sharon, of all people, and she doesn't even tell me she was scheduled to work a double." She took an unopened bottle of red wine from atop the fridge. Rachel waited with her pencil poised in her hand. She was averaging a B minus in calculus and needed an A on this test.

"And then"—Denise rummaged through a drawer to find a corkscrew—"one o'clock comes around, and get this: I get stuck with two four-tops, three two-tops, and a party of *ten,* including three fucking screaming kids flinging ketchup all over the goddamn place." She poked the cork with the cork-screw and turned it hard. "They didn't even make a reserva-tion."

She wriggled the cork until it came out of the bottle with a satisfying *pop.*

"I mean, what kind of French restaurant does brunch anyway? They don't do *brunch* in France." She poured the wine into the glass and lifted it to her mouth. "It's a fucking rip-off, I'll tell you that much," she said, and took a sip.

Rachel looked down at her calculus textbook again. She could sense that Denise was standing with her hip against the counter, sipping her wine and looking at Rachel, and so she was not concentrating on the numbers in the book in front

of her but instead feeling the profound annoyance of knowing her mother was watching her. Still, she did not look up.

"You eat yet?" Denise asked.

Rachel shook her head.

"You hungry? I brought back a burger. We could split it."

"Go ahead," Rachel said, standing. "I'll eat later." She
closed her book and headed toward her room. "I've got to
study."

Rachel could feel that her mother had more to say. She
waited on the threshold of her bedroom door for Denise to
come after her, to yell, again, about how lucky Rachel was
that she had a mother who didn't make her get a part-time
job, a mother who valued her daughter's education, a mother
who wanted her daughter to have all the opportunities that
she hadn't had herself. How lucky Rachel was that she had a
mother who would work two jobs for her, despite that prick,
that motherfucker, that dirty bastard who was trying to take
away all their chances at something better.

There was a time, when Rachel was a child, when her parents still saw each other. A babysitter would come over and
give her dinner and a bath and put her to bed. Her mother
never dated anyone else in all that time, and Rachel suspected
that maybe Denise had been waiting for him to leave his family and choose them, after all. But by the time Rachel was
thirteen, he stopped coming over, and Rachel saw him only
out of the house. Denise never told Rachel the particulars
about the relationship ending, and Rachel never asked.

Rachel sat on her bed for a few minutes looking at her

calculus textbook and began to feel guilty. Denise wasn't coming after her this time. She got up to go into the kitchen to tell her mother she would eat the other half of the burger. But as she walked through the living room, she saw her mother leaning against the kitchen counter with her face in her hands, quietly sobbing. Denise hated when Rachel cried; she said it was a sign of weakness.

Rachel turned around and tiptoed back into her room, shutting the door behind herself carefully, hoping her mother wouldn't realize that she'd ever left.

It had rained in the morning, but the night was clear and crisp, and Rachel knew there'd be a campfire on the beach. She walked down the trail to the lake with her flashlight. Her sandals squished into the damp ground, picking up mud and wet leaves on the bottoms of their soles as she walked. When she got closer to the water, she could hear someone picking the strings on a guitar and voices talking over the music.

When the trail ended, the ground turning from soil to grass to sand, Rachel clicked off her flashlight and stopped for a moment to look out at the scene: the fire crackling and blazing and the faces of the three counselors glowing with orange light. Everything else surrounding them was dark, and the lake had taken on a sheen of pure blackness that might make someone more superstitious than she wonder what lurked beneath.

Rachel walked toward the group, her usual crew: Fiona,

Chad, and Yonatan. Yonatan played the guitar aimlessly and nodded in wordless recognition of Rachel. Fiona moved over on the wooden bench to make room for her friend.

"Where've you been?" Fiona asked, more curious than accusatory, though Rachel could often sense an unwarranted jealousy behind such questions.

"Just had to call my mom," Rachel said. She pointed to Fiona's beer. "Any more of those?"

Chad, on the other side of Rachel, reached into a cooler next to the bench, pulled out a Heineken, and used an opener on his key chain to open it.

"Bottles today," Rachel said. "Fancy."

"Yonatan and I walked into town yesterday," Chad said. "We splurged."

She took a long sip. She loved beer. Cheap or expensive, it didn't matter. What she liked was that wheaty taste, like bread gone bad, the sourness that hit her as fast as a light switch turning on.

Chad grabbed Rachel's knee. "How's your mum?" he asked. They had become friends over the past three weeks. They had discovered that they were both children of single mothers and that Rachel would often check in with Denise before joining the rest of the group.

"She's fine," Rachel said.

"You're lucky you can call her just like that. The time difference is too hard here."

"I guess so."

"You are," Chad said. "I miss mine."

Rachel lifted her bottle, and they clinked. A "cheers" from one child of an absent father to another.

Rachel had been fifteen when she had last been at Camp Marigold. She and Fiona had decided that this summer, the one between their freshman and sophomore years of college, would be the perfect time to go back together. It would probably be the last fun summer they could have, the last time they wouldn't have to take on career-oriented internships or stay on campus during the summer to do research or take extra classes. At this point, neither of the girls knew what their careers would be, and they were holding on to that uncertainty for as long as they could.

Rachel couldn't exactly afford such a low-paying job as being a summer camp counselor, but her mother's waitressing gig had turned into a fairly lucrative second job, and she had encouraged Rachel to go back to Marigold one last time. Because she was still young. Because she'd worked so hard this year at Michigan between her work-study job and her full course load. Because it would make her happy. Denise was funny this way—she insisted she only wanted Rachel to be happy, but Rachel never knew when sacrifices her mother had made for her would be thrown back in her face.

Besides, Denise had reasoned, this was what loans were for. This was why they chose a public school, where the loans wouldn't be quite so debilitating. Postgraduation, Rachel would have her pick of jobs and pay them back in no time.

When they arrived back at Camp Marigold in Fiona's Jeep, elements of the place that Rachel hadn't thought about in years suddenly reintroduced themselves: the welcome sign, posted on a wooden placard at the camp's entrance, with marigolds painted a chipped orange and the ridiculous slogan (CAMP MARIGOLD: GROW WHERE YOU ARE PLANTED); the crunching of loose gravel underneath the car's tires; the strong smell of the fresh manure from the horse stables coming through the car's open windows. Rachel couldn't deny the immediate comfort and ease that came with the return to a place where it seemed like nothing had changed.

Of course, it was different being there as a nineteen-year-old. They were now the counselors, whose lives they had been only peripherally aware of as campers. The international counselors had always been there, the Australians and the Brits and the Spaniards and the Israelis, but now, as a counselor herself, Rachel learned what they were really like. They were uniformly adventurous types: partiers and drinkers or, at the very least, adrenaline junkies. They came through agencies, which took most of their already low salaries but paid for their plane tickets and gave them their chance to come to summer camp, that fantastically American tradition. For many, like Chad, it was their first time in America. He had come straight from JFK to Lakeville, Connecticut.

"Is New York City like it is in *Friends*?" Chad now asked Rachel as they sat around the bonfire.

"No one normal in New York would live in an apartment that big," said Fiona.

"What about *Seinfeld*?" Chad asked.

"I guess that's more realistic, yeah," Rachel said. "I don't watch it that much."

"I just love it," he said. "The humor is so New York."

"You mean Jewy?" Rachel asked.

Yonatan snickered.

The most Jewy thing about Rachel was her last name, Rivkin, and her *bubbe,* with whom she ate bagels in her house in Flatbush every other Saturday when she was growing up.

"You should come visit me in Tel Aviv, Rachel," Yonatan said, still picking at his guitar. "You would love it."

As Chad asked more questions about "real" life in New York, Yonatan began playing some songs Rachel recognized. He knew every word to "Redemption Song" by Bob Marley, and after a certain point, they stopped talking to listen to him sing in a charming Israeli-cum-Jamaican accent, totally engrossed in the lyrics ("How long shall they kill our prophets while we stand aside and look?").

When he was finished, they clapped politely. Yonatan seemed embarrassed. He put his guitar down.

"It's so hot," Rachel said, wiping at her warm face. "Anyone want to go swimming?"

Before they could respond, she lifted her shirt over her head, unbuttoned her shorts, and left them in a pile in the sand. She ran toward the water in her bra and underwear. She knew what she was provoking when she undressed fast and publicly like this, but she didn't, that night, have any end goal. Knowing that there were glances on her—that was enough. She kept going once her ankles hit the water—it felt warmer at night—and she swam out into the lake until she could float on her back and see only stars.

For a while, they left her there alone. The sounds of their conversation traveled clearly across the water. The boys were talking about soccer and the upcoming World Cup.

She thought of childhood summers on this lake. Night swimming when she would sneak out of her tent and meet boys there; they would kiss in the water and then roll around on the beach, the sand sticking to their wet bodies. She'd lost her virginity on this beach at fifteen years old to a seventeen-year-old junior counselor named Andy. After that summer ended, they never spoke again.

The clarity of the sky out here never ceased to amaze her.

She dipped under the surface of the water and then swam toward the dock. She pushed the upper half of her body against it and looked toward the group sitting around the fire, the orange embers of it crackling and slowly dying.

"Fiona!" she yelled. "Come in!"

Fiona waved from the circle. This summer, there was less room for spontaneity with her friend than there used to be. Rachel knew it had to do with Fiona's very minor, slightly noticeable weight gain. Everyone gained a little weight at college, but Fiona brought it up so often, making continual self-deprecating comments about her body that Rachel was tired of having to quell. Fiona called herself fat all the time, which was far from true; Rachel had little patience for that sort of self-pity.

"You guys are no fun," Rachel said, but she wasn't sure if they heard her.

———

Rachel wrapped her arms around herself as she walked from the lake to the fire. The sand felt cold on her bare feet. She tried to hide her shivers as she stood for a moment air-drying her body at the dying fire in her bra and underwear, noticing the clandestine glances from all three of them. Then she put her clothes back on and walked up to girls' camp with Fiona.

"What do you think of Yonatan?" Fiona asked.

"I think he's sweet," said Rachel. She also thought that he was handsome, but she could tell that he was the kind of smart, modest guy who didn't believe a girl like her would be interested in him. He probably thought that for her to date or even hook up with him would be playing against type. "Why?"

"I don't know," Fiona said. "Well, he asked if I would save a dance for him on Friday."

"That's cute, Fee!" Rachel feigned her best impression of enthusiasm. "What did you say?"

"I said yes," Fiona said. "I think. I was sort of embarrassed."

"You're adorable." Rachel put her arm around her friend. "You should hook up with him. That would be so exotic."

"I don't know if I can handle anyone seeing me naked right now."

Sometimes she hated this about Fiona, couldn't indulge her constant insecurities. Rachel wanted Fiona to understand how great she was: smart and insightful and loyal and kind. But explaining this over and over to her never seemed to work.

"That's the most ridiculous thing I've ever heard," Rachel said without a hint of sympathy, and Fiona did not argue with this.

———

It was a Monday morning, and the girls in Rachel's tent woke up excited. It was a new week of activities, many of which they had signed up for because they were coed. According to Rachel's rule, Wednesday was the last possible day the boys could ask them to the dance. It was go time.

At flag raising, Rachel watched the boys and girls making eyes at each other. Helen was far flirtier than Fiona ever was, but still so young. Prepubescent. She was interested in boys for the attention, not for the actual physical component of a relationship. Sheera seemed to be uninterested altogether. Sarah, with her newly D-cup breasts, had attention lavished on her by the more confident boys without much of a choice on her part.

Jack, the camp director, stood next to the American flag. He was probably in his early forties and had a certain masculine confidence. He was one of those men who seemed so traditional about gender roles, so insistent on the boys standing on one side during flag raising and the girls on the other, insistent that all the female counselors wear one-piece bathing suits, as if the infiltration of a woman's sexuality would cause mayhem and upset the order of everything. But he was handsome: tall, with tan, muscular legs and graying chest hair peeking out from the neck of his T-shirt. She'd never been with an older man; it was a bucket-list kind of thing. That spring she'd developed a crush on her married English professor, who taught pre-nineteenth-century American literature, an otherwise insufferably boring course. She hadn't acted on it, though. Married was one boundary she wouldn't cross. Jack, she knew, was divorced.

After they said the Pledge of Allegiance, the campers and counselors walked to the dining hall for breakfast. Rachel noticed Helen, who had been standing near her at flag raising, dart ahead to catch up with the boys.

"Mikey!" Helen called after him. "Wait up!" Rachel almost laughed at Helen's overt enthusiasm.

Mikey stopped for a moment, standing among the moving hordes of hungry kids until Helen caught up to him, smiling. Her smile, with its twinge of girlish flirtation, redeemed her overexcitement.

Helen walked next to Mikey with her arm purposely grazing his. But Mikey looked distracted, and Rachel followed his glance over to Sheera, who was walking near Sarah and the other girls in their tent, albeit slightly apart from them. Sheera was from the city, like Rachel, which gave one immediate bonus points at a mostly suburbanite-attended camp. She seemed to be straddling the line between wanting to fit in with the girls and wanting nothing to do with them, and they seemed to be trying to figure out the same with her.

So Mikey liked Sheera, Rachel realized. He was looking at her for just a beat too long for it to be otherwise.

After breakfast, Rachel's thoughts wandered back to her father. When she woke up, she'd felt okay, but as the new day settled, she let the gravity of the news sink into her bones, and it felt so heavy, so oppressive, that she found herself unable to say much at all.

Rachel and Fiona fed and washed the horses. Rachel's

mind was on one thing now, and that was the thing she wouldn't discuss. She knew that Fiona was sensitive enough to think Rachel's quietness had something to do with Fiona herself—maybe something minor Fiona had said or done—but Rachel didn't have the emotional energy to clarify the reason for it.

All morning, they led girls and bored horses around the fenced-in arena. Rachel and Fiona took the horses out for a longer trail ride during lunch. In the afternoon, Rachel taught older riders how to jump over bales of hay. They fed the horses again before dinner.

Over spaghetti and meatballs, Helen observed, "You're so quiet today, Rachel."

"I'm just tired," she said.

And at lights-out, much to the girls' disappointment, she skipped roses and thorns in order to make it to the computer lab faster to call her mom.

Since she hadn't heard anything yet, she knew things were more or less the same. But as she dialed the number, she felt a strange sense of hope bubble up inside her.

"Any news?" Rachel asked as soon as her mother answered.

"Hey, hon," Denise said. "He's stable. But he hasn't woken up."

"What does that mean, 'stable'?" Rachel asked. "That sounds sort of good?"

"They have him hooked up to life support because his heart is too weak to work on its own."

"Oh," Rachel said. She twirled the telephone wire around her finger. "Do they think it will start working again?"

Her mother paused on the other end of the line.

"Mom?"

"No, honey," she said. "They don't."

Rachel was standing outside the computer lab as Fiona came down the hill toward the staff lodge.

"Hey, hot stuff," Fiona called. "Wait up."

Rachel didn't move. Her arms were wrapped around herself, the summer breeze chilling her.

Fiona approached and looked into Rachel's face as she got closer. Rachel felt on the verge of crumpling, and tears were pooling in her eyes, like they would spill over if she moved just an inch, and all control would be lost.

"Come here," Fiona said, and took her friend into her arms. "That's it," she said to Rachel, stroking her hair. "Let it out."

Later, they sat down at the base of their favorite tree—the huge elm in the center of the flag lawn—and Rachel told her everything.

"How did you guys find out?" Fiona said.

"*She* called my mom. She thought we should know."

"Wow," Fiona said. "That was nice, I guess."

"I don't know why everyone keeps saying that," Rachel said. "He's my dad. Of course I should know."

A few British counselors passed by, noticing Rachel and Fiona.

"All right, girls?" one of them asked.

"We're fine," Fiona said in an overly cheery voice.

After the Brits went into the staff lodge, Rachel said, "I feel sad but like that's not how I'm supposed to feel."

"I don't think there's any 'supposed to' here," Fiona said, making air quotes.

"He cut me out of his life. Him dying doesn't change anything now." Rachel wiped away a rogue tear. "It should be just like any other day."

"Yeah, but, it does change things," Fiona said. "Death is not just not talking to someone. It's more real than that. It's final. You know?"

"I guess," Rachel said. "I guess until now I thought they were the same."

The girls stood and went into the staff lodge to find themselves some beers.

By the end of the day on Wednesday, only Sarah had been asked to the dance, by Danny Sheppard; the rest of the girls in Rachel's tent were dateless.

So on Thursday, Helen went ahead and asked Mikey herself. He seemed confident but mostly clueless in regard to girls; Rachel had noticed how he kept looking at Sheera at flag raising and free time without saying anything to her. He didn't ask Sheera to the dance, and so Helen, with her flirty smile, plucked him up first.

Helen was parading her dresses around the tent at bedtime, deciding which she'd wear to the dance the following night. She held a red polka-dot dress against her skinny body.

"Should I wear this one?" she asked, and then held up a hot-pink tube dress. "Or this one?"

"Mikey was my canoeing partner the other week," Sheera said. Rachel could not tell if Sheera's tone was genuinely innocent or meant to challenge Helen.

But Helen didn't miss a beat. "Yeah," she said. "I heard it was 'cause he didn't have a choice."

For hours on Friday, the girls primped in the bathroom with curling irons and straighteners, blue eye shadow and glitter lotion, perfume that smelled like cotton candy. Helen had never straightened her hair before, so Sarah did it for her—first blow-drying Helen's wet curls upside down, then drying each section with a paddle brush, then mechanically clamping and gliding the straightening iron over the entire head of blond frizz. In the end, Helen's hair was sleek and at least two inches longer, with a severe part down the middle. She wore the hot-pink tube dress.

Sarah borrowed the red polka-dot dress, which was too tight over her chest, and Sheera wore a simple black dress that fit her well. Rachel also was wearing black. As the girls began to leave for the dance, Rachel slipped a Poland Spring bottle filled with vodka—left over from their most recent night off—into her tote bag.

"You can never go wrong with an LBD," Rachel said to Sheera as they left the tent.

Sheera looked back at Rachel blankly.

"Little black dress?"

"Oh."

"I mean you look great."

"Thanks," Sheera said. They chatted about their real lives as they walked down to the basketball courts where the event was taking place. They were both from New York. They were both from single-parent homes. Sheera went to a charter school in the Bronx that was near the magnet school Rachel had attended.

When they got to the courts, Top 40 music was playing from a set of speakers, and clumps of boys and girls were standing separately, not yet dancing. "Promiscuous girl," the song went, "you're teasing me. You know what I want, and I got what you need." Rachel and Sheera had fallen behind, and the rest of the girls from their tent were already standing on the courts with one another, shuffling their feet and pretending not to be waiting for their dates to approach.

"Don't you want to go out there?" Rachel asked.

"Okay," Sheera said, though she hesitated for a moment. Of course, Rachel knew, if Sheera *had* wanted to go out there, she already would have politely exited their conversation.

Sheera walked toward the dance and then turned briefly back to Rachel, waving, like a younger girl leaving her mother on the first day of school. Rachel felt sorry that, up until now, she hadn't tried to get to know Sheera.

She saw Fiona then, standing with the counselors from her section in a simple white halter dress made of linen. Very preppy, probably from J.Crew.

"Look at us," Rachel said as she approached. "The devil and the angel."

"That's fitting," Fiona said, and hugged her friend. "How are you doing?"

"Fine," Rachel said.

"No word yet?"

"No."

"Keep me posted?"

"Of course." Rachel stood back to appraise her friend. "You look great," she said, meaning it.

"Really?" Fiona said. She looked down and straightened out the skirt of her dress.

"Really," Rachel said. "Let's dance."

As Rachel and Fiona danced—with each other, with Chad, with some of the other counselors they were friendly with—Rachel often found her thoughts turning to her father, and as a knee-jerk reaction, she would look away, as if to look away from the memories, and her glance would land fondly on her girls, who were beginning to dance with the boys now, or on Jack walking around the perimeter of the basketball courts with his arms crossed, or on Yonatan, who was DJing the dance, playing music from his iPod.

Some of Yonatan's friends or campers would go over and say hi to him or request a song, and he would bop along as he humored them, but he seemed mostly interested in picking what songs played next himself. He could very easily have made a playlist for the dance and left the iPod playing on its own so he could enjoy himself, but he was clearly interested in curating the music live. Rachel was dancing and also watching him, so curious about who he was, what his life was like back in Israel, when she felt a soft hand on her

shoulder. She turned around to see Mo, the British woman
who was her boss, the head of the Hemlock section.

"Rachel," she said, "you have a phone call."

Mo was an uptight person, aloof. She kept Rachel at a
cold distance as if she were Rachel's supervisor in a stuffy
office setting, not at a summer camp.

"Rachel?" Fiona said, understanding as quickly as Rachel
did. "Should I come?"

Rachel shook her head, and she walked to the camp office
with Mo in silence. She wasn't sure if Mo knew exactly what
had happened or not, but she was suddenly grateful for Mo's
silence. As they ascended the hill, the gleeful talk of children
and the blaring pop music receded while the truer sounds of
summer resurfaced: the birds chirping at one another from
their treetops, the evening breeze sighing over the high grass.
It was as if she and Mo were walking onto a higher, more
peaceful plane. If only for a moment, the landscape made
Rachel feel at ease. It was an ease that felt like the calm,
knowing moment before a downpour, when the leaves on the
trees turn upward and the clouds roll in and you know you
have a few minutes to find shelter. An ease entirely at odds
with what she was on her way to do: pick up the phone and
learn that her father, who had disowned her three years earlier, was now actually, heart-stoppingly dead.

When Rachel was fourteen, she didn't want to spend time
with either of her parents. She had started high school and
had begun to discover the joy of getting sexual attention, the

way it made her feel instantly powerful. Boys were such a quick fix. There had been a "Piece of Ass" list that went around the cafeteria during her first week of high school, with a list of the five hottest girls from each grade. She ranked as number two in her freshman class of four hundred girls. How easy it was to pretend to be offended.

Some weekend in the fall, not long after September 11, she and her father went for a hike an hour upstate.

"I wanted to take you out of the city," he explained in the car. Rachel was annoyed; she had been asked to go to the movies that day with an eleventh-grade boy.

"With everything that's been happening," he said, "I think it's healthy. Don't you?"

"I guess."

"I try to convince your mother to move to the suburbs. I think it would be better for you both."

"We would never leave the city."

"I know."

He exited the highway, and they drove onto a winding road that wrapped around and ascended the side of the mountain. About halfway up, he pulled into an inconspicuous dirt parking lot off the side of the road.

"Here we are!" he joked. "Hike's over!"

She didn't laugh.

"I'm kidding," he said. "This is where our trail starts."

He wasn't a healthy man by any means, and it was unusual for him to suggest something active for them to do together; meals and "cultural" activities, like going to museums or the theater, were much more the norm. He had a solid paunch around his middle and still smoked a pack a day, as he had been doing since he was a teenager. He was almost sixty now, and when he and Rachel went to dinners, he always ordered some sort of red meat and glass after glass of red wine, which he slugged back like it was water. So it was strange—sweet and a little sad—to see him in his version of active wear now: Adidas gym pants with the white stripes down the side, some sort of spandex-looking T-shirt that clung too much to his extra weight, and what looked like brand-new sneakers. He was carrying a backpack that was way too big for the two-mile hike they were about to embark upon. Rachel was used to seeing him dressed in an expensive suit.

"I brought sandwiches," he said.

They climbed mostly in silence. Once they got onto the trail, Rachel did not think as much about what she was missing in the city. She would not admit that it was, indeed, nice to get out. She was in good shape from field hockey, but her father often needed to stop, sit on a rock, and drink from his water bottle.

"I'm good. I'm good," he'd say after a minute, pressing himself back to standing.

When they got to the top, he poured some water over his head, like a football player who had just gotten off the field.

They sat on a boulder overlooking the Hudson River.

"That's Bear Mountain." Her father pointed to the other side. "See, there's the ice-skating rink. I took you there once, when you were really little."

"I don't remember."

"Your mom was with us." Rachel wondered, as she imagined the scene, which she didn't remember, if he had been nervous that day, taking his second family around so close to his first. Then Rachel realized he'd probably planned it all out; he'd made sure he knew where his real family would be that day so as to not run into them.

He took out the sandwiches from a white plastic bag in his backpack. "Turkey and pastrami on a roll, lettuce, tomato, mustard, banana peppers." He handed it to her.

She couldn't remember the last time they'd eaten deli sandwiches. "You didn't even ask if my order was the same."

"Is it?" A look of panic crossed his face.

She kept a straight face for a beat and then broke into a smile. "Yeah," she said. He smiled back.

They ate their sandwiches with their feet dangling in front of them, like children. The mountainside sloped dramatically beneath them, with thorny brambles and miles of woods leading all the way down to the Hudson. Across the way was the quaint Bear Mountain Bridge, with its drawbridge and its two lanes, and beyond it a range of blue and green mountains. A large tugboat was pulling a much smaller motorboat along the murky river.

He took another bite of his roast beef sandwich, chewed thoroughly, and swallowed.

"So," he said. "Your mother tells me you're starting to date."

Rachel glanced at her father and then fixed her gaze on the mountains ahead. "She doesn't know anything about me."

"I highly doubt that, my dear." He patted her knee. "She probably knows you better than you know yourself."

"Don't call me that." She moved her knee away. Sometimes this sensation of hot anger roiled inside her, even when she was having a fine time. She couldn't say where it came from, only that there was some sort of disconnect between what she wanted and what was happening in front of her. The mountains, the river, those were all fine, but it was this—this man next to her, her father, who could take her on a hike and memorize her sandwich order and call her pet names and yet had to be back home, back to his other home, by sundown.

"She's an intuitive woman, your mother," he continued. "She feels so much."

He looked so pathetic in those brand-new sporty clothes. The anger was alive; she could feel it wanting to erupt out of her.

"Where does your wife think you are right now?" Rachel asked, her face hot. She had never asked this before; that was part of the unspoken deal.

He swallowed again, his Adam's apple rising and falling. "What?"

"It's a Saturday. I can't remember the last time I saw you on a Saturday."

He bunched the wax paper from his sandwich into a ball. He took a deep breath.

"Golf," he said quickly and quietly. "But, Rachel, sweetie, there's no need to—"

"Don't call me 'sweetie.'"

He took another deep breath. "Sorry. Rachel. I don't think this is good for you, talking about this."

"How would you have any idea about what is good for me?"

He stood. "I think we should start heading back."

"You're just not going to talk to me about this?"

Now the anger was coming in its other form: that familiar wave of fragility that caused her voice to crack and tears to form despite her most intense efforts to make them stop.

"How come you're so ashamed of me?" she asked.

He shook his head and looked at Rachel with such sadness. It wasn't empathy; it wasn't like he could feel how she felt or was even trying to. It was pity. Like he was very, very sorry for her.

He put his hand out. "It's time to go."

She swatted his hand away and spent a few more moments facing the mountain landscape, though she wasn't looking at much of anything. She focused only on making the tears stop, on pulling herself out of the moment, so that she could get back down the mountain and get home and never have to think about this again.

When she was ready, she pushed herself up off the rock and began to walk in the direction of the trail. She watched her feet, putting one step in front of the other as she went down the rocky path. Her father followed behind her silently. He drove her back to the city, news radio playing through the car's speakers and neither of them talking over it.

———

When Rachel got back to the dance, she saw Fiona standing with some of the other counselors from her section. Fiona didn't notice that Rachel had returned. Yonatan was now playing an Israeli pop song, and the kids were surprisingly into it, letting loose, holding hands, jostling one another around the makeshift dance floor. Rachel went over to him.

"Who is this?" she asked.

Yonatan looked surprised to see her and then collected himself and said some Hebrew band name she'd never remember. She tucked a piece of hair behind her ear.

"Are you having fun?" she asked.

"Yeah!" He bopped his head in time to the music. "Are you?"

She shrugged. "It's fine," she said.

She grazed her fingertips over his shoulder, realizing only once the contact had been made that her brain had, somewhere below her consciousness, made the command: "Pick up hand. Touch shoulder with fingers."

"Do you want a drink?" she asked.

"Huh?"

Rachel took out the Poland Spring water bottle she'd been keeping in her bag. "It's vodka."

He laughed. He grabbed the water bottle from her and took a tiny sip. His face puckered at the taste of it as if he had just sucked on a lemon.

She took a sip herself and felt that familiar burning in her lungs. This was her MO, carrying vodka around in Poland Spring bottles: to high school dances, to college football games. When she got to Michigan, she had realized that the other girls mixed vodka with juice or with Crystal Light packets, and without her trying, the undiluted alcohol had become her trademark.

"Hold your nose," she said, and he briefly looked around the dance to make sure no one was watching, then took one more sip, doing as he was told.

He opened his mouth wide and let out a loud breath through it, like a lion exhaling.

"That is brutal," he said.

"Brutal!" she laughed. "Your American slang is improving."

He smiled at her. It was a slow smile of recognition, as if he was beginning to realize that he knew her or could grow to know her.

Then Yonatan turned away and put on an American song that everyone could sing along to. "I remember when . . . I remember, I remember when I lost my mind." Even the counselors at the dance were becoming more relaxed, more fun. Both Chad and Jack were dancing innocently with the shyer girls. Jack held one of Sheera's hands and spun her under his arm. It was the first time Rachel had seen such unabashed happiness come from the girl. Fiona was dancing in a clump with the girls from her section. She still had not noticed that Rachel was back, and Rachel was glad for it. Fiona was as close a friend to Rachel as any, but not close enough to eradicate the loneliness Rachel felt in this moment. When Yonatan turned back around and faced Rachel, she took his hand and began to dance with him. She swayed her hips left and right. "Who do you, who do you, who do you think you are?" They were only attached by their hands, but those two hands were a bridge, a now-permissible connection between them. She had given him, with her hand, permission to look at her the way he was now—his eyes suddenly open to the possibility that maybe they could, maybe they would.

He could dance, Yonatan. He had an innate sense of rhythm and a suggestive way about him as he moved, a confidence in his loose limbs. He was a musical person, and so it made sense that the music was a vessel for his sensuality that had, until now, been calmly, quietly hidden away. He took his free hand and put it in Rachel's hair—not long enough for anyone else to notice, but long enough to graze her scalp, to comb his fingers just once through the waves.

It gave her chills. Without thinking, she gestured for Yonatan to follow her and, leaving the iPod to play by itself, led him to the athletic shed, which sat just at the edge of the woods, about fifty yards away from the basketball courts.

She pulled the door open easily; nothing was ever locked at this camp. Yonatan looked behind them before they walked into the shed. No one saw. But they could so easily have gotten caught, at an event where the entire camp was present. That was part of the fun.

She closed the door and pushed him up against it. He responded eagerly, grabbing her whole head of hair in his hands. He kissed her tenderly, but in response, she pushed her mouth hard against his, biting his bottom lip.

"Ow," he said.

She didn't apologize but kept kissing him—more aggressively than she normally kissed—and reached into his pants.

It was larger than she had expected, and the discovery thrilled her.

"You're so big," she said into his ear, biting that too. "I want you to fuck me like an animal." She was a petite girl, and sex hurt her easily.

He pulled away and looked at her. She could tell that she was more than he could handle. She was a handful, especially now, and his face reflected it: surprise and apprehension.

"Rachel, I don't know if we should."

"You don't want to fuck me?"

"I do, I do." He kissed her once, tender again. "You just . . . you seem not okay tonight."

"I'm great," she said, and took his hand and put it between her legs.

They held each other with their hands, grinding and moaning. She wanted to feel only the physical, and her whole body ached with it, with the buildup toward something better than the now. She wanted to feel him inside her, and she wanted it to hurt.

She was pushing her underwear to her ankles, about to take him in, when a light from the outside cracked into the dark shed. The door creaked, and Rachel first saw only the outline of two younger people as she opened her eyes. Two young outlines holding hands.

Rachel pushed away from Yonatan as he scrambled to tuck himself back into his pants. She pulled up her underwear and straightened her dress.

"What are you doing?" Rachel said to Helen, standing in

front of Yonatan to shield his nakedness from the girl, though it was, of course, too late.

Helen had dropped Mikey's hand. The two children stood there waiting for the adults to say something else.

"Mikey," Yonatan said, putting on a deep counselor voice and stepping out from behind Rachel, "go back to the dance."

"We weren't—" Mikey began. "We were just . . ." He trailed off. Helen looked as if she was about to cry. As both counselors took in the desperation in her eyes, Yonatan seemed to realize that this moment was no longer his.

"Mikey," Yonatan said more sternly now. "Come with me." He guided Mikey out of the shed to return to the dance, saying something hushed to the boy as they walked away. Mikey turned back to offer Helen a helpless glance.

It was hard to tell if Helen was the type to tattle. She was so very much a girl still: a girl who was leaving a dance to fool around with a boy, yes, but still a girl. The look of shock and fear on her face suggested that what she had seen was far beyond her own desires and perhaps even beyond her own understanding. They had probably escaped to the shed only for the excitement that came from sneaking around. They were probably just going to make out. Yonatan, a grown man, had literally been holding himself in his hands. What, for this girl who thought playing four square counted as foreplay, who didn't need to wear a bra yet, could be more earth-shattering than that?

"Helen," Rachel said. "Please just do one thing for me."

"I won't tell anyone," Helen said, shaking her head back and forth as if she could shake the memory right out of it.

"Me neither," said Rachel. "But especially, please, *please* don't tell Fiona."

Helen wiped a rogue tear away. "Does she like him?"

Rachel nodded. She thought of Fiona's arms around her under the oak tree. Fiona asking Rachel if she wanted her to come for the phone call. Fiona, whom she was still hiding from. Fiona saying she couldn't handle anyone seeing her naked.

"Of course I won't," Helen said.

They walked back to the basketball courts in silence. Fiona, finally seeing Rachel, rushed toward them.

"I've been looking for you," Fiona said to her friend. "Should we go somewhere?" Fiona noticed her sister's stricken face and put on her own forlorn and sympathetic expression. "Did she tell you?"

Helen panicked, unsure what she was supposed to say or what exactly Fiona was referring to, and looked to Rachel for support.

"Give us a minute," Rachel said to Helen. Helen did as she was told, ambling unsurely toward the group of girls her age.

Fiona put an arm on Rachel's shoulder. "Do you want to talk? What can I do?"

Rachel shook her head. "Nothing," she said. "I just want to dance."

7

John and Amy Larkin drove up Route 22 for Visitors' Day. It was a clear, sunny morning, and Amy was surprised by how tired she was. As they drove, she realized that she hadn't been up before ten since they'd dropped Helen off at camp three weeks earlier. Her body should have still awoken at six like clockwork given all the mornings over all the years making breakfasts and shuttling the kids to school. But every summer, once the kids were gone, she could not stop sleeping. She'd hear John's alarm go off, roll over, and fall back asleep, only to reawaken some hours later to the late morning sun drenching her in its warmth. She wouldn't get up right away; sometimes she would spend another hour in bed just watching the sun fall through the window. On these late mornings, she felt like a girl waking up in her mother's bed—too small to have this thing all to herself and yet luxuriating in the feeling that this was a special occasion, that this could not happen on just any morning.

Her days were spent alone, planting flowers in the garden at home and then, later in the afternoons, driving to the community garden in town, where her vegetables grew, to harvest her cucumbers and tomatoes. Dinner was usually something simple, like a piece of salmon and a caprese with heirlooms and buffalo mozzarella. Sometimes John came home on time. Sometimes he did not tell her until the last minute that he wouldn't make it for dinner. It had been like this on occasion when the kids were around, but it happened even more when Amy was the only one home. She never told him that this bothered her.

She had packed thermoses of coffee for John and herself for the drive, and she was guzzling hers. John had tuned the radio to jazz. He was doing that annoying thing, humming along to a song even though he had no idea where the tune was going. Amy had long ago stopped telling him about the things he did that annoyed her. She'd known John since she was nine, and now she was forty-six; she knew every one of his habits and tics, as spouses in most marriages did, but the difference was that Amy had watched those tics grow as he did. Now the humming, which was once a boyish quirk, had developed into a full-blown grown man's assertion of himself. It was his way of taking up space in the car.

As they wound along the highway, she noted the breadth of trees flanking both sides of the road. There were no towns or even buildings in sight. Just trees. How quickly they had found themselves in the country. She felt a hint of jealousy of

Helen, of her daughter's still-intact childhood. She still got to attend camp, got to escape every summer, got to be a girl.

As soon as Amy drained the last of her coffee, she realized how urgently she had to pee.

"Honey, can we pull over?"

"We'll be there in half an hour," John said, his eyes on the road.

"I can't wait half an hour."

"You can't hold it?"

"No."

John sighed. "You and your tiny bladder." He did not say this affectionately. John had not learned to let go of trivial annoyances in the same way that Amy had. "I haven't seen any signs yet for rest stops."

Amy hadn't either, and she waited patiently, with her thighs pressed against each other, until she saw a blue sign with the stick figure drawings of a man and a woman and the block letters EXIT 31 over it.

"Exit 31," Amy said, pointing to the sign. "Five miles."

"I see it," John said.

In five miles, Amy made a conscious effort not to point out the sign again, and John remembered to take Exit 31, turning the wheel sharply around the tightly curving road.

They ended up at a stoplight and a T where their road met a perpendicular two-lane country road. There were no further signs for a rest stop.

"Turn right," Amy said.

"How do you know?"

"I just have a feeling."

John looked at her suspiciously. But he made the turn anyway.

They passed patches of thick woods, no people or homes in sight, followed by open expanses of farmland. Amy wasn't sure whether they were in New York or Connecticut at this point.

"Where are we?" John said, as if hearing her thoughts. He leaned over the steering wheel and looked out at the road and at the next farm they passed, with its red barn and silver silo towering over it.

"Beats me," she said.

They drove for a few more minutes, still not seeing a gas station or any sort of public restroom.

"Cows!" Amy exclaimed as they drove by dozens of them grazing. "I'll take the brown ones; you take the ones with spots?"

He grunted. So he wasn't in the mood today.

"Ame, let's just pull over," he said, already pulling onto the side of the road near a lush patch of trees and bushes.

"No," she said, pushing her knees closer together. Her bladder pulsed.

"We are in the middle of bumfuck Connecticut and now at least ten minutes from the highway. No one is going to see you."

"It's embarrassing, John." She sounded like a little girl to herself, the way she whined. Why didn't he have to go? He'd had coffee too.

"Well," he said, sitting back in his seat. This was his move, the lean back, which signified that he was reserving his right, as the breadwinner and patriarch of the family, to make the final decision. Once he did the lean back, that infuriatingly stubborn move—arms folded, satisfied scowl on his face—there was no bargaining with him.

Amy sighed and poked through her purse for a packet of tissues. She took one from the pack and made her way, with a frown, out of the passenger door and around the back of the car.

He had pulled alongside a rough patch, which dropped steeply from the road, and she stepped carefully down to a more secluded area, snapping twigs under her feet as she went. She found herself surrounded by overgrown bushes and the thick trunks of trees with lush summer coverings of green leaves overhead. She arrived at a clearing behind a wide-based tree, which would shield her from the view of anyone on the road, and, with the hand holding the tissue, lowered her underpants to below her knees and lifted the hem of her dress with the other.

She exhaled as the stream of urine gushed out of her, splattering on the dirt between her feet. She heard a car driving along the road above.

"Shit." Her pee had started to make a puddle on the ground, and a few drops splattered back up her legs. As the stream began to slow, it trickled onto the inside of her thigh and down the length of her calf.

She wiped herself and tried to clean up the mess she'd made on her leg with the one tissue, wishing she had brought the pack with her.

She heard some sort of crunching in the leaves on the other side of the tree, and she had a mental glimpse of herself as someone else would see her: squatted, panties down, bare-assed. *God dammit, John.* She scrambled to right herself, pulling her underwear up and letting her dress down.

As she did so, she heard the crunching come closer, a light pattering along the floor of the grove.

"Hello?" she said. She was almost certain it was an animal, but what if it wasn't? What if this was her last moment on earth; how would John explain it to everyone? To the kids? Even within her trepidation, she felt something akin to satisfaction that her disappearance would be John's fault.

She approached the tree and peered around it to look in the direction of the pattering. The animal's ears were sticking up, and its black eyes were open wide. The deer had stopped moving, startled by Amy. It was just a baby, though no mother was in sight. She was so used to deer digging through her vegetable garden and eating her lettuce that she knew them only as nuisances. This felt different. She felt a sympathy, an instinctual sadness for the fawn, worrying that it had been separated from its mother. But what would she do if it had?

The fawn was standing only a few feet away from her. Amy looked into its black eyes, wondering whether it was a boy or a girl. She took one small step forward, testing it, seeing if it would run away. It just stared back, unfazed. She thought it was supposed to be afraid of her.

She heard another scampering and then saw a larger deer

approaching the fawn. The mother. Instantly the fawn turned and followed it, leaving Amy, who suddenly remembered that John was waiting in the car.

They arrived at camp half an hour later, as John had said they would. She probably could have held it.

They drove up the hill, past the stables, and to the parking lot below the flag lawn.

"Do you remember our first kiss under that tree?" she asked him as they parked, pointing to the elm tree on the lawn.

"Of course," he said, not romantically but matter-of-factly, as if he was almost offended by her asking. But she liked how he said it like that, as if implying, "How could I forget?"

She and John had met as campers when they were nine years old. They were both from Westchester, she from New Rochelle and he from Scarsdale (Scarsdale was only twenty minutes away from New Rochelle but infinitely fancier). He had been a skinny boy with a pale complexion and freckles who bought a cherry Popsicle from the canteen every day after lunch, which turned his lips and tongue a bright red. Before he had braces, he had buckteeth, and he was goofy with his friends, always giggling in a way that felt, before Amy could put words to it, both masculine and feminine. He was great at archery. He called her by her last name, like she was another one of the boys. Amy liked this: She had brothers, and so it made her feel at home, safe. She and John goofed around like this for three summers, and then when they returned for their fourth, when they were twelve, John had sprung four inches, and his voice had changed, taking away any scraps of that latent femininity. Amy's denim shorts and V-neck T-shirts clung differently, though it took a comment from a girlfriend ("That V is mighty deep, huh, Ame?") for her to realize she looked any different. She and John kissed under that elm tree that summer. They lost their virginities to each other two summers after that, in the oar house down by the lake, when they were fourteen (it sounded so scarily young now, and she took pause when she thought of her own daughters, thirteen and eighteen, almost nineteen). Amy thought about those times often, how simple it all was, how easily it all came to her.

People, when they heard their story, thought it was romantic. But she often wondered: *Did he fall in love with girl me and then fall out of love with adult me? Or is adult me still the same as girl me?* Both possibilities were depressing. Though she felt the second was more true and that he was both happy she had not changed and disappointed in her for it.

They had taken some time apart to date other people when they went away to college, but when they graduated, it was clear to the two of them that there was no other person with whom either wanted to spend a comfortable, reasonable life. They never fought, simply because it felt like they never had anything to fight about. John was a kind, moral person; and yes, he was occasionally stubborn about something like what movie they would see on a date or where they would go to dinner, but these were unimportant things: What did it matter where they went to dinner, anyway, so long as they were together? One boy she dated in college was something of the opposite: He let *her* make all the decisions, always saying something like "lady's choice" when she asked what they should do that night. Rather than provide her with a sense of autonomy, the pressure of being in charge filled her with dread. She much preferred it when her partner took control.

The break had made her want John more, and him her. Amy knew nothing about the girls he had dated in college, though her imagination of them caused intense amounts of jealousy and desire to build over the years she and John were apart. She had never seen him so excited to rip off her clothes as he was the first time they had sex after they got back together (and to her delight, he did literally rip them, popping a button off her blouse). And so she moved with him to D.C., where they knew no one, for him to attend law school there, and she took a job as a waitress at an upscale oyster bar in Capitol Hill. She was so good at that job; she could have done it forever. She could tell you the difference between each oyster on the menu—of which there were normally around two dozen, depending on the month—and not just which were larger and which were smaller, but she could also extoll the virtues of the sweet and meaty bluepoints or the tender, briny Malpeques. She could carry a tray of four martinis and place each one in front of its respective customer, remembering who had the twist and who had three olives, without so much as spilling a drop. She remembered the names of her regulars, and once they had begun to request her, she remembered the names of the grandchildren they gushed about too. At Christmas, she received store-bought greeting cards with cash inside.

She remembered one night before she was pregnant: It was after a particularly busy shift, and she was sitting at the bar drinking a white wine and organizing her credit-card receipts. There were a couple of older men on the stools around her, and her co-worker and friend Jill was tending bar.

"How'd you do tonight, Miss Fancy Pants?" Jill asked.

Amy tried to give a sly grin, though she was sure it didn't look as cool as she wanted it to. "I did okay."

Jill reached across the bar to refill Amy's glass. Jill was in her forties, with decades of restaurant experience, much like the other bartenders and servers. They'd made fun of Amy at first for being innocent and somewhat prissy—which, until then, she hadn't realized was the case. She hadn't known, for instance, that she was expected to roll silverware at the beginning of every shift, and this made the other servers take a slower liking to her than she would have hoped. But she proved herself quickly: She was small and fast; she had killer timing and killer instincts, always seeming to know exactly when that kitchen door was going to swing toward her.

"That husband of yours ever gonna come see you at work?" Jill asked.

"Nah," Amy said. "He knows this is my thing." The truth was she'd never invited him, and he'd never asked to come either.

Then law school was over, and Amy got pregnant, and John got a job at a New York law firm, and they bought a house in Westchester, and Amy's regulars gave her one last card before she left and patted her growing belly on the way out. She never did share the tips with him.

Amy and John walked up the hill to the Hemlock section, Amy relishing the memories this place produced, as she always did. This camp was a marker for all her firsts: a bunk in the Hemlock section, where Helen lived now, was where she'd woken up one August morning and found blood in her underwear; in the bathroom in the same section was where Jenny Smalls had coached her, from outside the bathroom stall, on how to put in her first tampon; and down in the oar house, that was where she had sex for the first time and where, a summer later, she had her first orgasm. Now those things felt so long ago. She did not want her girls to grow out of the camp life, because that would mean the end of their firsts too.

Helen's blond curls bounced as she bounded over to her parents. Physically, Liam was a miniature version of his father and Fiona an amalgamation of both parents, but Helen was all Amy. They had the same toothy, uninhibited smile, which John had said was one of the first things he noticed about Amy when they were kids: that she smiled no matter what was happening, even if it wasn't something particularly delightful. Helen, like Amy, gave her smiles away easily, to anyone and everyone. This made them both likeable people.

It had taken longer than it should have for Amy to learn that it also gave the impression that they were simple people.

"How's Dandelion?" Amy asked. "How's Josie?" These were Helen's and Fiona's horses, which the Larkins kept at camp during the summer. Amy missed spending time with them like she was able to during the school year. Now that Fiona was away at college, Amy had taken on the care of Josie as if she were her own, and she and Helen would go on rides together on weekend mornings. The Larkins had bought the horses for their girls because they could. This was the consolation that came with being married to a man who didn't touch you anymore but who did well: At least you could give your daughters what you never had.

"She's so good," Helen said. "There's a horse expo later, so you'll see everything I've been working on. I want to surprise you."

"Okay, sweetheart," Amy said, running a hand through her daughter's hair.

She then realized she had forgotten Helen's goodies in the car, things she thought Helen might miss: magazines, nail polish, and hair scrunchies; provisions such as peanut butter and ramen noodles; necessities like face wash and sunscreen.

John put an arm around Helen and playfully pulled her closer. Helen beamed as she looked up at her dad. Amy loved how much they loved each other, because she was their link; she had everything to do with it. She had chosen this man, and she had birthed this girl.

"I have a few things for you," Amy told Helen, still glowing at the sight of the two of them. "I guess we were so excited to see you, we forgot to bring them up." She turned to John. "Keys?" He nodded, reached into his pocket, and tossed them to her. She caught them effortlessly.

She walked back down the hill, smiling at the kids running ahead of their parents.

"Luke, slow down!" a man yelled. The woman next to him was cradling a tiny bundle to her breast. Amy could not stop herself from peeking into the sling as she passed. The baby's face was tiny, red, wrinkled. Fast asleep.

"How old is he?" Amy whispered to the mother.

The woman smiled, that tired smile exchanged only between mothers, which contained so much intrinsic knowledge, and happiness, and pain.

"Three weeks," the mother said. "It's a girl."

Liam was Amy's first, a baby with bright eyes who was so easy that he cried only when it was something Amy could easily fix and almost always slept through the night. At first, she did not understand all the fuss about babies being hard. But then came the girls: Fiona, who had an inquisitive, worrying face—such a serious girl—and who, between her third and fifth months, refused to be put down even once. When feeding her, when taking her out, even when puttering around the house, Amy had to be standing and holding Fiona in her arms and moving in a back-and-forth motion, or else Fiona's unhappiness would be irreparable, and Amy would have to pay for it in painful, deafening screams that could last for hours. And so she paid in constant, tireless attention and chronic low back pain instead. Fiona eventually got excited by her own crawling, an immense relief to Amy until the baby started eating paper and chewing on remote controls and drinking water from the toilet bowl.

Then long after Amy thought she was done—six years after—Helen came. She was not planned—this was when Amy and John still had sex—but how Amy loved being pregnant again, how she loved having a second girl, how she loved that she would have two daughters and they would be sisters. She had never had a sister of her own.

Yet her girls did not like each other. As a baby, Helen did not like anyone, in fact, except Liam. Helen would let herself be held by Amy only when she was feeding, and then she wanted to spend the rest of her time with her older brother, who doted on her so much that Amy worried for Helen's future with boys. There was no way to explain why she was smitten with Liam and yet so uninterested in Fiona, who wanted desperately to be Helen's friend. When Helen was six months old, Fiona wanted to bring her into her first grade class for show-and-tell, and Amy suspected how it would turn out, but she took the chance anyway—hoping, against the odds, to be proved wrong. At the entrance to the classroom, an excited Fiona, wearing a new pink dress, took Helen from Amy's arms carefully, the way she had been taught, holding Helen's butt with one hand and her head with the other.

Once she was transferred to her sister, Helen cried so passionately and flapped her arms and legs so violently that she literally wriggled herself out of Fiona's tenuous grip and fell, butt first, onto the linoleum floor. Fiona was still small, so Helen's fall to the ground was neither too far nor too hard, but it was enough to startle the baby, enough for her to stop, look up in that surprised, delayed way that children do, in the moment of confusion between being fine and being hurt, and then break into a stunning scream.

Amy took Helen home before Fiona could show her sister off. Helen would not stop crying. Amy fed her, changed her, sang to her, rocked her. She was inconsolable. Two hours later, Amy drove back to the school and had the principal call Liam, who was in third grade, out of his class. When he saw his crying sister, he very calmly sat down in the chair across from the principal's desk and put his arms out for Amy to place the baby in them. Helen fell asleep within minutes.

"Thanks, sweetie," Amy whispered, kissing Liam on the forehead and placing Helen gingerly into her carrier.

The whole drive home, with Helen fast asleep in the backseat, Amy wept quietly. She had never felt more useless.

Amy opened the trunk of their SUV and unloaded the shopping bags onto the ground. As she was about to close the trunk, she heard the distinct bleep of John's cellphone. Odd that he had left it in the car; he was always so connected to work, even on the weekends. But she thought perhaps he was trying to unplug by leaving it, and that thought was heartening to her.

She shut the trunk. She was walking away with the bags

when she stopped and thought, *Maybe John didn't mean to leave the phone in the car.* Maybe he'd meant to slip it into his pocket and had forgotten. It might be best to get it in case something important came up.

This was the narrative Amy was telling herself, though she knew she wasn't going back for the phone for John's professional well-being. She knew she was going back to check the thing that she never checked.

Amy opened the driver's-side door and looked at the display panel on the phone. It read, "Molly: One New Message." It was not the first time she'd seen this name pop up on John's phone. He thought Amy was so clueless that he didn't need to take any precautions to remain discreet. Or perhaps he simply didn't care.

But this time, she did not turn the phone over and pretend she hadn't seen the notification. This time, she opened the phone and read the message.

"Are you staying in Connecticut tonight?" it read.

Amy's heart pounded as her fingers rested on the keypad. Then she moved them along the keys, the answer coming to her quickly, thoughtlessly.

"Yes," she responded, though this was a lie. They would drive back to Larchmont when the day was over. "Don't wait up."

She hit SEND. She held the phone open, watching it, waiting for a response. It came fast.

":(Tomorrow night?"

Again, she did not hesitate. "Yes," she typed. "I'll say I have to work late." Sent.

"Okay :)" Molly responded.

Amy closed the phone fast and threw it across the car like it was too hot to hold. She had things to bring Helen, a day to spend with her daughter. She hoped Fiona would at least stop by and say hi. She carried the shopping bags up the hill.

And as she approached the section, she could see Fiona was already there, wearing her navy camp staff polo. John was standing at the entrance to Helen's tent, and the girls were standing close to each other, and—could Amy believe it?—they were laughing.

Fiona looked over and noticed her mother. "Mom!" She waved. Amy felt that uninhibited smile come on.

She placed the bags on the ground and approached the girls.

"Hi, sweetheart," she said to Fiona. "You look marvelous."

"I've missed you, Mom," Fiona said. She had not said that once during her first year of being away at college.

"I've missed you too," Amy said. She put an arm around each of her girls' shoulders and kissed each of their foreheads and held them close to her breast.

Since she was a teen, she had been afraid of what had, long ago, become true: that she could, at any moment, lose her luster. That for John, she could so easily become old news.

8

There was something rebellious in Nell that Mo did not have an iota of in herself. Nell did not do things because she was supposed to; she just did what she wanted. She decided very quickly whom she liked and whom she didn't and never pretended otherwise. She did not buy into the scene at the staff lodge where, every night after lights-out, the counselors made out with one another and in front of one another on the seedy couches, drank cans of cheap beer, and filled the basement with clouds of smoke. Sometimes Mo went to be social, but often Nell convinced her to do things as just the two of them, like walk down to the lake with bottles of beer.

One evening, with their bottles of Heineken—which they'd bought on their day off and hidden in the back of one of the kitchen's industrial fridges—they sat with their denim shorts in the sand and their feet in the temperate, murky

water. On their third beers—more than they usually drank—
Nell began to talk about her life at home. They were about
four weeks into camp, though as Nell began to talk about
her conservative parents, about the oppressive boarding
school she had attended, Mo realized how little they had
told each other about their outside lives. What they had
bonded over was their Englishness, their newness to the
camp, their love of horses, and, perhaps most profoundly,
the feeling Mo had that both of them didn't really belong
there. They were different somehow, not just because they
were foreign or new—because plenty of the counselors were
foreign or new—but because they both, for reasons Mo
couldn't quite explain, couldn't assimilate into the Camp
Marigold universe.

Nell was explaining how her parents had tried to put her
on an antidepressant a couple of months earlier.

"It was all a secret, of course," she said in her posh accent, and took a swig of her beer. "They're too upper-crust
for anything like that to get out."

"What was wrong?"

"I was 'unstable' after graduating school," she said, using
her fingers to make quotation marks in the air. "And my A
levels weren't good enough to get into any uni they liked."

"So you're not going to uni?" Mo asked.

"I am," Nell said. "Just not to one they think is good
enough."

Nell looked like a classic beauty—long red hair, porcelain
skin, thin but curvy—but didn't act like one. She was dis-
dainful of other pretty girls, as if she didn't know she was

one of them, and of men too, like they all had some agenda she wasn't buying into. She had a dirty mouth, and Mo, who was in charge of the section of thirteen-year-old girls, often had to remind Nell, the head horseback-riding counselor, to watch herself in front of the campers. Mo wasn't actually sure what had appealed to Nell about working with kids to begin with or if she had just come to the camp to get away from a life back home.

"What does that mean, 'unstable'?" Mo asked.

"I cried a lot. Even when I felt fine, I couldn't stop," Nell said. "And then after crying all day, I would go out, drink too much"—she lifted her bottle—"and go home with someone. Then same thing all over again the next day. You know."

Mo nodded, though she didn't know.

"So this was my solution." She swept a hand toward the lake and toward the camp behind them. "I never took the medications. Threw them in the trash."

"And what do you think? Did it work?" Mo asked, already half-knowing the answer.

"Camp? I don't know. I'd hardly say it's won me over."

The next morning, Mo left her bunk sometime before dawn and went down to the stables. She had to move slowly in the darkness down the sloping hill from girls' camp. She cut across the athletic fields, thick with unkempt dandelions and slick with midsummer dew, to the red-roofed barn.

She normally did not ride in the early mornings, as she didn't like to deprive Micah of any sleep before his full days with rowdy kids. But she had stirred in her bunk all night, the anxiety of the approaching day resting heavily on her, and this was, and always had been, the only way to alleviate such anxieties. Today, she had a certain impression to make: that her girls were happy and well fed, active but staying out of trouble. She had to meet parents and be much more gregarious than was her nature.

She saddled Micah, who was waking slowly, and led him outside into the lightless morning. It was miraculous, riding's immediate effect on her: the slackening of her limbs, the slowing of her heartbeat, and the deepening of her breathing; even the full return of her senses—the realizations of the smells of fresh hay and the loamy arena and Micah's lemon-scented, freshly washed coat, of the feel of the firm but supple leather reins between her fingers.

Most of the kids at Camp Marigold didn't like riding Micah. He was a brown dun past his prime, and he looked stocky and dull next to the sprightly, shiny Thoroughbreds. The unskilled and impatient riders found him stubborn; the rich ones found him common. But Mo took a liking to Micah and he to her. She'd been riding since she was a child, but she had never been a prizewinner; she felt sure that Micah had never been one either.

She looked across the arena to the dining hall painted the same burnt red as the barn and beyond to the beginnings of the trails leading to boys' camp and the lake. In the distance were the Berkshires with their fleshy treetops, the mountains rounded against the now dark blue sky. Mo had heard about a lot of beautiful places in her life, but no one had ever mentioned Connecticut.

She was lost in her thoughts until she spotted Jack, the camp director, jogging up the hill below the stables and waving as he got closer. She sat upright and brought Micah to a halt. Mo waved back to Jack, then began to trot Micah to the barn so she could put him in his pen and return to girls' camp before she needed to explain herself. But Jack continued toward them, then stopped at the fence and beckoned her over.

"Morning, Mo," he said, cheerful and out of breath, leaning against the fence for support.

"Hiya, Jack," Mo said. "Have a good run?"

"Mmm." He stretched a calf against the wooden fence's bottom rung. Jack was in his forties and handsome. He had a head of thick graying hair that he was always running a hand through.

"And who's this?" he asked, outstretching his hand above the fence to pet between Micah's ears. The horse leaned into the touch.

"This is Micah," Mo said, hopping down. "I hope it's all right I'm out. I'll get back before anyone wakes up."

"Yes, yes, of course. Alone time is important, Mo." He kept his eyes on the horse, scratching the top of its head. "Hi, Micah," he cooed.

"He's a sweet boy," Mo said.

Jack often played poker or billiards in the staff lodge with the younger counselors; he clearly wanted to establish himself as some sort of cool avuncular figurehead by drinking and staying up late with them. She had trouble with this sort of boundary crossing, but she liked Jack anyway; he asked questions and made friends easily. She was slightly ashamed that, though she was at least ten years his junior, she normally went to bed before him.

The orange sun began to rise over the Berkshires. Jack took a deep breath and looked around the camp's sloping greenery. "Ready for today?"

"I suppose," Mo said. "Not quite sure what to expect." It was time to get back to her section to shower off the equine smells before the rest of the counselors woke up.

"You'll be great," he said. "Just be yourself."

Back in December, Mo's twin brother, Benji, and his fiancée, Jade, were home from London for the holidays. They were sipping wine in her parents' kitchen, cleaning up after a dinner of roasted chicken and root vegetables, and Benji and Jade were trying to convince Mo to come out with them that night.

"It'll just be us, Paul, and Oliver," Benji said. "Maybe David."

"Where are you going?" Mo asked, drying a dish and handing it to him to put away.

"Dunno." He shrugged. "Probably just O'Shannon's or something." That was the local pub, where they always went when they were all home and caught up on old times while they got obliterated.

"You should come, Mo!" Jade was nice enough, and enthusiastic about everything. She and Benji had met at some swanky bar in London: He was a banker, and she worked in marketing. Mo thought Benji was too smart and too interesting for Jade, who seemed to have no bite to her; she appeared to be the kind of person who breezed through life having never second-guessed a decision, having never been anxious about an unforeseeable future. She was pretty and agreeable, as she seemed to know, and so why wouldn't things come to her?

But Mo was tired and full, and she knew she'd likely be expected to stay somewhat sober and drive them all home at the end of the night, and as much as she loved Benji's friends, she would have liked to catch up with them without Jade there, as Jade seemed so conscious of gender divides that she always clung to Mo as the only other woman at such events. She would make pithy asides about lads being lads and roll her eyes at their dirty jokes, jokes that Mo actually enjoyed.

"Mo," Benji said, a wide grin on his face, preparing to tease her, "if you keep saying no to every social invitation, we are eventually going to stop asking you." He sipped his wine, and Jade playfully swatted him on the arm.

"He doesn't mean that," she said.

"I know," Mo said, miffed because obviously she understood Benji's sarcasm much better than this girl who'd only known him for two years.

"Hey"—Benji put his wineglass down on the counter and raised his hands, grinning, as if to say "Not guilty"—"Not my fault if you die alone."

She was used to his bone-dry humor, and had been conditioned to laugh at or at least shrug off the most brutal teas-

ing from him over the years. She was surprised to find that
this last remark hurt. And she could see from Jade's stunned
expression that Benji had most definitely crossed a line.

Benji took note of the silence in the kitchen. "What?" he
said.

What Mo hated most was Jade's apparent distress, as if
Jade too was truly afraid that Mo dying alone was an absolute possibility.

"I'm going to bed," Mo said, abruptly placing her wine-
glass down and retreating to her childhood bedroom.

As a kid and a teenager, Mo had latched on to her brother in
school and become an accessory to him and his friends,
which she had hoped made her seem like a cool girl, who
mostly spent her time with boys, instead of a desperate one.
On the weekends, she rode at Silvershoe Stables, keeping to
herself, intimidated by the tight-knit clans of prissy girls
there. She wasn't as wealthy as they were; her family knew
the owner of the stables, and they got an even better dis-
count due to Mo's additional volunteer hours there, which
she performed happily.

Her parents were outgoing people—both of them teachers and popular in their respective schools—and she was an
introvert in a family of extroverts. But despite her discomfort around her contemporaries, she enjoyed the honesty and
transparency of kids. It was like they did the work of being
outgoing for her. They were easy to get to know, to understand, because they said what they felt and thus encouraged

her to do so too. She became a teacher herself, intent on feeling as if she was doing something more productive and beneficial with her life than just riding horses. And she was good at it.

For seven years now, Mo had taught eight-year-olds at the same Montessori school in York. Every day, she went for a run after work, came home to her studio apartment, made dinner, ate it in front of the television, graded homework and prepped for the next day, and was in bed by ten. On the weekends, she stayed with her parents in the suburbs and went riding at Silvershoe, where she now knew all the horses intimately.

But as the holidays ended, after Benji had long ago apologized, and he and Jade had returned to London, his comment continued to eat at her. Suddenly, when she woke up on a Monday in January and taught the same lesson in long division that she'd taught the year before and the years before that, she saw her life going on this way forever. And the most unbearable part was that, now that she was aware she was likely going to die alone, she realized that everyone else in her life must have been aware of it too. When she went for her run in her neighborhood after work, she felt exposed, as if the shop owners who waved to her as she passed were actually silently judging her for her boring reliability, for the fact that they knew they would see her at five P.M. each day like clockwork. All along, she'd thought her dedication to routine was commendable, but really, it was pitiful. When the parents at Silvershoe were asking about her personal life, they weren't doing it to make conversation; really, they were curious as to whether her answer would, just once, be different, include an allusion to a man or even a friend, anything other than "I just spent the holidays with my parents." A woman her age who didn't seem to have any attachments unnerved people.

All her friends, from work and from university, were married or in serious relationships, and she was growing tired of them trying to fix her up with someone every time they knew of a single man, no matter his intelligence or looks or potential compatibility with Mo.

It wasn't that she didn't want to meet someone. She just felt like it was too late. A thirty-year-old virgin: Who wanted to deal with that? She wasn't exactly a knockout—not ugly, but nothing special—and she was shy too. Boys began to come on to her when she was a teenager and continued to through university, but she'd found she was always inexplicably afraid of them. She felt fiercely protective of her body and herself, as if someone coming into her space—literally entering her—would feel violating and wrong. She could not understand why this was. She would develop crushes sometimes, but she rarely had desires beyond kissing. She did not even learn how to properly masturbate until she was twenty-five. It was as if she was so afraid of doing the wrong thing when it came to being naked with someone else that she avoided the prospect entirely. And now it was too late for her. Now if she engaged in anything, she'd only be making a fool of herself.

She finally told her brother her secret about a month after his comment, in a fit of lonely desperation. He had pointed out the bleak nature of her life from the outside, and sarcastic though he was, the petrified look on Jade's face had confirmed it all. Everyone would continue to pity her unless she made some sort of a change.

"You're kidding," he said over the phone.

She hoped that her silence indicated that she wasn't.

"How does that even happen?"

"I don't know," she said. "I didn't want to for a long time. And then it was too late, and I was embarrassed."

"Well," he reasoned, "maybe you're a lesbian."

"You can't just decide to be a lesbian," she said, although the thought had indeed crossed her mind. Once, in a particular kind of mood, she had sought girl-on-girl porn online and then, immediately afterward, panicked about her sexuality. In a tizzy, she had read online that it was common for straight girls to watch lesbian porn.

It wasn't like anyone she knew would have a problem with her being gay. The thing was, she didn't know what sex was like, so how could she know if she liked it with a man, let alone with a woman? One time when she was drunk at uni, a girl had kissed her, but the anxieties about not knowing what to do, the fears of failure, had felt the same as they would have been with a man, and she had gone back to her dormitory alone that night.

This was how, at age thirty, she ended up at a place where no one knew anything about her. A place where people could suspect her life was actually full of excitement and possibility. This was how she came to do the most impulsive thing she had ever done: taking a job as a "section leader" at an

American summer camp, the same camp that her brother had worked at years earlier, some five thousand kilometers from home.

The girls in the Hemlock section had been preparing all week, sweeping the floorboards of their platform tents, straightening up the belongings in their cubbies, and removing stray socks and bikini bottoms from the clotheslines. As the returning counselors explained, Visitors' Day meant the girls having free time with the boys while the adults socialized, getting to leave camp, enjoying a meal beyond the dining hall, and most significant, it meant the counselors relinquishing their power for one day to the higher powers: the girls' parents.

Mo put a wake-up mix in the CD player at seven-fifteen. She'd made dozens of these mixes before coming to camp and agonized over the song choices. *Is this song still popular, or is it overdone now? Is this one only big in England, or do they like it in America too?* Unlike on most mornings, today she didn't need to raise the volume at the second song to get the girls out of bed. By the end of the first track, they were already beelining toward the showers in their towels and flip-flops. She sat on the wooden step at the entrance to the head tent, where she and Nell slept, and watched the procession unfold.

Sheera, one of Mo's favorite campers, stopped in front of the head tent on her way to the showers.

"Mornin', Mo," she said, swinging her shower caddy.

"Good morning, Sheera."

"Mo, what are you going to do while we're all with our visitors today?"

"I'll be down with the horses. Helping Nell."

"Are you going to watch us ride?"

"I hope so," Mo said. "Also, when all of you are having fun outside camp, I'll probably rummage through your trunks and eat your new snacks."

"Mo!" Sheera opened her mouth in faux shock. "Appalling!"

"Where did you learn such big words?"

Sheera rolled her eyes. "My daddy's coming today," she said. "He's bringing me Starbursts and baby 3 Musketeers. Huge bags of them." She looked hard at Mo. "I'm locking my trunk." She turned on her heels and sauntered toward the showers.

Mo liked that Sheera could joke with her; the rest of them treated her like she was too old to be fun.

The cafeteria building was split into two single-sex dining halls. Apparently, the boys and girls sat on opposite sides of the same room years ago, but there had been too many distractions—the kids didn't eat, just socialized—so they built a wall to separate the two sides. Mo felt grateful for any same-sex separations like this; she had had the idea that maybe she would meet a man that summer, and yet the more divisions there were between the genders, the more excuses she had to not meet one.

The girls sang some sort of grace before every meal. This

morning they sang "The Birdie Song," linking their thumbs
together and fluttering their fingers above their heads.

"Way up in the sky, the little birds fly,
While down in their nest, the little birds rest."

The girls made beds for the invisible birds with their arms,
rocking them back and forth like infants.

"With a wing on the left and a wing on the right,
The little birds sleep all through the night."

Rachel, the counselor for tent three, led her girls, putting
her hands together against her ear and resting her head on
them like they were a pillow.

"The fuck is she wearing?" Nell whispered.

Rachel and her friend Fiona were Americans who grew up
going to Camp Marigold. Normally, Mo would have said
something bitchy to Nell about the girl's too-short dress. But
Mo knew, because she was Rachel's boss and had to deliver
the news from the outside world, that Rachel's father had
died just a few days earlier. She was shocked that Rachel
hadn't left, let alone seemed cheerful and happy to still be at
camp. So instead of making a snide comment to Nell, she
simply shrugged.

The campers raised their voices at their favorite part of
the song and yelled: "Shhh. . . . *You'll wake the dang birdies!*"

They laughed, clapped, and sat, and the kitchen workers
came out of the swinging doors wheeling carts filled with

identical breakfast trays. Mo and her table of camp leadership were served the sausage links and French toast sticks first.

"Of course breakfast is good on Visitors' Day," Nell said, dousing her meal with syrup. "So the first thing a Maple kid will tell their parents is, 'Mom, we had French toast sticks for breakfast!'" she said, mimicking an American accent.

After breakfast, the parents began to arrive. They parked their SUVs on the lower fields and carried picnic baskets, balloons, and shopping bags to the boys' and girls' camps. The weather wasn't ideal: The sunny morning had quickly morphed into a gray day, and a uniformly cloudy sky had cast itself over the camp, the freshly cut grass appearing a dull, dirty green.

"This makes me miss my mom," Rachel said to one of her counselor friends outside the head tent, where Mo was also standing. The dads stayed outside their daughters' tents, peering in, while moms straightened up bunks and took items out of shopping bags: shaving cream, gum, Pixy Stix, cups of ramen, *Seventeen* magazines, nail polish, Snapple iced teas.

Mo noticed two parents standing silently outside tent three. The older girls all welcomed their parents' initial arrival but seemed to remember quickly afterward—now ignoring their parents and giggling over magazines with one another on their tents' front steps—that it was not cool to spend too much time with or to be too excited by the presence of one's family.

"Hey, Rachel," Mo said. "Could you go over and chat up the parents over there? They look a bit . . . idle."

Rachel stood still for a beat and then, without looking at Mo, strolled over to the tent. Mo watched her put on a saccharine smile as she shook the parents' hands.

Sheera came up to Mo's tent hand in hand with a tall man in slacks and a fedora. "Mo, this is my dad," she said proudly.

"I've heard so much about you," the father said, taking both of Mo's hands. Then he said more quietly, "Thank you for watching over my girl."

Sheera stopped by Mo's tent every morning. The other girls in tent three didn't seem to understand Sheera, who lived in an apartment in the city instead of a house in the suburbs. Those girls had yards and dogs; they lied and said they had their periods to avoid swimming in the lake; they never signed up for activities at the nature lodge. Sheera ran from one activity to the next, hiking and going horseback riding and swimming in a lake all for the very first time.

"She's a pleasure," Mo said. Over Sheera's shoulder, Mo saw Rachel laughing with the father at the tent, throwing her head back.

After a picnic lunch on the flag lawn, activity demos began. Each girl chose her favorite activity and participated in a show for the parents—a dance performance, a horseback-riding expo, a swimming or boat race. After the section was cleared of campers and parents, Mo walked down to the stables to help Nell.

Parents stood around the wooden fence of the arena with

cameras around their necks. In the dim barn that smelled of leather and manure, Nell, Rachel, and the other riding counselors had already lined up the twenty campers from youngest to oldest. Since there were only twelve horses, they split the expo into two age groups. The counselors would walk alongside the younger group for the show; the older campers could go unspotted.

"God, there you are," Nell said to Mo, pulling her by the arm. "Stay here."

Mo watched the older girls in the barn while Nell and the other riding counselors went out with the younger girls. "Hi, Mo!" Sheera waved from the back of the line.

"Hi, Sheera," Mo said, distracted by two ten-year-old Buckeyes shoving each other and bickering over who was first.

"Mo, I'm riding Micah!" Sheera called. "Your favorite!"

"Girls!" Mo approached the shrieking Buckeyes and physically separated them from each other. "You're acting like kindergartners!"

Now she turned her attention to the arena, the ambling procession of horses and the girls sitting proudly atop them. The small girl riding Micah looked timid, unsure of what to do. He stood out from the pack, moving at a slow, almost lethargic pace, his eyes toward the ground. Every now and then he shook his head or blew out air or stamped an erratic hoof. Nell walked beside Micah and the girl; even though Nell wasn't even touching the horse, you could sense her poise and her comfort in the arena. One could easily imagine her as a serious English riding competitor, showing horses in gray jodhpurs and freshly polished boots, a long red braid falling from under her helmet.

Behind them, a girl rode Firework, a younger horse with a shiny black coat, and Rachel stood by, chin up. The families clapped and snapped photos. The younger girls retreated to the barn.

"It's gonna rain any fucking minute," Nell muttered to Mo, and only then did Mo notice the clouds had grown darker. "Let's get this over with."

The younger campers dismounted, and soon after, the older ones cantered out to the arena alone. Helen led the procession, sitting up straight as she'd been taught in many years of lessons, jumping her horse, Dandelion, with seeming ease over the haystacks and hurdles. The other girls followed behind with slumped postures. Parents leaned against the fence with rapt attention. Someone's digital camera flash illuminated the arena from the crowd.

"No flashes, please!" Nell strained in the parents' direction.

Sheera, looking over to her father, slacked on Micah's reins. The girls in the barn were squealing from the excitement of having just shown off what they'd been working on for the past four weeks—one of their first instances of an adrenaline rush; Mo remembered the feeling well—and pulled at their shorts, at the bottoms of their shirts, asking to go see their parents. "Not until it's over," Mo repeated while keeping her gaze on Sheera and Micah. Nell, at the edge of the barn, was grimacing at the clouds.

When the thunder clapped, deafening and explosive, like it was retaliating against its daylong silence, Micah let out a yelp and reared onto his hind legs. Sheera fell off her horse with her legs in the air and landed helmet first on the dusty ground, her body following like a rag doll. Mo didn't wait for the audience's collective gasp to rush onto the field where Sheera lay motionless; her fiftysomething father jumped over the fence and ran at full speed toward them, his hat falling behind him. The rain began to pour in violent sloshes.

Mo heard herself yell that someone should call for an ambulance.

Someone else yelled from outside the arena that it was on its way, and Mo realized that her call for help was minutes later than anyone else's.

Mo and the father knelt over Sheera while the rain soaked their bodies and made pools around them. The girl, her eyes closed, made no sounds. By the time the paramedics came, Nell and the other counselors had cleared the area of horses and children. Some parents, unable to be managed, still stood around like this was part of the show.

In the ambulance, Sheera remained unconscious. Her father asked Mo to take his hand, and they each joined their remaining hands with Sheera's. The red lights and sirens circled around them as their ambulance sped down an empty country road.

"Oh Father, the source of all health and healing, please fill our hearts with faith, oh Lord, and heal our Sheera according to your will," Sheera's father said. Mo quickly looked up to see the man's eyes closed tight and shut her own again. "Please stay with her, and give her the strength she needs to wake again. In Jesus's name we pray. Amen."

"Amen," Mo said.

Mo woke up on a hard plastic chair under fluorescent lighting that gave no hints as to what time it was. Her pulse was erratic and all encompassing, like it could break through the skin of her throat.

Sheera's father was in the room with his daughter. No one had come out to give any updates. Sheera's father shouldn't leave her side, after all, and no doctor or nurse had any responsibility, really, to relay messages back to Mo. She was not family or even a close friend. She was a foreigner to these people and to this place.

A quiet American hospital on a Sunday night in rural Connecticut. Mo had not had many moments in life when she looked around and thought, *How did I end up here?*

She looked at her watch. It was only eight P.M.; the horse expo, Mo remembered, had been at one. She'd fallen asleep in the middle of the day, exhausted by a trauma that wasn't even hers. Then she realized that it was hers, that she was responsible for the well-being of these girls and that being at the hospital at all was, in itself, a failure.

She walked up to the reception window and asked if she could use the desk phone.

"There's a pay phone down the hall," the woman at the desk said without looking up.

Mo searched her pockets, realizing she had nothing on

her. "I was so frantic when I left . . ." There was a quick, sharp feeling of fear and desolation. The overhead lights buzzed and reflected off the shining linoleum floors—clean, sterile, lifeless.

"Please?" Mo asked the nurse, who looked up and around and, seeing there was no one else there but a man anxiously pacing the waiting room, rolled her eyes, sighed deeply, and pushed the phone across the desk.

"Press nine to dial out."

"Camp Marigold, this is Nan," the camp secretary said on the other end of the line.

"Nan, it's Mo."

"I'm so glad you're calling, dear. How is she?"

"I don't know. No one's come out yet. I'm just sitting here waiting."

"Shit," Nan said. "We're praying with all our might over here." It was odd how religious Americans were. "Do you need anything?" she asked. "Should someone come and pick you up?"

"No, I'm going to stay," Mo said. Her voice shook. "Could you do me one favor? Could someone go fetch Nell and get her on the line?"

Nell sounded breathless when she came on several minutes later. "What's going on?"

Mo explained the situation again. "I just feel so tired," she said. "Everything in my body feels like it's working on overload."

"Of course it is," Nell said. "This is terrifying."

"I hate that I can't do anything."

"Just try to breathe, love. It's out of our hands."

She imagined Nell in her hoodie and shorts on the other end of the line, twirling the phone cord around her finger, her mouth close to the receiver.

"I will," Mo said.

"Call the office first thing in the morning, okay?"

"Sleep tight," Mo said in a quiet, tender tone that surprised her. "I'll see you soon."

Jack arrived at the hospital in the morning and, in his authoritative way, gleaned the important information about Sheera from the on-call doctor. She had woken up as soon as they'd put her in the hospital bed, confused and crying, complaining of a terrible headache. She'd thrown up once in the middle of the night. But the CT scan showed no signs of bleeding or permanent damage. These were just symptoms of a moderate concussion, and she should be feeling like herself after a few days of rest.

Jack took Mo back to camp in his two-door sedan, which smelled like body odor and cut grass. He drove fast; she rolled down her window and watched the woods and the green farmland blur by.

When they arrived at Marigold, Mo noticed neon yellow caution tape around the fence of the horse arena. DO NOT ENTER, it read.

"Is that really necessary?" she asked.

"Unfortunately, yes," Jack kept his eyes ahead of him.

"It's just temporary. Just to show our concern to the parents and donors."

"What will the horses do?" Mo asked.

"I've talked to Nell and Rachel," he said. "The three of you can still ride them as normal to give them some fresh air and exercise. Just no campers for the time being."

He parked his car in front of the camp office. Mo opened her door but Jack remained still.

"Micah's lived a good life," Jack said. "He's our oldest horse here. Did you know that? Twenty-eight years old."

"Yeah. I did."

"Mo," he said, turning to look at her, "we'll be putting him down tonight, after the campers are asleep. It will be easy and painless."

"It's not because he's old, though," Mo heard herself saying. "I woke him up too early yesterday morning. You saw. It was a long day, and he was tired."

"I know you're upset, Mo," he said. "We all are." He put his hand on her knee. "You can come down to the stables while we do it if that'll make you feel better. Maybe it will give you a sense of closure," he said. "I know how you loved him."

She pushed his hand away. "Don't touch me." Before he could respond, she got out and slammed the car door.

When she got back to the Hemlock section, she found the girls running around getting ready for breakfast and Rachel standing on top of the picnic table in the center, shrieking out warnings. "Five minutes to flag raising!"

Mo approached Rachel. "You can get down," Mo said. "I can take over."

Rachel looked startled. "I didn't realize you were back. Is she okay?"

Mo nodded.

"What about Micah? Is he hurt?"

Mo hesitated. "Really, I can take it from here," she said, stepping onto the bench of the picnic table.

But Rachel shook her head. "What's going on?"

Mo was not equipped to deal with as much catastrophe as she had had to that day. She took a deep breath and said in what she hoped was a calm but empathetic tone, "They're going to put him down tonight."

A gasp came out of Rachel, and then she put a hand over her mouth, as if doing so would hide her reaction. "Oh," she said, composing herself.

"I'm so sorry," Mo said, putting a hand awkwardly on Rachel's forearm. She hadn't known that the horse had meant anything to Rachel.

Rachel looked down at Mo's hand.

"Why don't you get some rest?" Rachel said. "You must be exhausted."

It was true; she'd hardly slept in the brightly lit waiting room.

Rachel turned away from Mo and called out to the girls again: "Five minutes till flag raising!"

Mo descended from the picnic table, then walked into the head tent. Nell was just rousing herself from her bed; she was a late sleeper.

"How is she?" Nell asked, and stood.

"She's going to be okay," Mo said. "I don't know if her father will let her come back, though." She decided not to tell Nell about Micah just yet.

"That's really sad," Nell said. "You look so tired."

"I am."

"Go to sleep," she said. "I'll take care of the girls."

Mo nodded and climbed into her own bunk, across from Nell's. But just as Nell had been getting up, Mo had realized that Nell did not look the same to her. Nell could not look the same, not after Sheera's fall. Not after Micah had been sentenced to death and Mo had seen Rachel's reaction to it. Not after they had talked on the phone the night before and Mo had imagined Nell's mouth near the phone's receiver. Mo's thoughts felt thick with exhaustion, but she understood thoroughly, instinctively, that everything had changed.

"Nell," Mo said from her bunk, and Nell walked toward her.

Mo did not say "Come here," because she already sensed that Nell knew to do so. She knelt down to Mo's eye level. Mo had always assumed that she would be the one pursued and not the other way around. She could tell, by the way that Nell's face looked so open and pure, like a blank canvas ready to be painted over, that Nell too was surprised to be the pursued, not the pursuer. When Mo pulled Nell's chin toward her face, Nell exhaled, as if a sense of relief came from the submission itself.

9

Nell and Mo heard the gunshot because they were listening for it. They were lying in Mo's bunk together in the tent they shared, side by side. Their fingers were intertwined. When the shot rang out—it easily could have been a car back-firing or fireworks to any unsuspecting ears—Mo jumped.

Nell and Mo had no beers of their own left, so when they were finished crying, they went down to the staff lodge.

They didn't go to the staff lodge often because they didn't like any of the other counselors. There were the Americans, the Brits, the Australians, and a handful of more exotic foreigners, whom the Anglophones were drawn to like mosquitoes to sweet blood. Marco from Portugal, who taught mountain biking, was short but tan and compact, and Philippa S. and Philippa J. sat with him at picnic tables on the athletic fields when they should have been watching campers and taught him "blow job" and "rim job" and other jobs they wanted to perform on him. Chloé, from France, ate everything, in moderation, and still looked thin in a bikini, and Devon and Alex and Blake chased after her, asking, *"Voulez-vous coucher avec moi ce soir?"* though Finn from the Netherlands, who was apparently a basketball star in Ukraine, was already fucking her in the oar house every night.

Nell sat down on one of the couches with a can of beer. Devon, a lifeguard, sat next to her and offered her a joint.

Nell took a hit and blew smoke toward the ceiling.

"I'm sorry about your horse," he said. He had a shaved head and a thick Manchester accent.

"Thanks," she said.

"Fucking brutal, watching," Devon said. "Wonder if the kids heard it." Nell was the lead horseback-riding counselor, and Jack had asked her to be there to bring the horse out into the open field. She had refused. So a few of the men, including Devon, had done it instead.

Earlier that night, they'd also learned that Sheera's father had decided not to let her return to camp.

Micah's age had been his death sentence. Any horse could have done the same thing in reaction to such a loud clap of thunder, but twenty-eight was senior enough to make senility plausible, and a good camp just couldn't keep around a senior horse that had given one of its campers a concussion. And, though no one would ever say it aloud, the fact that

Sheera was one of the camp's few black kids—well, that hadn't helped his case either.

Nell took a deep swig of her beer.

"Tell me something, Red." Devon leaned back, appraising her, the joint burning between his fingers. "When you started riding, you ever have that thing happen to you that you hear about?"

"'Thing happen'?"

"Ya know, like"—he moved closer; his breath was coated with weed and whiskey—"you ever bleed some? Down there?"

Nell took the joint again. "I think that's an urban myth."

"I don't believe you, Red." He yelled across the room: "Philippa! Come here for a sec."

The Philippa with bleached hair and a fringe tottered over.

"You rode horses as a girl, yeah?"

"Yeah, why?" Philippa sat down on one of his knees, then reached across to take the joint from Nell. He placed a hand on Philippa's back, just above her ass.

"Did you ever, ya know, *bleed* when you got on the horse?"

Philippa broke into a cackle and swatted Devon on the shoulder. "You're a fuckin' pervert, Dev, ya know that?"

He grinned. "So you did, eh?"

"Wouldn't be telling you if we did now, would we?" She threw Nell a glance of female solidarity.

Nell stood. "Gotta use the ladies'."

It was too warm in the staff lodge. She stepped outside onto the front porch and sat on the top step. It would be four A.M. at home in Surrey. Nell wanted to call her mother, but she would be asleep. She hadn't wanted Nell to go to camp; instead, she had thought that Nell should have stayed home in the months leading up to university and taken an internship in the city, as if spending that extra time in the upstanding home she came from would literally set her straight.

Months earlier, Nell had been suspended from school, but her father didn't know why. Only Nell's mother knew; only Nell's mother took her to that doctor. He prescribed an antidepressant, but she wasn't depressed; she was just gay. For the remaining months of that spring, she worked at the local stables where she'd ridden as a girl. Nell carried the medication with her at all times, and every morning on her way to the horses, she threw a single pill into the dumpster.

A co-worker from the stables had worked at an American summer camp a few years earlier, and it sounded like the right kind of escape: warm weather, cheerful strangers, anonymity, horses. A chance to visit America for the first time. Nell was eighteen now; she could go where she wanted. She applied through an agency, and they placed her at Camp Marigold in the lower Berkshire Mountains of Connecticut, where she was given the role of head riding instructor. She was surprised, considering her young age and lack of camp experience, but her pedigreed English riding education seemed to be a major draw for wealthy American families. When Nell told her parents over dinner one night that she'd be going, that she had already bought her plane ticket, they begged her not to. "But we're a team," her mother had said.

A team united against the wayward winds of homosexuality, which, her mother seemed to believe, were much stronger in America.

It was a family tradition to go away to boarding school at the age of fourteen, and Nell's parents had sent her to Wentworth Academy, the same all-girls school that her mother had attended. It was a stuffy academy in the Midlands with several acres of land and—the reason Nell had agreed so readily—a fantastic number of purebred horses. As a fourth year, she was the student riding apprentice and had keys to the stables. She would have girls meet her there late at night; the mornings were reserved for her own riding with her favorite horse, Henry, a chestnut Arabian, when they would wander off campus onto trails and hills and back roads.

She became known for these late nights in the barn, which the other girls called "appointments." For the others, the appointments were only physical, not an experiment, not love, just a way to make it from one coed dance to the next. One could say to one's roommate, at eleven in the evening, "I have a French tutoring appointment in fifteen minutes," and the unusual lateness of the meeting would never be questioned; perhaps the roommate had had a similar appointment just a week earlier.

Nell learned that her code name was "Red," coined by a whispering bunkmate or a curious member of the tennis team. Not exactly original, but maybe that was the point—that her scandalous role in the school could be communicated through the mention of that seemingly innocuous color. It became known through the school's more secretive channels that Red would meet with whomever, and would keep things quiet too.

One morning, she arrived at the barn to take Henry out, and Sasha was waiting there. She was a tall second year with gray eyes. She always wore her brown hair in a perfectly contained braid falling over one shoulder. They'd spoken only a few times, but Nell often had fantasies about the girl. She was so poised and proper on a horse, so in control.

"What are you doing here?" Nell asked, thinking that Sasha had come to ride or, even worse, to threaten her. She seemed posh enough, conservative enough, that she might have actually cared to stop it—as if an underground lesbian community at her own boarding school would bring scandal on her just by association. There was certainly a reigning old-fashioned homophobia at Wentworth; Nell's appointments needed to be so secretive because the girls' proper reputations were always at stake.

The girl walked toward Nell and said, sarcastically, "Hi, Red."

Nell did not normally feel nervous, but Sasha made her nervous. It was something in the way she was looking so intensely into Nell's eyes. It was imploring, but also challenging, the way those gray eyes squinted and studied Nell like the eyes of a cat ready to pounce.

"Nell is fine," Nell said.

"I'm Sasha," the girl said, not breaking the eye contact.

"I know."

Nell looked around. Did she have backup, girls ready to attack, waiting just outside the stable doors?

Sasha approached Nell. She put a hand out and reached it toward Nell's face. Nell flinched and closed her eyes, bracing herself for the contact, until she realized that the hand was moving through her own hair.

She opened her eyes and saw that Sasha's intense look had gone away, and now it was nervous and unsure: all imploring, with no challenge, and at the mercy of whatever Nell decided to do next.

Normally Nell wouldn't have taken the risk in the morning—it was about to be bright out, and time was limited before the school day started. But Nell had a feeling that Sasha was different, that she wanted this from *Nell,* not from Red, judging by how nervous she seemed. Or so this was what Nell told herself as she took Sasha by the hand and pulled her onto the ground in an empty stall.

Sasha leaned in to every touch. They kept their boots and tops on; Nell pulled Sasha's jodhpurs down just past her knees and took her time. Sasha's thighs smelled like baby oil and cardamom. When Sasha finished, she made a high-pitched squeal, which Nell thought was the most beautiful sound she'd ever heard.

Henry, in the stall next to them, stamped his feet. Sasha was standing, brushing the hay off her pants and pushing her hair behind her ears. Nell opened the door of the stall they were in and made her way around to give Henry a kiss on his wet nose.

"Should we ride?" Sasha said.

Most of the girls barely spoke afterward, embarrassed or ashamed.

Nell looked at her watch. "We don't have much time."

"That's okay," Sasha said. "Just a little jaunt could be fun."

Sasha took Dove, the albino, and Nell led them behind the barn and through the thick woods that sat on the edge of campus. The horses seemed to awaken in the unfenced terrain. Henry was happy to lead the way, to navigate between trees and to jump over fallen logs. Nell hated seeing him later in the day in the arena, plodding around the circle. Now he stopped to drink from a mud puddle.

"Is that the headmistress's house?" Sasha asked while they waited for Henry to finish drinking.

They were at the top of a hill. The tangled forest stopped at the bottom of the slope, butted by a tall brick wall and a manicured lawn on the other side. Nell checked her watch again—five minutes to seven. "She'll be going up to the school soon," she said. "We should get back."

"I'm not worried." Sasha looked away from the stone mansion and then did something Nell could have never hoped for: leaned over and gave her a kiss. A sweet, short kiss. The sort of kiss a real couple would share.

"Are you blushing, Red?" Sasha asked as she pulled away.

"No," Nell lied; she could feel her face was warm.

"Okay," Sasha said. They were both smiling like idiots. "Let's go."

———

The screen door creaked and shut behind Mo as she took a seat next to Nell. That morning, Mo had kissed Nell for the first time. She was wearing jeans and a hoodie and had her hair in a ponytail, the only way Nell had ever seen her wear it. Her tan had settled nicely over the four weeks they'd been there. Nell thought of her as "all-American"—athletic, wholesome, pert—even though she was also English.

"You wanna look at the stars with me?" Mo asked.

"Sure," Nell said, and tilted her head toward the sky.

"No. Over here is better."

Mo led them toward the middle of the green where the American flag was raised every morning. She lay down, and Nell lay next to her. The grass was damp, but neither of them complained about it.

"I can't find the Plough," Mo said.

"Me neither," said Nell, though she wasn't really looking for it. She felt distracted somehow by Mo's presence. She had been lost in her thoughts about home and didn't feel ready to come out of them.

"I think there's the little one there"—Mo pointed—"so if I just trace along"—she moved her index finger aimlessly around the sky—"it's got to be nearby."

"Do you need to know where everything is?"

"I don't *need* to." Mo dropped her finger then. "I just like to," she said sheepishly.

"Well, that's the Milky Way," Nell said, feeling bad now. She used her finger to trace the cloudy galaxy in her own line of vision, knowing that pointing out constellations was useless—that in an expanse as wide as the night sky, it was nearly impossible to show someone else what you were seeing.

"I know what the Milky Way looks like."

Mo turned onto her side and faced her friend.

"Nell?" she said.

"Hm?"

"Do you want to go home?"

Nell felt alarmed, as if Mo had been attuned to her own thoughts about her family and Sasha just minutes earlier. "Do I want to go home?"

"Do you want me to say first?"

"No, that's okay. I know you want to go home."

Mo frowned. "No, I don't."

"You don't?"

"No. Yes. I don't know. I asked you first."

"So my wanting or not wanting to go home would affect your wanting—or not wanting—to go home?"

"I don't like it here anymore," Mo said, quieter. "I just don't want to leave you."

It made Nell feel good and safe to know this, but the safeness also made her bristle, as if she had to quickly push her way out of it. She knew what had happened the last time she had allowed herself to feel safe. Here was this lovely, kind person, who did, in more than one way, make her feel safe; and up there was the night sky, open and endless and full of far more possibilities than the ones on this provincial earth.

"Do you want to leave because of Micah?" Nell forced

herself to ask, though she really did not want to talk about
the horse anymore.

"Micah. Sheera. All of it." Mo swept a hand around the
camp. "I swear this place is cursed."

"Maybe it is," Nell said. The idea of an escape had been
faulty, of course. Here there was just another set of problems
that required yet another escape.

Nell and Sasha met at six A.M. on every Monday, Wednesday,
and Friday, first in the barn, and then, if they had time, they
went for a ride. Soon they started meeting at five-thirty instead in order to be able to go farther into the woods each
time, staying out longer, arriving back later, coming upon
streams and clearings and once at the fence of an oat farm.
The sun was rising then, and Nell had a moment of rever-
ence watching the fields turn gold.

"You'll remember me when the west winds move." Sasha
started to jokingly sing the Sting song, and Nell laughed and
felt (perhaps naïvely, she noted even at the time) that they
understood each other in a deep and real way.

Nell began to make eye contact with Sasha in the dining
hall. She tried to make their mornings last longer and longer.
She asked Sasha questions about her life—about her divorced parents, her troubled younger brother, her stupid and
trivial Wentworth friends. Sasha wanted to be an actress; she
believed she was destined for much greater things, and Nell
agreed with her. She entertained fantasies about the two of

them riding Henry and Dove into the woods one morning and never coming back.

And most astonishingly, Sasha reciprocated favors in the barn, almost every time. The other Wentworth girls would only occasionally and, even then, not very well, but Sasha actually asked what Nell liked, what she wanted. As Sasha snaked down Nell's bare stomach, kissing her belly button, her hips, her inner thighs, Nell felt entirely sure that she was desperately, unequivocally in love.

And then one morning late in the fall, after almost a full term of their appointments, Sasha wasn't there. Nell took Henry out anyway, worrying the whole ride that Sasha had been caught leaving her dorm.

Nell tried to make eye contact with Sasha in the dining hall that night, but she looked away. She was with her friends, the girls who scrunched their kneesocks down to their ankles and wore baby blue bows at the bottoms of their braids.

She wasn't at the barn the next morning either. A week later, a tiny first year was waiting outside the stable doors when Nell arrived. Nell asked her what she was doing there so early and sent her back to her dorm.

At the coed dance with St. Joseph's that weekend, Sasha spent all night dancing with Charles Mitting, who was tall and famously rich. On Monday Nell's roommate leaned over to her at breakfast, looking at Sasha standing tall with her lunch tray and her braid falling down over her shoulder.

"She and Charles Mitting are an item," Nell's roommate said.

"Is that so?" Nell sipped her coffee.

"Yeah." The roommate stuffed a piece of toast into her mouth. "Lucky bitch."

It was late. Counselors were walking out of the staff lodge and back to their sections, some looking curiously at Mo and Nell as they passed. Nell was sure that the counselors gossiped about them because they hadn't made any other friends.

"Here," Mo said, and pulled a handful of Laffy Taffys out of her pocket, placing them on the grass in front of them.

Nell unwrapped a yellow one, stuck the candy in her mouth, and read the joke on the inside of the wrapper with the light from her mini LED.

"What did the finger say to the thumb?" Nell asked.

"What?"

"I'm in glove with you."

Sticky pieces of fake, plasticky banana lodged themselves in her molars.

"I've never asked," Mo said. "Did you leave anyone back home?"

"Leave anyone?"

"You know, like a boyfriend," Mo said. "Or girlfriend," she added. This had been, up until then, the unspoken thing. *Who do we like? Does it matter?*

Nell chewed hard. "Free as a bird."

"Same here," Mo said.

Nell unwrapped a strawberry Laffy Taffy. "What's brown and sticky?"

"A pile of shit?"

"Close," Nell said. "A stick."

Nell had not slept with anyone at camp, and neither had Mo. Becca and Logan had been sneaking into the vacant bunk rooms in the nurse's office for six consecutive evenings. Steph and Brett had apparently fucked in the pool house around two the night before. Four weeks into camp and they had all regressed completely—like they had to act the way the kids did, like they were good only for gossiping and pushing boundaries in the most predictable of ways.

The last weeks of the semester, just before Christmas, most girls spent their nights in the library studying for exams. Nell spent hers in the stacks. It was too cold by then to meet in the stables.

She had an appointment with a blond second year late one night in the poetry stacks, authors A–D. The girl was quiet and jumpy, as they always were. Nell performed what was rote by then, the intimacies, if she could even call them that.

The girl's eyes were shut so tight, presumably to help her forget where she was and whom she was with. Nell looked at the book spines while her hand worked. Baudelaire. Bishop. Blake. Just as the girl's back started to arch and she started to make the sounds that signaled she was nearing the end, a soft and damp object grazed Nell's shoulder and landed in her lap.

The blond girl opened her eyes and looked down at Nell's

lap, her face turned ashen. She stood up fast, straightened her skirt, and ran away from Nell, out of the aisle and out of the library.

Nell picked the thing up by its cotton string. It was soaked in blood, still wet. As she looked up, an anonymous hand launched a paper airplane over the bookshelf. She caught it before it landed, staining the paper with the blood on her fingers, and opened it.

"A gift for Red," it said, "who loves pussy more than anyone we know."

Nell looked at her watch. "We should be getting back."

Mo was focusing on Nell intently now; she had this crazy look in her eyes and the batting eyelashes of a girl who didn't know how to flirt. As they walked up the hill to their section, Mo stayed close and let the sides of their pinkies brush against each other, the sides of their knees.

When they got to their tent, Mo sat on the edge of her bed.

"Do you want to sleep in my bunk tonight?" she asked.

Of course, Nell did. She would be lying if she said she hadn't often thought about the convenience of their living in the same tent and was partly surprised that she hadn't propositioned Mo much earlier in the summer. But something had always stopped her: this understanding that, despite being much older than Nell, Mo was younger in so many ways. She was inexperienced and naïve. She needed a teacher.

"No, thank you," Nell said. "I'm really tired."

And they lay in their respective bunks, alone.

That morning, Nell had allowed herself to hook up with Mo—she too had been caught up in the drama and the danger of Sheera's fall. And she had wanted Mo. But something about Mo's continual closeness now, her transparent desire for intimacy, made Nell recoil. She didn't want to have to get so close to just be the teacher again, this champion for confused girls. For them, it was a game, an experiment. But for her, it was all too real.

The silence settled uneasily between them.

"I don't know what you think about me," Nell said some minutes later—just for good measure, just to get her point across clearly. "But whatever it is, it's wrong."

She thought she heard Mo sniffling later that night—it was likely she was crying. Nell herself had trouble sleeping; she felt cruel pushing away her only friend there. But it needed to be done.

Early in the morning she left the tent and called her mother on Skype in the computer lab.

"Hello?" Her mother was looking closely into the webcam that Nell had installed on the home computer before she left. She searched Nell's pixelated image on the other end as if in disbelief that such technology—the ability to see her daughter in real time across the Atlantic Ocean—was possible.

"Hi, Mum," Nell said. She'd Skyped with her mother only once earlier in the summer, even though she'd originally promised that she would a few times a week.

"I was just sitting down to lunch." Her mother, delighted, lifted up a salad and a fork to the camera. But when she put the bowl back down and said, "So what's going on over there?" her face got stuck, mouth ajar and fork aloft.

"Mum?"

The sound came across in unrecognizable tidbits and bleeps, and then those cut out too.

"Mum, they killed a horse last night," Nell said.

Now her mother's voice moved in super, undecipherable speed, catching up. Then it stopped. Her face began to move again, peering too closely into the camera.

"Nell? Are you there?"

"I'm here."

"Nell?"

The face froze again, up close, imploring.

"They killed a horse last night," Nell repeated to her mother's motionless, expectant expression.

10

The staff lodge was a decrepit place that hadn't been refurbished in at least twenty-five years. The felt was coming up at the corners of the pool table downstairs, its wooden sides splintering, and the vending machines were unplugged and unstocked. There were a few plastic tables and folding chairs where the counselors played poker and drinking games, though they never had a full deck of cards to work with. Upstairs, stuffing burst from the seams of secondhand couches.

The counselors cheered when Jack walked in. One of them offered him a Coors Light. He sat down next to Yonatan at the card table and played a couple hands of five-card draw. There was only one air conditioner in the lodge, on the bottom floor next to one of the card tables, and though most evenings grew cool enough for open windows to suffice, that night was so hot that the counselors took turns crowding around the AC.

"Fuck, Jack," Yonatan said, folding again. "I forgot how good you are."

Jack allowed himself a momentary feeling of pride.

Yonatan lifted his empty beer can in the air. "Another?"

Jack shook his head.

After Yonatan left his seat, Rachel replaced him in it. Jack nodded at her and took a sip of his beer.

When he was going through job applications during the winter, he'd stopped a beat too long on Rachel's passport-sized photo. It was objectively a bad photo: She stood against a white wall, unsmiling and washed out by the drugstore's fluorescent lighting. But she still looked glamorous in an off-hand way: She wore her thick, dark hair over one shoulder and was looking up, surprised, from beneath lowered eyelashes, as if someone had just called her name. Her most notable feature was a slightly oversized nose. It was distinguishing, regal; it set her apart from the prototypical Pretty Girl.

He had noted the age: nineteen. From her résumé, he learned that she had been a camper at Marigold and then a CIT, a counselor-in-training, at age fifteen. Now she was back after four summers away.

She looked somewhat bored at the poker table watching the men play, though she expressed no interest in joining the game. She was wearing a white ribbed tank top and no makeup and had gotten darker since the beginning of the summer. Good-looking young men like Chad and Yonatan were more her speed, more age appropriate. Jack himself was forty-four. She was a kid; his own son was seven years older than her.

"Jack, you want in this round?" someone asked.

He glanced at his watch but didn't register the time, acutely aware of Rachel's presence. "One more, then I've got to hit the hay."

A counselor split up the chips—checker tiles and pieces from a Connect Four game—and they threw in the ante. Jack felt self-conscious knowing that Rachel was looking at his shitty hand: two threes, the queen of hearts, the eight of diamonds, the five of clubs. One of the threes was a club. He switched out his eight and got the two of hearts back. He folded.

"Smart move," she said.

"You missed my straight," he said. Immediately, he felt ridiculous for wanting to impress her.

They watched the rest of the round in silence. He felt the perspiration on his palms; it was so hot in the room. He wiped his hands on his shorts, and as he did so, his pinkie finger accidentally grazed Rachel's thigh. He took note of how thin the sliver of space between their legs was, and then he felt her closing in, pressing the edge of her thigh against his. Did she think that he had done that on purpose?

He played one more distracted round this way, not daring to move his leg, because if he did, he'd be admitting to the contact. He checked his watch again, noting the time now—

close to midnight—and separated from her. Underneath the table, she grabbed his wrist and slid a piece of paper into his hand.

He stuffed the paper into his pocket and stood. "Have a good night, guys," he said with a grin. "Don't stay up too late."

The counselors promised they wouldn't. Jack could hardly wait to get outside, where, underneath the dim light above the lodge's screen door, he read the note: "Tennis courts @ 1." Had she just had it ready all night to give to him?

Of course, he didn't go.

By noon the next day, it was ninety-seven degrees in the shade. Jack spent as much of the day as he could inside his air-conditioned office. He sat in a swivel chair at his desk, which was cluttered with stacks of overstuffed file folders and a clunky PC, and scanned through emails, mostly from parents and forwarded by his secretary, Nan. ("Why can't our daughter keep a cellphone at camp? I'd really just feel better about having her away for eight weeks if we were able to text her now and again." "Allison tells us the horses are not purebreds—we were not made aware of this when we initially decided on Camp Marigold.") He put the emails in his "Answer Later" folder and pulled up his bank account. The birthday check he'd sent to his son a month ago still had not been cashed. He had even written a note in the card this year: "It's really beautiful here. I don't know if you're a fan of nature, but I think you'd love it. You're welcome to visit at any time. I'll pull out all the stops."

A fan of nature? Pull out all the stops? He felt ashamed of his transparency, imagining the three of them—Junior and Laura and the doctor husband—laughing over the note.

He left the office right before lunchtime. He saw Rachel over in the stables, brushing a brown-and-white-speckled horse.

He went to the staff lodge again that night and played some rounds of poker. He drank his one Coors Light, and halfway through the night, Rachel took the empty seat next to him, pressed her thigh against his—that same crisis of inaction eating away at him—and, as he was leaving, grabbed his wrist and passed him a note. He read it outside: "Barn @ 1." Again, he didn't go.

Before Laura got pregnant, Jack had had ideas for himself. He wouldn't be so bold as to call them dreams. He was an okay student, okay enough to get into a Connecticut state school, the only thing he'd be able to afford to pay back. (Single mom; college was on him.) Not good enough at football to get a scholarship somewhere, but his future wasn't hopeless. He imagined a big school, maybe one with a study abroad program. London intrigued him; the English countryside intrigued him. It seemed far and foreign enough but manageably similar to home. He liked the idea of a place so heavy with gray fog that, on the occasion that it lifted, the sun would feel that much more earned.

They were high school sweethearts, and they got married fast, three months into the pregnancy. They were seventeen. It was the right thing to do, yes, but also, as they were going through all the motions of picking a place (her backyard) and an officiant (their local pastor), never once did he feel like it could turn out to be a mistake. She was bright; she made him laugh; she poked fun at his stoic nature, brought him out of his funks. Her family had more money than his, and Jack began to work in construction for her father's company. Laura had the baby: John Michael Pike, Jr. They lived in Laura's parents' house, in the windowless basement. Sometimes the darkness at night made Jack want to scream out. But he got a lot of sunlight during the day at least. Neither of them went back for senior year.

They lasted almost until Junior's first birthday, when Laura left Jack for her ob-gyn. She told him tearfully, sitting him down on the edge of their bed in the basement apartment, that they never would have worked out. Dr. Whatever-the-Fuck was, unlike Jack, her "intellectual equal."

He left the job with his father-in-law, moved out of the basement. Moved back in with his mom. Got his GED. Bagged groceries, took night classes at the community college. Was promoted to assistant manager at the Stop & Shop. Saw Junior once every two weeks, picking him up from the doctor's mansion in West Hartford. Jack's mom died— lifelong smoker, lung cancer. He sold her one-floor house, which turned a surprisingly okay profit. Moved to his own apartment in the same shitty part of Hartford. Was promoted to manager at the Stop & Shop. Got his bachelor's, graduating with a degree in physical education. Got a job as a PE teacher at a local elementary school. Twenty years hopping around schools until he eventually became the director of PE at one.

He knew Al Billings, the head of athletics at Marigold, from one of his previous schools. Al reached out because he thought that Jack could be a great fit for the open camp director position: hardworking, tons of experience in schools, a real self-starter. Great with kids but tough when necessary. Al's call came at just the right time; Jack was just getting out of, or trying to get out of, something with one of the kindergarten teachers at school. She was his age, never married, pretty but slightly overweight, unbelievably insecure. A history of abusive boyfriends, Jack learned, and he was the first who wasn't. It had initially been an arrangement of two lonely people, he had thought, but she had begun to treat him like some sort of savior, to dote on him, ask questions about their future together. He would have rather been lonely than trapped. He took the Marigold job.

It came with a pay raise and a year-round cabin. He'd looked forward to the mix of social and solitary aspects, for he thought of himself that way, as someone who liked to be around people but, after some time with them, needed to retreat, recharge. During the summers, he would be surrounded by campers and counselors; but from Labor Day to Memorial Day, he'd live in his house in the woods, put in a few morning hours in the office, and spend the afternoons running along the trails, hiking in the snow, and reading books he'd never bothered with before. Maybe he'd start a vegetable garden. Maybe he would get a dog.

He just hadn't anticipated how long that first winter would be. The action-packed summer went fast, and the cold days dragged on. Lakeville was a seasonal town; the local men were drunks, and the local women were ambitionless, cloying. It did not take him long to realize it was less lonely to stay in and get a good night's sleep than it was to drink his Jack Daniel's neat in a mostly empty tavern. Before spring's first thaw, he found himself anxious for the summer again. In early April, using a book from the Lakeville library as his guide, he planted cucumbers, tomatoes, and red peppers. He built a trellis and waited for the vines to start climbing.

Weekends at camp were more unstructured than the weekdays, so Jack rode around in his golf cart that Saturday, the day after Rachel passed him the second note. He was so distracted that he had to brake quickly to stop himself from hitting two older kids on their bikes.

"Watch where you're going, boys!"

He went back to the staff lodge that night because, he told himself, it was a Saturday. He had never gone two nights in a row before, let alone three.

At the poker table, she sat next to him, pressed her thigh against his, and made brief but imploring eye contact with him. She was older than her years, he began to tell himself.

She must have been. She was self-possessed, mature. She knew exactly what she was doing.

She passed her note. He left and read it outside: "Oar house @ 1."

He wouldn't just be fired if the board found out; his nascent career as a camp director would end nearly as soon as it had begun. He'd probably never get another reputable job.

He wasn't even the type to go for younger women. It felt creepy, unseemly, the difference in their ages.

And yet.

Somehow.

He suspected that to Rachel he was a conquest—an authority figure, a commodity. Her youth reflected his own aging self back at him. It made him grasp his own mortality more clearly, feel simultaneously free of and shackled by time.

So nothing really mattered. And therefore, everything did.

Inside the shed, it smelled like dust and overgrown dandelions. They knocked down paddles leaning against the walls, life jackets from their hooks. He felt too serious to laugh. It had been a while, and he finished too fast, but then he worked on her and took them both by surprise. They lay on a plastic tarp after, and he let her sleep for half an hour before waking her and telling her it was time to go back to her section. When she woke, there was no glimmer of regret as he'd expected there to be. She simply stood, brushed herself off, gave him a long kiss, and left the shed without a word.

———

The next day, Jack rode around on his golf cart feeling high. He kept thinking about Rachel and at one point rode past the girls' Hemlock section—for the thirteen-year-olds, where she was a counselor—just to catch a glimpse of her. He saw her chatting with a pair of campers, and when she saw his golf cart approaching, she looked up and shyly smiled. The thought of that smile distracted him throughout the day, but it also gave him a certain levity and confidence as he spoke at flag lowering, at dinner, at the opening campfire.

Later that night, she slithered so swiftly around his bedroom and under his sheets, knew exactly what to do in a way he hadn't experienced in half the grown women he'd been with. But then came the reminder: She mentioned that she had just completed her freshman year at Michigan.

He already had a son when he was her age, he told her.

"Where is he now?" she asked.

"Medical school."

"Were you married?"

"Briefly," he said.

It continued like this for three more nights: Monday, Tuesday, Wednesday. The heat still had not broken. She spent each night in his cabin and left early in the morning in order to make it back to her tent before the campers awoke. The sex was good for both of them. And he was getting used to the pillow talk, which he hadn't had with anyone since the kindergarten teacher over a year ago. She was a smart girl, Rachel. One night he asked her, postcoitus, what she was studying at school. She said she was thinking of majoring in gender studies.

"You're not one of those militant feminists, are you?" he joked as he twisted a piece of her hair between his fingers. In truth, he felt intimidated by her intelligence. Why did he always do this to himself, go for the women he was too stupid to actually be with? Sometimes he felt like a token to them: a working-class guy, athletic, dumb, good with his hands.

She jerked her head away. "You have no idea what you're talking about."

"I was kidding."

"Feminists believe that men and women deserve the same rights. How is that militant?"

"There are just some women who get crazy about it. You know, like . . . the really butch ones. Who basically look and act and talk like men. There's something unnatural about that."

"What's *unnatural*," she said, getting riled up in a way that excited Jack, "is supporting women's equality in the social stratosphere but also wanting them to stay stunted in their appearance. There's this reigning mentality that women can be successful and at the top of their game so long as they still look like women, so long as they're still hot and youthful and thin while maintaining their childbearing hips. If women look too much like men, they're a threat. If they still look like women, they can do whatever they want, because men are technically safe from them."

"Don't put words in my mouth," Jack said. "I don't believe that all women need to look and act a certain way. But men and women are different for a reason, biologically. Can you agree with that?"

"Of course," she said. "But that's not what we're talking about."

"So what are we talking about?"

She looked Jack over once like she felt sorry for him. "You're lucky you're handsome," she said, resting her head on his chest and falling asleep soon after.

Jack slept through Rachel's departure on Thursday morning and awoke to an empty bed. It was only six but already oppressively hot, almost too hot for coffee. After one slam of the snooze button, he got up and stood over the kitchen sink in his boxers, considering the coffee issue for a moment before putting the kettle on. As the water boiled, he dragged the fan from his room into the kitchen until he felt the resistance of the extension cord.

The kettle hissed. He poured and drank his coffee and pulled the dusty blinds open. The camp was still empty, and the morning was hazy; he could not see the lake from his cabin as he could on clearer days, only the downward slope of the green hill leading to it.

The coffee was heating him from inside. He was a glutton for punishment.

He considered not going on his four-mile run but quickly quashed the thought. He ran the same route in snow and rain. If Jack believed in anything, he believed in routine. So he went, jogging down the road, its two lanes marked in faded paint, that ran along the southern edge of camp, out to the gas station and back, counting three trucks, four deer, and zero people. The air was thick, heavy, like he was running against a current.

Back at camp, he ran up the main drive, passing the empty horse arena and cutting through the dew-slippery athletic fields. Still not a person out. He turned the knob on his shower all the way to the right and stood under the ice-cold water for several minutes.

At flag raising, he stood beside the flagpole with his hand at his heart. An Aspen boy was unfolding the flag, and Chad watched from behind the boy, overseeing the whole thing. Jack wondered, in a brief patriotic moment, if he should instate a rule that would reserve that right for American counselors.

The girls were on one side of the green facing the flag and the boys on the other. They were ordered by their age sections, which were named, idiotically, after trees, from the young Maples in the front to the fourteen-year-old Evergreens at the back. He looked out at Rachel from the flagpole; her face was glistening in the heat, her cheeks adorably pink.

After the pledge, he asked, "Are there any announcements?"

Chad raised his hand, then ran it through his messy hair while he announced the coed boat race on Saturday night. Jack resumed his place in front of the flag, and the campers waited.

"I don't need to tell you all it's hot out today." He told

them to drink a lot of water and stay in the shade. He told them to take it slow, take it easy today. He remembered Rachel telling him, "You don't look a day over thirty-eight."

He clapped his hands together. "Let's eat."

Jack walked somewhere in the middle of the pack to the d-hall, watching the boys and girls sloppily flirting, nudging shoulders and elbows with one another, some girls pretending to be annoyed by it, before they split into two groups to go to their separate dining halls. Rachel walked arm in arm with Fiona, ignoring her campers, wearing those short denim shorts that shouldn't be allowed. He was careful to watch her walking for just a few seconds, her narrow hips swaying back and forth, her pert ass contained in the tiny shorts. He had a moment of ego-stroking disbelief that he got to be the one to sleep with her night after night.

At breakfast, Jack sat at a table at the front of the boys' dining hall with the male activity and section heads.

"Looks great," he said to the kitchen boy serving plates of powdered eggs and cubed potatoes.

"You're too nice," Chad said to Jack once the kitchen boy had gone to the next group. "I have to eat these shit eggs one more time, I'll be sick all over this table."

Jack waved his fork at Chad. "These shit eggs buy you an extra few bucks in your paycheck."

Chad changed the subject: He had found a bong made from a plastic water bottle, duct tape, and a hollowed-out pen in one of the Evergreen boys' bathroom stalls. Jack was supposed to crack down on this sort of thing, but the truth was, the rebellious kids were from the richest families and had been going to Marigold forever; their parents sent them there summer after summer so they didn't have to deal with them. Unless the board caught wind of it, you turned a blind eye.

"It wasn't poorly done," Chad said. "But I would have used an apple from d-hall. Less apparatus."

"You still have it?" Brett, the head of swimming, asked.

The kitchen boy came to refill their coffees.

When he left, Brett asked with his mouth full of potatoes, "You all see Rachel's shorts today?"

Chad nodded, raising his eyebrows, and went back to his shit eggs.

"Hey," Jack said, louder than he'd intended, then lowered his voice, "this isn't a locker room."

Brett put his hands up. "Just saying what we were all thinking."

"Well." Jack stabbed a potato cube. "Keep it to yourself."

He spent the rest of the breakfast in silence, except for an occasional request for someone to "pass the ketchup" so he could disguise the taste of the powdered eggs.

Sometime after lunch, he got in his golf cart and took a ride to the lake. Chad was sitting close to Rachel on the dock, their feet dangling over the edge. A dozen canoes and kayaks were out, kids rowing them unimpressively in circles.

Jack parked his golf cart and walked down the dock.

"Hiya, Chad," he said. "Rachel."

They looked up, sunglasses covering their eyes.

"Hey, Jack," Chad said.

"You guys got some counselors out there on the boats?" He surveyed the scene, listening to the giggles and the unruly splashes coming from the lake. "Doesn't look like it." This was important, this act of establishing authority at the appropriate times.

"There's some CITs out there," Chad said. "Not to worry."

"CITs aren't counselors," Jack said in his camp-director voice.

Rachel stood. She was wearing a simple black bathing suit, still sexy despite being a one-piece, and her hair was wild from the humidity.

"I can go out," she said, seeming unfazed by Jack's presence. "We were just discussing strategy for the boat race Saturday."

"Strategy?" Jack smirked. "It's a boat race. You've got your boats. You've got your start. You've got your finish."

"Right, but . . ."

"Just get out there," he said, nodding toward the water. Then he stayed standing at the edge of the dock and watched them approach an empty canoe on the shoreline. Rachel walked to the front of the boat and sat on the bench at the bow as Chad, ankle-deep in muddy water, pushed the boat out of the muck. She craned her neck toward Jack, briefly—had he been too much of an asshole just then?—and he began to nod in recognition of her, but as Chad lumbered in, she turned around and faced the water, picked up a paddle, and rowed.

———

Jack went to the staff lodge that night. Rachel shared a chair with Chad at the table nearest the AC, one butt cheek on him and her other leg dangling, her toes tapping the ground. They were giggling as Jack pulled up a chair, sat across from them, and began to shuffle the cards sitting on the table. Eight other counselors, guys and girls, sat at the round table.

"Five-card draw," Jack said. "Who's in?"

Both Rachel and Chad played. Jack won two of the four rounds. The first was a lucky hand. Chad won the second round only because he had somehow landed a full house; the guy had no poker face. The third, Jack stayed in, and everyone else backed down, and he collected without revealing his hand, nothing but a pair of threes. The fourth hand, only Rachel and Jack were left in a showdown. Her face stayed dispassionate as she placed her hand on the table faceup, showing a straight.

Jack had three kings. He'd thought he had her.

"Can't win 'em all, Jack," she said, and scooped up the chips.

"Good thing it's not real money." He winked, because even though they all kept tallies of their wins and losses, it was accepted knowledge that everyone went in on a staff party at the end of the summer and called it even.

"Good thing," she said. She whispered something into Chad's ear; he kissed her on the cheek, and she stood and waved to the group. "I'm going to bed, guys," she said, and made toward the back door.

Usually she went back to her section with the other Hemlock counselors at the end of the night, then snuck down to Jack's cabin after everyone was asleep.

He counted to thirty in his head. "Ya know what? I'm beat, kids."

Outside, he caught her halfway up the hill and grabbed her elbow, entirely unconcerned with being seen. This was, he was learning, part of the fun of it—he felt like he was invincible, like he was getting away with it, over and over.

She started before she turned. "You scared me," she said, eyes wide, then looked around. "Not a good idea for you to follow me."

"We're fine," he said, gesturing at the dark, empty camp and then tracing his fingers down her arm. "I'll see you later?"

She let out a loud yawn. "I'm exhausted, Jack."

"We can just sleep if you want," he said.

She shook her head. "I'm really not in the mood."

"Of course," he said, nodding emphatically. "Next time, then."

She frowned; Jack couldn't tell, as he searched her darkened face, whether she was regretting her answer just then or regretting that anything had happened at all.

And so she did not come to his bed that night or the next. By Saturday, the heat still had not broken.

At the boat race, Jack welcomed everyone, and then Chad set the ground rules ("No horseplay. No going past the buoys. No going before my whistle. No standing in the boats."), and the kids went out in coed teams: a girl and a boy from the same section in each canoe.

Jack stood on the dock, wearing his Camp Marigold polo and cheering for the kids. Al Billings walked over and stood next to him.

"Some heat we had this week, huh, boss?" Al said.

"You're tellin' me."

After they exchanged a few more pleasantries, Al lowered his voice. "I wanted to ask you—well, Lucy wanted to ask you, really—are you seeing anyone?" Lucy was Al's wife.

Jack looked over Al's shoulder—he hoped imperceptibly—at Rachel standing on the shoreline in her bathing suit and shorts, hands cupped around her mouth as she cheered on her girls.

"Well," Jack said, "it's complicated."

"Recent breakup?"

"Not quite," Jack said. "Just going through a rough patch."

Al nodded. "A long time since I've been single," he said. "But if you change your mind or things don't work out, Lucy's friend has a daughter, recent divorce. A bit younger than you. Very pretty."

"Thanks, Al," Jack said. "I think this is just a bump in the road."

That night, Jack decided to get beer for everyone as a thank-you for doing what they could with the heat that week and for making the boat race happen without a hitch; it also might loosen things up between Rachel and him. He drove to the nearest gas station and picked up two cases of Natty Light. He didn't care if it tasted like water; it reminded him of high school parties after football games and of the early nights of his and Laura's marriage, when he would drink three, four, five while watching a game on TV in the basement, and she, pregnant and glowing, would lay her swollen feet on his lap.

"The party's here," Jack said, entering through the downstairs door, lifting one of the cases. The glistening teens and twentysomethings cheered from near the AC. It was like the first time he had come into the lodge during staff training, but then they were cheering just for him. Now it was for the beer. For a second, Jack felt like a corrupter, like a creep, but then he reminded himself: *They'd be having fun anyway, without you.* Jack caught Rachel's eye, and she quickly turned her head. Chad, who had his hand on her waist, was looking in another direction.

This time they played Kings, which got everyone drunk fast. As Jack drank, he felt himself leaning too far across the table, talking too loudly, pointing fingers at people who weren't drinking enough. He kept reaching into the case of beer next to him. Rachel sat across the table from him, drinking steadily. Her chair was next to Chad's, and their knees were touching slightly, but she had a bored look about her and seemed moved by neither man's presence.

She eventually got up without a word and walked to the bathroom down a darkened hallway off the downstairs room. Jack stood. "Gotta piss." He caught the bathroom door before she closed it. He shut and locked it behind him, turned her around, and pinned her against it, thrusting his tongue into her mouth.

"You're drunk, Jack," she said when he pulled back. But then she smiled as if to say she didn't mind.

"I've been wanting to fuck you for days," he whispered into her ear, then licked it.

"This is interesting," she said.

He slid his hand up her dress and between her legs, and she fell into the touch. He worked furiously, panting. At the end, she let out a sigh and then stood straighter, as if suddenly remembering where she was.

"You're so beautiful," he said, putting his arms around her and nuzzling his nose into the side of her face.

"Stop, Jack," she said, straightening out her dress.

"I'm serious," he said, using one hand to move her chin so she faced him. "Watching you just then was the most beautiful thing I've ever seen." He didn't mean for it to sound like a line. In that moment, he meant it.

She moved the hand away and walked to the mirror above the sink to check her reflection. She ran cool water from the faucet and splashed it onto her face.

"Am I missing something?" he said from the door while she cleaned off her eye makeup with a paper towel. She stopped with the towel between her fingers and looked at him in the mirror. "What the hell is your problem all of a sudden?"

When she turned around to face him, he saw her sad, pitying face—still pink from the orgasm or maybe from the heat. Right then, he knew it had ended, that he had ruined it at the very moment he had shown he was angry, and hurt. He wanted to believe that this had to do with her age and nothing to do with him, but he knew that wanting what you couldn't have and not wanting what you could never really stopped. He'd taken it that one step too far, and now he was no longer a confident older man but a lonely one.

"I just . . ." She bit her lower lip and shifted her weight unsteadily. "I can't sleep at your house every night, Jack. I don't want anything serious. I'm nineteen."

He stood against the door.

"Jack, I'm really drunk."

"What makes you think I do?" he said, feeling his body shaking.

She shook her head. "I have to pee." She watched him until he had no choice but to leave.

He walked out of the bathroom, got back to the table, and drank another Natty Light. The game had ended, so he sat there drinking while the others were laughing with their heads back and jaws hanging loose. A few were leaving, and he mumbled good nights as they passed him, offering quick, shifty nods. Rachel appeared who knew how much later from the bathroom and walked upstairs. Chad got up from the poker table and dutifully followed.

Soon after, Jack followed too, bringing his case of beer with him and splaying himself out on one of the lounge chairs. Chad and Rachel were sitting next to each other on one of the couches.

Jack slurped from can after can, wiping his brow with the back of his hand and pretending not to watch Chad and Rachel talk and inch closer to each other. Soon it was only the three of them in the upstairs lounge. Rachel looked distraught and wasted, and started falling asleep on Chad's shoulder.

"You all right, Jack?" Chad said at one point.

"Fine," he said.

"All right." He jerked his head toward a dozing Rachel. "I'm gonna walk this one back. I think we're the only ones left."

Jack belched. Chad shook Rachel awake, took her arm, and led her out. Jack counted to twenty and followed, taking a beer with him.

"I need to go to bed," Jack heard Rachel whine.

Chad said, "I'm taking you there," but he was leading her toward the woods behind the performing arts building. Jack started to walk down the slope toward his cabin but stopped at the edge of the forest. He hid behind a giant sycamore and watched Chad and Rachel move into the woods.

They walked ahead a little longer, and Jack kept a close but respectable distance, fifty feet or so, just close enough to make out the outlines of their bodies under what he figured had to be a full moon ahead.

Soon the crunching of leaves beneath their feet stopped, and he could make out their two bodies against the base of a tree. He stood still, his breathing shallow and almost silent. He could see the silhouettes of their writhing bodies: Rachel's head moving left and right against the tree, her entire figure anchored to the trunk save for the arched small of her back, which Chad held with one hand. His other arm was outstretched and steadied against the tree's base, the hand landing just next to her lolling head. Her hands roamed from Chad's head to his neck to his shoulders and lower back and ass, and her hips moved forward and back as Chad held up the folds of her dress.

Jack could hear Rachel whimpering and Chad grunting. Soon the grunts began to quicken as he thrust into her faster and faster until finally he let out a low, drunken moan.

Afterward, Chad moved his face into Rachel's neck, but she pushed him away. She tucked her hair behind her ears and brushed dirt off the back of her dress. She said something to Chad and began to walk ahead of him, toward the edge of the woods. Chad buttoned his pants and followed.

And then, Rachel stopped. She held herself still, and Chad, probably thinking she was waiting for him, put his arms on her shoulders from behind. She shrugged them off and said something else, and then he dropped his hands at his side and stood like a soldier at attention.

Jack savored the moment. He walked toward them slowly, deliberately, suddenly sober. He was breathing heavy now, filled with purpose, an old man in charge.

He looked into Chad's eyes and then Rachel's.

"You're both fired," he said, and he let those words hang

in the air. He watched them fall onto Chad's and Rachel's stunned faces—Rachel's incredulous, crestfallen, beautiful face. Chad began to open his mouth, but Jack did not let him speak.

"Pack your things," Jack said, already walking away.

Jack got back to his cabin and surveyed it, austere and modest and his. He turned on his fan, dropped onto his bed, and immediately fell asleep, sound and alone, on top of his sheets.

In the morning he found himself in the previous night's clothes, the sheets soaked with sweat. He turned on his transistor radio—today, the heat would break, the man said—and put on clean boxers, made himself coffee, and looked out onto the still-quiet camp. Today he took his coffee cup and walked around the back porch, which faced his vegetable garden.

His garden. He had somehow forgotten about it, neglected it over the last week. For a moment, he worried the heat had killed everything.

He walked down the few steps to the garden. Miraculously, his cucumbers were still growing in greens of all shades. The peppers too were fleshy and full, and there were little baby peppers growing from new stems on the same plants. He went inside to get his colander, then returned and pulled the greener cucumbers and the redder peppers from their stalks.

And the tomatoes: The vines were crawling up the trellis he'd built. Was it possible the vines had grown almost a foot since the last time he checked? The fruits were orange and yellow and red, plump, their skin shining. They had multiplied, maybe quadrupled in the last week. They had never looked better.

11

"Do we have to go?" the girls asked Fiona as they reluctantly took their dry bathing suits down from the clothesline.

"It'll be over before you know it," Fiona said.

That night was a camp-wide, coed boat race, but her girls were too young to care about coed activities, still in the stage where being with one another was much more fun than anything a boy could provide. She didn't blame them; at nine years old, the Maple boys ignored the Maple girls entirely, unsure of what to do with the girls' precociousness and femininity, thinking them too smart or too delicate to appreciate a good fart joke.

Down at the lake, teams were already assembling: one boy and one girl on each, each competing against another coed twosome from the same age section. The competitors for the older sections, the Hemlocks and the Evergreens, were already pairing up, groups that had probably been conceived a week earlier, boy-girl pairs based on whoever was "hanging out" this week. She saw Helen and Sarah standing with Mikey and Danny—tall, magnetic Danny appearing to tell some story bombastically while the other three listened, ready to laugh.

Rachel was standing nearby, chatting with one of her fellow Hemlock counselors.

Yonatan was a counselor for the Maple boys, and he beckoned a group of his boys toward her group of girls.

"Hey," he said, smiling kindly, as his boys shuffled in the sand behind him. "Are your girls on teams yet?"

"No, they aren't," she said, raising her eyebrows at the girls, because she knew that she and Yonatan would have to coordinate this, that these kids were not going to take any initiative themselves.

"Billie," Fiona said to one of the girls standing behind her, "is there a boy you'd like to be teamed up with?"

Billie shrugged.

Yonatan turned around to survey his group. "Avery," he said to the lanky boy standing off to the side. "Do you want to be on Billie's team?"

"I think you guys would make a great pair," Fiona said, which was true: both were quiet, smart kids. Average in terms of athleticism.

"Okay," Avery said to his feet, and he walked toward Billie but landed a good foot away from her.

Emily and Marley's arms were linked—the two did everything together—and it took some cajoling just to get them to separate from each other, let alone pair them up with boys. Fiona and Yonatan continued to create teams, conferring with each other on the matchups. It was fun, this part of working with young kids—the absolute authority one had. They finished the teams with few arguments from the kids and sent them off to the boating staff to get their life jackets and their paddles.

Yonatan was still standing next to Fiona after their kids had gone to the dock. He hadn't saved that dance for her at the dance like he'd promised. He had seemed more into Rachel that night, which was unsurprising, of course. Fiona never asked Rachel if anything had happened between them—better to leave it alone, considering that was also the night Rachel's father had died. Besides, she didn't want to know the answer.

"I think we did good," he said.

"Yeah," she said, looking over at their groups. Some boys and girls whom they had paired up stood next to each other, awkward and silent, while other campers, like Emily and Marley, gravitated toward their same sex again, refusing to acknowledge their partners until the moment they had to get into the boat.

"Give it three years, and we won't be able to pull them apart," he said.

"I like this group for that reason," she said. "Their innocence is so nice. Refreshing, kind of. I can talk about real things with them: their lives at home and their friends and the things they like to do—ride horses or swim or dance or draw. Rachel says her girls only talk about boys."

He turned to her. "You're right. It is refreshing."

Something about the intensity in his stare made her uncomfortable, and she had to look away.

"You're very insightful, Fiona," he said.

She didn't know how to respond to that.

"Are you blushing?" he asked.

She put a hand to her face.

He very gently pulled her hand away from her cheek. "Don't hide it," he said. "It's cute."

"He was flirting with you!" Rachel exclaimed later that night, beer can in hand, in the staff lodge.

"No, he wasn't," said Fiona. "He was making fun of me."

"Jesus, Fiona," Rachel said. "You wouldn't know a come-on if it fucked you in the ass."

Rachel stumbled away to sit on Chad's lap. According to Rachel, there was still nothing happening between them, despite the fact that they flirted perpetually. Fiona didn't understand why anyone would be into him; his nose was always sunburned, and he wore the same army-print bucket hat every day.

Fiona slowly followed Rachel to the couch and sat on the other side of Chad. Rachel slumped farther onto Chad, her body limp. Its whole weight rested on him. He traced the fingers of one hand up and down her spine while he took a hit of a joint with the other.

Fiona put her hand out. "May I?" She let the smoke fill her lungs, and that instantly familiar sense of calm came over her.

Rachel nuzzled her nose into Chad's neck. He passed the joint to her and then whispered something into her ear.

Fiona sat quietly for a few more minutes, uninvolved in their private conversation, until Chad finally passed the joint to her again. After that second hit, she stood.

"Night, Rach," she said.

Rachel looked up, as if she'd just noticed Fiona was there.

"Where are you going?" Rachel asked.

"Bed," Fiona said. "Don't stay out too late."

"What are you, her mum?" Chad said, but Fiona was just high enough to not retort.

She left the staff lodge and walked up the hill to girls' camp. It was almost midnight, and there were few lights on now. After so many summers, she could have made it from any one point to another barefoot and blindfolded. She looked up as she walked. She found the Big Dipper, then the Little. The Milky Way. When one looks up at the stars alone on a quiet night, it's very easy to feel insignificant. She didn't know any other constellations and made a resolution to study more of them when she could. Then she made a resolution not to forget to do this just because she was high.

She got back to the Maple section and crept into her tent. Sometimes, in the middle of the night, her girls whimpered and cried, homesick, and she stroked their hair, wiped their tears away. Billie had a lovely voice and sometimes sang to the other girls at night to assuage their sadness.

Fiona lay in her bunk for a few minutes, thinking about her own summer as a nine-year-old, her first summer at Camp Marigold. She remembered the Fourth of July from that summer the best. After the fireworks, they'd gone back to their section, and her tentmates had begun to sob in their bunks, one after another, a domino effect of hysteria. Fiona had tried to make herself cry, but nothing came out. She'd liked the fireworks over the lake; she wouldn't have wanted to be anywhere else.

Now she was hungry. She couldn't sleep when she was hungry. As quietly as she could, she got up, opened her trunk, and rifled through her T-shirts to find the bag of granola and the jar of peanut butter she kept in there, raccoons be damned. She took them out, closed her trunk, and walked to the bathroom, a moldy cabin filled with millipedes and spider webs. She sat on the dusty floor and, with her fingers, reached into the bag of granola and dipped the bits into the peanut butter. At the first bite, she made an involuntary groan. The combination of sweet and salty was better than anything else, better than being drunk or high, better even than the one orgasm she'd ever had (in her childhood bed, seventh grade, by accident, and it had been so powerful and unruly that she was afraid to experience it again).

At flag raising in the morning, Fiona looked for Rachel but didn't see her. She wondered if Rachel was hungover and had faked sick to sleep an extra hour or two.

Their friendship was like this. Fiona was reliable and predictable. Rachel knew where she could find her friend in most moments. But about Rachel the opposite was true: She was so often inaccessible, unavailable. Fiona had realized sometime during this summer that they actually liked each other for these reasons; each one fulfilled what the other lacked. Fiona was steady, and Rachel was spontaneous, and for so many summers, they had thrived in their roles.

But this summer, Fiona was beginning to feel that something had shifted and she couldn't get it back, like being the paragon of steadiness had begun to wear her down. Maybe more of it was required of her now, after Rachel's father had died, and at first she had thought she was okay with that. But ever since the night at the motel, Fiona had wondered how Rachel would react if Fiona wasn't there for her. Fiona wondered how good, how freeing it might feel. Even just for one day.

Fiona walked down to the stables after breakfast. Normally she and Rachel groomed and fed the horses before the campers got there, and gossiped about whatever had happened the night before.

She opened the heavy door to the barn and filled a bucket from the supply station with soap and warm water from the hose. She strained to carry the heavy bucket as she walked along the cement floor to Josie's stall. Josie was the palomino that Fiona's parents had bought for her for her thirteenth birthday. Both Fiona and Helen kept their horses at camp during the summer. Before the Larkin girls, this had been unprecedented at Camp Marigold.

Josie approached the edge of her stall when she saw Fiona

and peeked her head out. Fiona opened the stall and let her-self in. She squeezed a sponge onto Josie's golden-hued coat and let the soapy water drip into the mounds of hay.

When she finished washing Josie, she began working on the other horses. She checked her watch; without Rachel's help she was running out of time before the campers would get there for the first activity period. She stopped with the washing, even though she'd gotten to only four of the horses, and began to fill the feed buckets.

Nell, the lead horseback-riding counselor, entered the barn and propped the door open to let the light in. When Fiona first met Nell, Fiona thought she was cool and no-nonsense, with her tough exterior and her posh British ac-cent. She loved Nell's long red hair. But then Fiona and Rachel found out that Nell was a year younger than them, and it bothered Rachel especially that Nell was their boss. She observed that Nell was a "dyke." "She walks with her legs so far apart," Rachel had said, "like she has a dick in between them." After that, Fiona had not been able to think of Nell in any other terms.

Nell peeked into the first stall. "They're not saddled yet?" she asked.

Fiona shook her head. "I'm on my own right now," she said, putting a bucket of feed in Firework's stall.

"They didn't need to be washed today," Nell said.

"I haven't seen Rachel since last night." Fiona suddenly felt like her friend's disappearance was her own fault.

Nell didn't respond to this, though she looked at Fiona

curiously. Nell opened her mouth like she was about to say something but then she shook her head, reached down to pick up an armful of saddles, and began to put one on Firework, whose snout was entirely submerged in the feed bucket.

The Hemlock girls came to first-period riding. This included Helen.

She entered the barn with her bevy of friends. Her deceptively angelic blond curls were loose around her face. She walked ahead to Dandelion, her horse, whose stall was next to Josie's.

"How's my girl?" Helen said to Dandelion. She kissed her horse on the nose and scratched between her ears.

"You're so lucky," one of Helen's friends said to her, which was what they always said.

Helen looked up at Fiona, suddenly realizing she was right there in front of Josie's stall.

"Hey," Helen said to her sister, an unreadable expression on her face. Fiona knew Helen well enough to know how unusual this was.

"Hey," Fiona said. "Have you seen Rachel?"

Helen's hand stopped stroking the horse. She looked at the other girls, who looked at Fiona and then back at Helen.

"You didn't hear?" Helen said.

"Hear what?"

Helen bit her bottom lip.

"Where is she?" Fiona said. "Is she okay?"

"She's gone, Fee," Helen said.

"What do you mean, *gone*?"

"I mean gone. She left before we woke up this morning."

Fiona looked around at the other girls, hoping someone would contradict her sister. No one did. "What are you talking about?"

"Mo didn't say why," Helen said. "She just pulled us all into the middle of the section this morning and said that Rachel had to leave and that we'll know by the end of the day who our new counselor is."

"It's so crazy," one of the girls chimed in.

"I can't believe she didn't say goodbye to you," Helen said to her sister.

Another Hemlock girl entered the circle. "I just heard Chad's gone too."

By lunch, it was all anyone was talking about.

"I heard they were caught doing drugs in the oar house," Fiona heard one Evergreen girl say to another on the salad bar line.

"Like pot?"

"No, like, hard stuff."

Fiona asked her section leader if she could leave to make a phone call in the office. They weren't allowed to use their cellphones at camp, but Rachel wasn't at camp, and hers might be charged and on by now. Fiona went to the front desk and dialed the number she knew by heart, but it went straight to voicemail.

All day, rumors swirled around the camp: "I heard they were skinny-dipping in the lake." "I heard they left camp when they weren't supposed to, and Jack found them ordering Chicken McNuggets at the McDonald's in Salisbury." "I heard they were caught hooking up in the backseat of someone else's car."

Fiona taught riding all afternoon as if she were floating on a cloud above the camp. She watched the girls and gave them orders, but the words felt disconnected from her. All she could think of was the theories about Rachel. Any of them were possible.

When the day was over, Fiona took the saddles off all the horses and fed them again. The campers buzzed at flag lowering. She could sense a seriousness in Jack as he made his evening announcements. At dinner, she picked at the salad on her plastic plate, surprised to find she didn't have much of an appetite.

At bedtime, she tucked her girls into their bunks.

"Fiona?" asked Billie, who was one of the youngest girls.

"Yeah, sweetie?"

"Can I sing us a bedtime song?"

"You want to sing for us?"

"Yeah," Billie said. "I learned it in music class today."

"Does everyone want a bedtime song?"

Yes! the girls said. Of course we do! Which was how it came to be that Fiona cried silently in her tent of nine-year-olds while Billie sang, like a prescient little angel, "All the lonely people, where do they all come from?"

———

At the staff lodge that night, Fiona learned the truth: They were caught. In the woods. They were fucking. Jack had found them.

"But were they obvious?"

"How can you not be obvious when you're fucking like animals?"

"But how did he find them so late and in the dark?"

"Who cares? Sounds like they were asking for it."

It felt odd to be at the staff lodge without Rachel, as if Fiona were suddenly naked and on display. She was deeply embarrassed and hurt that she wasn't the one who had known what had happened first.

"Have you talked to her?" people kept asking.

Fiona lied and said yes. She had.

"How is she?"

"She's fine," Fiona told them.

She smoked more than usual that night. She sat in a lounge chair high and watched everyone. Sometimes the right high made her careless and free. This one felt like a swirl of uneasy existential dread. She watched Yonatan pinch Steph and Becca make out with Logan and Nell drink a beer alone, and it was like watching all these people who seemed to know, so much better than Fiona, how to be alive. They were all playing their roles perfectly; weaving in and out of groups seamlessly; saying the right things, making the right quips, at the right times, as if they were performing just for her as an example of What She's Done Wrong. It felt so at odds with her own existence, fraught with that insecurity that she didn't *get* it, didn't ever know the right thing to say or do in a situation, when it seemed like everyone else did.

And then she remembered! Oh God, that memory. It pricked right at the center of her chest. It was earlier in the summer, on their first day off, the night when they got kicked out of the Super 8. She had been drunk and peeing, and she'd heard Rachel and Chad and Yonatan and Steph talking shit about her.

Chad had called her a "narc." Rachel had said, in response, something like, "Yeah, but she has a car."

How the fuck had Fiona forgotten that memory?

She stood, too high and faltering on her feet. Yonatan was talking closely to Steph. Fiona tapped him on the shoulder.

He turned around and beamed at her. "Well, hello, Miss Fiona."

"I am not a narc," she said.

Steph looked up at Yonatan with a grin.

"What?" Yonatan said.

"I said. I. Am. Not. A. Narc."

"A narc?" Yonatan played with the tab on his can of Coors Light. "What's a narc?"

"It's, like, someone who's kind of lame and who tells on people," Steph explained to him.

"Yeah," Fiona said. "That. That's what you guys called me."

"I don't know what—"

"At the Super 8," Fiona said. "I heard you." She shoved Yonatan now, and he stumbled backward a few steps, not from force but from surprise. "I heard you!"

Now a crowd was forming around them. Steph put her arm on Fiona's shoulder. "Fee, I know you're upset that Rachel's gone, but you don't have to go making up things."

"No." Fiona pushed Steph's hand away. "Don't call me Fee."

Jack approached the commotion.

"Maybe someone should walk you up to your bunk, Fiona," he said. "You seem a tad worn out."

"I'm fine," she said. "I'm *fine*."

She stormed out of the staff lodge anyway and up to her section without her flashlight. She got to her tent and opened the flaps. Inside, it was quiet. Billie was asleep in the bunk above Fiona's.

Fiona touched the top of the girl's head.

"Billie," Fiona said quietly, stroking the child's hair. "Billie."

The girl whimpered.

"Billie, can you sing that song again?" Fiona asked.

"What?" the girl asked, still half-asleep.

"That song. The lonely song."

"Do I have to?" Billie asked.

"Yes, sweetie," Fiona said. "You have to."

12

By the eighth and final week of camp, Helen still had not gotten her period, which was just fine with her.

That last week was always a sad one for Helen. Camp was so much better than her life at home and her boring house and her boring friends, especially now that Marla was gone. But the summer had been a good one. She had been a color wars captain, and her team had won. She had kissed Mikey Bombowski underneath an oak tree. She had gotten really good at waterskiing. Sarah had suddenly become mischievous and brought pot that summer, and they had smoked it in the woods behind their tent at night without getting caught. They spent the following two hours giggling on a mossy log.

Sarah had gone from having the smallest chest in their section of girls to the largest over the course of one year. It was only Sarah's body that had changed; her face remained more or less the same, so she looked like a little girl with a woman's body, and she had the confusing mix of affectations to match: with boys, the prolonged glances and light touches of a young woman who had just learned of her power, the sudden confidence and claiming of responsibility that came with having to wear bras and change tampons. But she still had girlish tendencies, like the fetishizing of celebrities (Zac Efron was a favorite, and they had tacked up posters of him in the bathroom cabin) and the bouts of homesickness and the fun that came with making skits or playing four square just with the girls, though none of them ever wanted to admit that they often had more fun on single-sex activity nights than they did during the coeds.

On the last night of camp, all the girls from all the age sections made a campfire down by the lake. They sat around it in a "Kumbaya" sort of way with their blankets and their flashlights and their snacks. They sang the same sappy hippie songs every year and mourned the end of the summer and the friendships that would surely fade.

When Helen went to Sarah's house during the school year, they would stay up late, watch R-rated movies, and steal Bud Lights from the back of the fridge. Sarah was an only child, but her parents never seemed to know where she was, what she was doing, and whom she was doing it with. Mr. and Mrs. Larkin implicitly trusted Sarah's parents, who were white and well dressed and inhabited a large, clean home. But the specialness of Helen and Sarah's relationship was never as special when not surrounded by other girls they could exclude or by the lush, endless trails and woods of Camp Marigold. Watching *Wedding Crashers* with a Bud Light buzz lost its luster after the third time they saw the movie, but getting lost in the forest at night would always be exciting.

By the first chorus of "The Circle Game" ("We can't return. We can only look behind from where we came"), Helen and Sarah were clutching each other's hands and letting the tears fall unabashedly down their faces. At these campfires, it wasn't about fighting your tears; in fact, it was the opposite. The more you cried, the more you cared. Tears were a marker of how feminine, how much of a girl you were.

Fiona led the girls from her tent in singing "In My Life" by the Beatles. Fiona never cried at these things. In two weeks, she would go back to college, and she'd forget all about this summer.

Another group sang "Puff, the Magic Dragon," with the sign language that corresponded to the lyrics.

When they all had exhausted their sentimental-song repertoire, Helen's favorite tradition began: the floating wishes. Each girl was given a paper lantern with a votive candle inside it. As each candle was lit, the girl made a silent wish, then sent the lantern out into the lake where, legend had it, her wish would materialize and eventually come true. When all the candles were lit, the lake glittered with the golden-yellow wishes, floating aimlessly as they burned.

"I'm not done with camp," Helen whispered to Sarah that night in their bunks.

"What do you mean?" Sarah said.

Helen snuck out ten minutes before Sarah did; they met down at the stables. Without saying anything, Helen hopped over the fence and into the horse arena. Sarah didn't have any choice but to follow.

"Isn't the barn locked?" Sarah whispered.

Helen wasn't sure how it was going to go, but in fact, the barn door had been left open, and she acted as if she'd known this all along. Truthfully, if she had known earlier that the barn was never locked, she would have snuck out to ride earlier in the summer.

She opened Dandelion's stall and then Josie's. Sarah could ride Fiona's horse.

They saddled the horses in the dark and crept out into the night. They trotted behind the performing arts building, down the hill to the lakeshore. The paper lanterns were still burning.

"Look," Helen said. "Our wishes."

They kept going along the lakeshore until they got to the other side. When they were in a desolate enough area, they turned their electric lanterns on and continued to cross through the trails that traversed camp bounds and began in the foothills of the Berkshires. They stayed up in those hills for an hour or so, climbing up the narrow pathways between the trees.

"Do you know where we are?" Sarah asked, sounding worried.

"Of course," Helen said, and she did. This wasn't her

first time in this part of the woods; earlier in the summer, she and Mikey had hiked up there one night, just to talk.

Finally, Helen suggested they take a break. They hitched the horses to a tree and then sat on a rock to drink from their water bottles.

"What was your favorite thing about the summer?" Sarah asked her friend.

"Color wars," Helen said. "No question."

"That's a good one."

Helen took another sip of water. It was a cool night, but she was warm from the ride, and the breeze felt good on her arms. "What was yours?"

Sarah was silent for a moment, thinking. "Well," she said, giggling, "I think it would have to be hooking up with Danny."

"What?" Helen swatted her friend on the arm. "You didn't tell me."

"He told me to keep it a secret," she said. "But the summer's over, so, whatever."

"Why'd you have to keep it a secret?" Helen asked.

The wind was getting stronger; a heavy gust came over the mountains, and Helen gathered her arms around herself.

"Oh, I don't know," Sarah said.

Helen was silent.

"Okay, I'm lying," Sarah said. "It's because we did it."

"You *did it*?"

"Yeah," Sarah said. "It was kinda fun."

"Why wouldn't you be allowed to tell me that?"

"Well," Sarah said, "I didn't want to do it at first. But then he convinced me."

Helen could hear a rustling sound from farther away, a crunching on the forest floor.

"I was worried that if we were gonna do it, he would go and tell people about it after. So he assured me that wasn't the case."

"I'm not just people."

"But then we made a pact not to say anything, because fair is fair, you know?"

"Do you hear that?" Helen said.

"What?"

She could hear the rustling growing closer, and then she saw two beady eyes, almost at ground level, glaring at them.

Sarah shrieked and jumped off the rock. "What is that?" she shouted.

"Calm down," Helen said, glancing over at the horses to make sure they weren't startled. "It's just a raccoon."

The raccoon, scared too, turned around and scurried back into the forest, its gray and wiry tail disappearing into the bushes.

"Let's go," Sarah said. "I don't want to know what other sorts of crawly creatures are up here."

They went back to camp the way they came, down the foothills toward the other side of the lake. When they got back to the lakeshore, all the candles had burned out, and the lake just looked like it was littered with wax paper bags.

———

Back at the stables, they put the horses in their stalls and left the barn unlocked.

"That was fun," Sarah said, draping her arm over Helen's shoulders. It wasn't as fun for Helen as she had thought it was going to be. The raccoon and Sarah's weird confession had cut it all short. Helen couldn't explain why, but she felt uneasy now about Danny, about the way he had told Sarah to keep things between them a secret.

"You okay?" Sarah said, stopping and turning to her friend. Helen was starting to get that dizzy feeling again, the one she'd had with Marla in the woods back in the spring, right before she'd fainted.

"I'm fine," she said, "just tired," and they walked themselves up to their bunks, tucked themselves in, and whispered good night.

Helen had a dream that she was in the swimming pool in Florida with her brother, Liam, again. She was grown, but he was holding her like a child, rocking her back and forth, and singing "The Circle Game" to lull her to sleep.

"Take your time, it won't be long now
Till you drag your feet to slow the circles down."

She fell asleep in his arms, and then they went underwater, where he continued to sing.

13

The new counselor for tent three—the one who had replaced Rachel—opened the front flaps of the head tent so
wide that Mo knew, even in her just-awakened state, that
something was wrong.

"What is it?" Mo croaked. Nell, in the bunk across from
Mo's, stirred and turned toward the wall.

"I don't—" the counselor began. "I think—"

"What?" Mo said, though she was already pulling herself
out of bed, readying herself for a crisis. Over the past eight
weeks, she had come to know, almost instinctively, if someone was panicking for no good reason.

"I can't—" The counselor shook her head, unable to say
what she really needed to. "Just come to the tent now."

Mo stood and followed, in her pajamas, across the section circle to tent three. She saw that five girls were standing

outside, also in their pj's, bleary-eyed and disoriented and shivering, even though it wasn't very cold that morning. This tent seemed to her a glutton for tragedy. Sheera hadn't come back to camp after her accident, but the girls in her tent talked about her often, as if she were their martyr, as if they had been friends with her the whole time. And then after Rachel left, they did the same thing—idolized her, talked about her like she had died.

Four of the girls were huddled together, but Sarah, the fifth, was standing away from the group with her arms wrapped around herself.

"Mo's here," Sarah said. "Mo. She's not waking up, Mo."

The other girls looked up at Mo as if she could make it better. Staring at the begging faces and with possibilities swirling through her own mind, she took quick stock of the girls in front of her and then came a razor-sharp thought: *Helen is missing. Helen is in there.*

Helen seemed like a confident, happy girl, the kind who was so fun and carefree that other, more anxious girls flocked to her. Mo had observed her spending a lot of time with Mikey Bombowski, but it seemed so innocent. The way she stood apart from him when they were together, like she was afraid to touch him, afraid of what might happen to her if she did. Mo understood the feeling well.

The girls watched Mo as she walked into the tent with what she hoped was a fearless expression on her face. She did feel a certain power come over her; it would be crass to call it an adrenaline rush, but it was something akin to being entirely out of her head and in her body. All she experienced was that she was moving—not like she was willing herself to do it, but like her body was progressing on its own, one step coming after another. Not unlike the way she felt when she had run onto the field after Sheera had fallen off the horse. She watched her feet ascend the two steps to the tent and her hand opening the flap. She briefly let the light in before letting the flap drop. Then it was dark again aside from the thin slivers of light coming in through the cracks in the canvas.

She could just make out Helen on the top bunk. Perfectly still. Mo stepped onto the wooden frame of the bottom bunk to gain some height. She put her ear to the girl's mouth. Mo touched the girl's forehead, half believing that all it would take for her to wake up was for Mo to place a hand on her sleeping body.

She wasn't warm, but not cold either. As Mo's eyes adjusted to the darkness, she was able to make out Helen's face: eyes closed and lips turned upward in a closed-mouth smile, as if she were in the middle of a nice dream.

Mo had the dual sensation of both wanting and not wanting to do what she did next: take her own hand from where it was resting on the forehead and move it along the jawline and to the pulse. There was nothing.

Was her hand on the wrong side of the girl's neck? Perhaps it was.

Mo traced her hand across the neck to the other side. She put her two fingers where a pulse should be. Surely she still wasn't trying the right place. She put her fingers on her own pulse to remind herself what a healthy heartbeat felt like.

Then she put them back on the girl's neck, searching every inch of skin to find it.

She put her ear to the girl's mouth, to see if there was some sign of breath, and then to her nose. She moved her ear to the chest, listening for a heartbeat, though of course logic would tell her later that when there's no pulse, there's no heartbeat either. She was jittery, on edge, because she was sure that Helen would awaken at any moment and startle Mo, and Mo would jump and say, "Jesus Christ, you scared me." She took her two hands and pumped the girl's chest: right in the center of her chest, between the nipples, just as she had been taught in staff training. She pumped forcefully, creating a steady rhythm, working up a sweat. She paused to open the girl's mouth and breathe some life into it. She pumped again.

She sensed light coming into the tent while she worked.

She heard Nell's voice. "Oh my God."

Mo looked up. "Call an ambulance," she managed to say.

Mo had no idea how much longer she was in there by herself, but at some point, men in navy with stethoscopes around their necks came into her line of vision.

"Someone keep that thing open," she heard one say, and the light stayed.

"Ma'am, how long have you been here?" they were saying, and "Ma'am, please step aside," and "Ma'am, what happened to her? What can you tell us?" So many words being thrown at her that she couldn't begin to respond or do anything they were asking of her. Arms were pawing at her, but she just kept pumping.

"Mo, stop," she heard. But it wasn't until Nell took Mo's hand and physically pulled her out of the tent, and Mo saw the men in navy carrying Helen prostrate on a stretcher and no one in the section but Nell and Jack and Fiona and the ambulance parked there and the men in navy putting the stretcher in the ambulance and Nell and Jack and Fiona climbing in and pulling Mo up with them and someone shutting the ambulance door behind them, that she understood.

※

They tried to move as fast as the paramedics did, which was, of course, pointless. The paramedics pushed Helen on the stretcher through all the double doors until a doctor and two nurses appeared. The doctor was asking the paramedics questions filled with medical jargon that Nell couldn't understand, and then they were gone, through doors to the hallway marked AUTHORIZED PERSONNEL ONLY.

The four of them stood there in the ER waiting room, the senseless chatter gone through those last double doors and everything now silent. Mo had lost all color. Nell knew that the situation was bleak, that there was nothing so disastrous as no pulse for that amount of time—and who knew when in the night it had stopped?—but she also kept thinking, *The girl's thirteen. She'll wake up somehow. Don't young bodies just know how to do that?* It was an idiotic thought, but she wouldn't let go of it.

She took Fiona and Mo to two plastic chairs in the waiting area and sat in between them. Fiona was shivering and intermittently gasping for air. Nell found herself rubbing circles on Fiona's back with one hand and keeping her other arm around catatonic Mo. Somehow Nell had become, in the past ten minutes, the caretaker of these women. What was it in her DNA that allowed her to remain so stupidly calm in the face of disaster? She realized this was the first time she had touched Mo in weeks—the two had been speaking only out of necessity—and then she hated herself for thinking about something trivial like that. Jack paced across the linoleum floor, back and forth.

Helen and Fiona's parents lived two hours away. Nell tried not to think about what that car ride might be like; she didn't know how much Jack had told them. They would have already been coming to camp that day; it was the last day of the summer. The only other person in the waiting room, besides the four of them, was the receptionist. She was typing away at her computer as if it were any other kind of morning. Nell watched the clock above the desk. She counted the second hand making its rotation six times around.

During the seventh rotation, the doctor, a squat man in his fifties, came back through the swinging doors for authorized personnel only. He looked around as if getting his bearings, as if he didn't work in this same emergency room day after day. Jack approached the doctor. Nell realized that she should stand, and she pulled Mo and Fiona up with her.

"The parents?" The doctor looked between the three of them. "Are any of you the parents?"

"No," Jack said. "They aren't here yet."

"This is her sister," Nell said, putting her arm now firmly

around Fiona's shoulder. Fiona worked for Nell at the stables, and although Nell had never taken much of a liking to her, she now wanted to protect her like she'd never wanted to protect anyone before. The fact that Fiona's mother wasn't there—it was too sad, on top of all the other sadness. The doctor took his thumb and forefinger and squeezed his temples. He took a deep breath.

"I'm so sorry," he said, unable to look at Fiona. "There was nothing we could do."

Nell was suddenly very aware of how she breathed in and out. She focused on reminding herself how to do that, like she would stop altogether if she didn't. In, and she held it. Out, and it came sputtering. She wondered if she'd ever be able to breathe normally again. Would she always just monitor her breath all the time now, reminding herself she was still living?

"We think she had been . . ." He struggled to find the right words. "We think it happened many hours ago. Probably not long after she went to sleep."

Fiona made some sort of gasping, choking noise, and Nell held on to her tighter.

He tried to look at Fiona now, but his eyes landed somewhere above her head, as if looking at her directly would cause him too much pain. "Look at her," Nell wanted to say to him. "The least you could do is look at her."

"Okay," the doctor said to everyone's silence. "Does anyone want to . . . ? Does the sister want to . . . to see her?" He glanced at Nell.

Nell shook her head. "Let's wait until the parents get here."

"Again, I'm so sorry," he repeated to the space above Fiona's head. "Please let me know when the parents arrive." He nodded in defeat and walked slowly back through the swinging doors leading to the emergency room.

Fiona too seemed to have forgotten how to breathe. She was trying to get words out, but they kept stopping at her throat. It sounded like she was choking.

"Deep breaths," Nell said. "Deep breaths."

The girl's mouth was wide open; she was making a rasping sound as she struggled for any sort of air. She put a hand on her stomach.

"Are you going to be sick?" Nell said. Fiona nodded. Nell took her by the arm.

"Bathroom?" Nell asked the receptionist, hearing the urgency in her own voice.

The receptionist pointed, wordlessly, down the hallway to her right.

Fiona could not wait until they got to the bathroom stall and, as soon as they entered the room, vomited all over the tile.

"It's okay," Nell said, keeping an arm around Fiona, who was staring at her own sick on the floor. Nell grabbed a paper towel from the dispenser with her free hand. She took a corner of the towel and wiped it carefully around Fiona's mouth.

Fiona was struggling to get air again, and it sounded like she was desperately trying to say something.

"What is it, Fiona?" Nell said. "You can say it. It's just me." As soon as she said this, she felt disingenuous. "Just me"? They weren't friends, nor had they ever been. Why would Fiona want to say something to Nell, in this moment out of all moments, over anyone else?

"I—" she stammered. "I can't—"

"I know, I know," Nell said, moving in to place the girl's head on her own chest.

But Fiona shook her head. Nell didn't know. Fiona's eyes opened wide in fear. "My mother," she gasped, as if she had just remembered her.

They sat in the waiting room longer, Nell in between Mo and Fiona again. Both catatonic now. It felt both brave and foolish to still be there, to be one of the people the Larkins would have to see first. What could it have been? Did anyone know Helen might have been sick? She had ridden with Nell; she had seemed like the healthiest girl.

And what would happen to Dandelion, her horse? Another petty thought.

Nell turned to look out the window of the waiting room. It was a small hospital; Jack was sitting right there on the curb where the ambulances were parked. His hands were covering his face.

Today, everyone was supposed to go home. This was supposed to be the timely, tidy end. Mo and Nell had flights back home on Monday; once, they had planned to spend the rest of the weekend at a hostel in New York City. They were going to try to see the Sunday matinee of a Broadway show. But after Nell rejected her, Mo had changed her reservation to stay in an actual hotel, and now Nell would be at the hostel by herself. Now they would be two once-friends wandering at the same time through the same foreign city.

Still, Nell had been dreading their goodbye to each other today. She knew how she'd hurt Mo. She would apologize, she decided. All that trite bullshit about how life is too short to not apologize came into sharp, painful focus. It was the most awful way to realize your mistakes.

She heard the wail then, outside the tiny hospital window. She could hardly bring herself to turn and see it: a mother on her knees and the ugly gasps of a weeping man. Fiona stood, as if in a trance, and walked out of the hospital doors, which automatically opened for her. As if approaching a stranger, she put one stiff arm on her mother's shoulder.

But her mother pulled Fiona onto the ground. She would not weep there alone. The men stood beside them, and Jack put an uneasy arm around the father. They looked like accessories to the tragedy, still able to stand on their feet.

14

It was evening by the time Rachel and Denise arrived, and they parked behind the long line of cars leading up to the house. Denise carried a container of pasta salad they had picked up at a grocery store in Larchmont, and Rachel held a bouquet of half a dozen white roses—one of the few flower arrangements that had been left in the grocery store, many of the petals already browning.

A woman with a round face and highlighted blond hair answered the door; she turned out to be one of the Larkins' neighbors, and she led them inside, where they found about a dozen more women who looked like her, plus Liam, shuttling between the kitchen and the dining room, carrying aluminum pans with potholders and placing them on the table among several pots and bowls and dishes of food. Denise made room for the store-bought pasta salad between a Pyrex pan of some untouched orange casserole and a crockpot full of meatballs. Liam saw Rachel, placed the Dutch oven that he was holding onto the table, and opened his arms, the hands still inside potholders.

"Rachel," he said, and took her into a hug.

"I'm so sorry for your loss," Denise said. "Is there anything we can do? You should rest. We can help in the kitchen."

He shook his head. "You two should have something to eat," he said without looking them in the eyes. "Rachel, Fiona is upstairs." He turned away from them abruptly and went back through the swinging doors to the kitchen.

Denise made herself useful in the kitchen anyway, and Rachel walked up the carpeted steps to the second floor of the house. At the top of the stairway, she looked down the darkened hallway in both directions; all the doors were closed: the doors to the master bedroom and each child's bedroom as well.

She approached Fiona's door, with the ornamental, cursive *F* hanging from the doorknob, and knocked.

There was no answer. Rachel waited a few moments for some sort of a response. She put her ear to the door; there was silence. She knocked again.

"Fiona? It's me."

After a few beats, Fiona told her to come in.

Fiona was sitting on top of her bed, her back leaning on the wall that the side of her bed rested against. She was holding a worn paperback novel in her lap. She looked oddly, suspiciously normal.

"Hey," Rachel said. She sat on the bed and took her friend

into a long embrace. Fiona melted into it, leaning her weight into Rachel, an action that seemed to contain as much relief as if Fiona were letting out a long-held breath. "I'm so sorry," Rachel said into Fiona's neck.

When they released each other, Fiona said "Hey" back.

"It feels dumb to ask you how you're doing."

Fiona shrugged.

"So, how are you doing?" Rachel said sadly, self-aware.

"I'm fine," Fiona said, not returning any glimpse of emotion. She had an unreadable, stoic expression on her face.

Rachel stroked Fiona's hair, combing each finger through the strands. She had thought it would be clearer what she had to do; she'd thought that Fiona would be so distraught that Rachel would need only to sit there and hold her while she cried. Rachel had not been expecting this sort of opaque quietness. She did not know if it was appropriate to ask questions or to talk about Helen or if she should instead pretend they were there for any other reason but the actual one.

"Are your Larchmont friends here?" Rachel managed to ask.

She nodded. "Cooking, I think. They keep coming up to bring me tea." She gestured to an untouched mug on her bedside table. "I told them I wanted to be alone."

They sat for a few more moments in silence.

"*Do* you want to be alone?" Rachel finally asked.

Fiona thought for a moment. "Yeah," she said.

"Okay," Rachel said, nodding too much. "I totally under-stand." She took Fiona's hands in her own. "Call me when-ever you need me, any hour; it doesn't matter. Okay?"

"Yeah," Fiona said, but for some reason, Rachel knew that she wouldn't.

"I'll see you Wednesday," Rachel said. Wednesday was the funeral.

Things had not been good between them. After Rachel left camp, Fiona had called her several times, left desperate voicemails, sent emails from the computer lab, but Rachel hadn't responded to any of them. She felt incapable of it; she was too angry. Angry that Fiona was still at camp, as if she was somehow betraying her through the sheer act of staying, even though Fiona was unaware of what had hap-pened. In the days that followed, Rachel didn't leave her apartment, numbing out to bad TV and eating junk food in order to not have to piece together the events of that night, to not have to think about her father, about Micah, about this disastrously terrible summer. She was being punished for something, she was sure. But for what? She kept saying to Denise, "I don't want to talk about it," and she counted the days until she could go back to school. Eventually Denise turned off the TV and sat on the coffee table in front of the couch and made Rachel sit up and took Rachel's face into her hands and had to physically shake her in order to get her to talk.

Drunk as she had been at the time, she knew she never would have wanted to sleep with Chad. He was her friend, and she had begun to find safety in that, having a male friend who didn't seem to want anything more from her than loyalty or trust or comfort. In the past few weeks, she had started to rethink her behavior around him, replay their summer together as if she could find a place where things had turned, where things went wrong. Maybe it was something that she could have stopped. She had been affectionate with him, as she was affectionate with all her friends, though now she wondered if he'd confused her affection with flirtation or a genuine romantic interest. The thought made her deeply upset, and angry with herself, that something terrible could have been avoided had she only smiled less, kissed his cheek less.

And so she had not told Fiona, had not even spoken to Fiona until now. Rachel had thought naïvely that somehow Helen's death would overrule everything, that something of this magnitude would erase the less tragic things that had happened to herself. But as she walked down the stairs in Fiona's house, Rachel realized that Helen's death only compounded the pain. It was the greatest loss to heap on top of an already broken summer.

Downstairs, Denise was carrying a bowl of pretzels into the living room. Rachel stood in the open doorframe and peered into the room: men, including Mr. Larkin, sitting on the couches and watching baseball, silently, each one with a bottle of beer in hand. Mr. Larkin, in a reclining leather chair, was watching the game but not watching it, his legs up and both hands holding the beer tightly and his gaze fixed, also tightly, on the vivid moving images ahead, as if he was looking at something inside the TV, or behind it, which no one else in the room could see.

＊

A week after Helen's funeral, an envelope was delivered to the Larkin home, addressed to Fiona. It was a manila envelope postmarked from York, England, with Mo's name and return address written in the upper left corner; there was a letter inside, along with another envelope addressed to Helen at camp. Fiona looked at the letter in the manila envelope first. It was typed on a piece of computer paper.

Dear Fiona,

This came to camp the day Helen died. I took it back to England with me and have been holding on to it for the past few weeks, afraid to let it go, like if I put it in the mail, then the last vestiges of her would be gone from me. She was only in my section for eight weeks, along with thirty other girls, so I hardly feel like it's my right to say I miss her or that she was any sort of "part" of me at all. She wasn't, not before she died. It would be a disservice to you to pretend otherwise. But I want you to know that her smile has stuck with me, the way it was always coming out so girlish and easy, like she held some perennial secret to happiness that we forget about when we grow up.

Fiona stopped reading there and opened the smaller envelope, which was postmarked from Sacramento, though there
was no return address.

Yo, Helen!

*I called your house, and your mom gave me this
address. I knew you were at your favorite place—
CAMP! So I just wanted to say what's up. I can't remember the last time I wrote a real letter! Too bad
you guys don't have email there.*

*Anyway, sorry I'm sending this so late in the sum-
mer. I know I've been quiet a couple months. Josh got
in trouble, so we picked up and hit the road. We're in
California, but I'm not really supposed to tell people
that. You can keep it a secret, right?* ☺ *I will say there
are some hotties in my new town. I hang out at the
public pool in a bikini every day, and let's say I've become "friendly" with some high schoolers. LOL.*

*What's going on in YOUR love life? Did you get
your period yet? Write me back! Hope you're having
fun in the woods, you weirdo.*

Love, Marla

❇

They had a second memorial service at camp, at the lake, a
month after Helen's death. It wasn't the Larkins' idea. Jack
had suggested it in a phone call to the family, using words

like "grieving" and "closure." Fiona's father was adamant about never returning to camp again, and her mother had lost all ability to argue, to make decisions, to even speak more than was absolutely necessary. She stayed in bed, and Liam—the only one in the family for whom moving was easier than staying still—brought her a plate of scrambled eggs and toast with butter and blackberry jam every morning. Amy would not touch it, and eventually, starved himself, Liam would eat the cold eggs while leaning against the kitchen counter before figuring out his next task.

It was congenital heart disease, they learned from the autopsy, something so random and unavoidable that it caused undue amounts of torture. They couldn't have known, Helen's pediatrician told them when he called to console the family, voice wobbly and full of unease, as if he'd never had to make a call of quite this magnitude. The occasional fainting was a warning sign, yes, but they'd tested and found she had low blood sugar years earlier, and that had been enough to explain it. How could they have known that it might have been something additional, something so rare and deadly that no one would have dared to imagine it?

They wanted desperately to blame him, to have someone to blame. But it was a genetic defect that could happen to you or me or anyone we know, he assured them, and they believed him: There was no one to blame even if they tried. And so the pain had no outlet, had nowhere to go, and each member of the Larkin family recoiled and looked inward as if they might, somewhere inside themselves, find the seed of the tragedy.

For the parents, it was easy: A genetic defect meant they had somehow failed her with their very core, their very DNA. Someone down the line, in one of their families, was not supposed to have procreated with someone else. Maybe, Amy reasoned, they had been too old by the time they'd had Helen. She was a mistake, after all. Or maybe, Amy's thoughts spiraled, this was proof that she and John hadn't been meant to procreate at all; maybe they were the ones who weren't supposed to procreate.

It was Fiona who had thought a second memorial at the camp would be good. She had not spoken at the first service, partly because it had been too early for her to process anything and partly because she hadn't felt she had anything worthwhile to say. It was, she knew, a terribly wrong thought to have, that she didn't have anything good to say at her own sister's funeral, and so she had pushed it away. But as their aunt spoke, and then Liam, and then—astonishingly—their father, she found that she was not crying. What was wrong with her? She felt a heavy, impenetrable sorrow, but it didn't feel like her own; it felt like an extension of her parents' sorrow. Seeing her otherwise healthy mother now need help walking everywhere she went: That was where the real sorrow came from.

Fiona's sister—her beautiful little sister, who had once made Fiona into a forgettable, petty middle sibling—was gone. Fiona was the youngest now, and the change was swift. Immediately, she was no longer forgettable or petty; instead, she experienced the attention lavished on a girl who had just lost her only sister, and in a perverse way, she accepted it. She had, without having done anything, become a sort of elevated figure: the girl, the poor girl, who had gone from middle to youngest sibling. She was pitied; she was put on a sad pedestal. And she was more loved. Was this the most horrible thing in the world, to acknowledge that she didn't hate this attention? She believed that it was.

And so, camp: Maybe she could feel there, finally. Maybe she could cry there, be less selfish there. If any place could bring it out of her, that would be it.

So she convinced them, using the same words Jack had. Helen would have wanted it that way, she told them. There was no place she had loved more. And ultimately, everyone was too tired to argue with her.

❇

It was mid-September and strange to be back so soon after the summer had ended and to be there for a reason other than for camp itself. The weather hadn't changed much, but there was a slight chill in the air, and when a fall-like breeze came through, it gave the campers and counselors shivers— not because it was particularly cold, but because it felt incongruous with the warmth they associated with the place.

There were over three hundred people there: campers and counselors but also members of the Larchmont community who had driven en masse to the Berkshires to pay their respects once again.

For the first time, Rachel did not want to return to camp. Not just for the obvious reasons—the way she had left and the reason she was returning—but because of the mismatched nature of it all. You didn't leave camp in July. You didn't go back to camp in September. And you didn't return for something like this. The natural order of everything was thrown off. Camp used to be the one place where you could trust that the only thing to change every year would be you. Now it seemed that even camp couldn't be trusted.

She had not gone to her father's funeral, and neither had Denise. But Denise insisted they attend Helen's memorial at camp—she told Rachel she would regret it if she didn't go, and she was right—and so two weeks into her sophomore year, Rachel returned, flying from Michigan to New York for the weekend. They drove up to Lakeville in silence; there wasn't a lot to say.

People were gathering quietly on the beach, all of them standing, arms crossed around themselves. Some adults were exchanging quiet words with one another. Rachel was surprised by the campers who had returned, though of course, when she thought about it, she shouldn't have been. Sarah had taken her shoes off and was standing with her bare feet in the water. She looked so unnatural wearing black. Danny Sheppard and Mikey Bombowski were standing next to each other a few feet behind Sarah, awkward, not talking. They were supposed to be home, back in their real lives, missing camp and gearing up for a new school year in which they would hold their pure memories of the summer close, a sunny reserve of simplicity to turn to on colder days. Rachel remembered Mikey and Helen outside the athletic shed, how Helen had dropped his hand when she saw her.

Denise stood next to her as they looked around for any member of the Larkin family.

"Is that him?" Denise whispered, pointing to Jack. He was wearing a suit, and he was standing off to the side of the mourners. He had a piece of paper folded in his hand; he would probably deliver some sort of speech.

"Don't," Rachel said to her mother.

Rachel then spotted Sheera, wearing the same black dress she had worn the night of the dance. Rachel had been certain that she would never see the girl again. Sheera was standing next to her father, both of them erect, patiently waiting.

Rachel left her mother where she stood and approached them. "Hi, Sheera," Rachel said.

Sheera started. "Hey, Rachel."

"Thanks for coming," Rachel said. She put an arm around the girl, and Sheera leaned into it.

"I had to pay my respects."

This made Rachel tear up. "That's very kind of you," she said.

She removed her arm from around Sheera and shook her father's hand. "Thank you for being here, Mr. Jones." He nodded. Rachel had not seen him, either of them, after Sheera's accident.

"I'm sorry about what happened," she added, but as soon as she said it, it felt trivial. She felt trivial.

He shook his head. "Let's not," he said, and he put an arm around Sheera, taking her back.

✳

When Fiona saw Rachel at the beach, the first tears came. She suddenly felt it all: the anger of Helen leaving her early, and of Rachel leaving her early too, as if she was realizing for the first time that the two things might somehow be related. As if it could, maybe, somehow, be Rachel's fault. How easy that would be, to be able to blame Rachel, to believe that the two of them had conspired with each other to leave Fiona there all alone on the day that she needed Rachel the most.

Rachel too began to cry as she approached her friend. They embraced for a long time, their arms held tightly around each other while they heaved in and out.

When Fiona finally let go, the first thing she said to Rachel, face stained with tears, was "Why did you leave?" Fiona was so angry she almost couldn't speak. She was spitting out her words like chants, as if she were possessed. "You should have been there," she kept repeating. "You should have been there."

"I wish I could have," Rachel said, as gently as she could. She went in to stroke Fiona's hair, but Fiona pushed Rachel's hand away.

"It's always about you, isn't it? How did this still manage to be about you?"

"What do you mean?" Rachel asked cautiously.

"The hospital. You weren't there."

Rachel shook her head. "I wanted to be. So badly. Believe me."

"You should know better than anyone," Fiona said, so incensed, she knew she was about to say cruel things. "I was there for you when your dad died. I got it, before anything even happened to Helen. I got that it was so hard and complicated. But where have you been since this happened? Gone. You left camp without a word. I got one measly five-minute visit. You didn't even bother to talk to me at the funeral."

"You didn't want me to," Rachel said, her voice quiet, trying not to think of her dad anymore.

Fiona was right: Rachel's relationship with her father had been complicated, but so had the one between Fiona and Helen. Rachel was the only person who knew the extent to which the sisters never got along. When they were younger, Fiona had told Rachel that she wished Helen had never been born—both of them remembered the sentiment clearly now. Rachel knew it couldn't suddenly feel so uniformly tragic and simple, and Fiona hated being reminded of how much Rachel knew about her.

Fiona kept going, possessed. "Do you know how stupid I felt, pretending like I knew where you went but actually having no idea?"

Rachel took a deep breath. "Do you know why I left camp?" *Oh,* she thought, *maybe this isn't the time.* She knew it wasn't the time, but the bait had been too tempting.

"No, and I don't even care anymore."

And that was when they heard it: Denise's harsh New York accent raised above the din of the three hundred mourners.

"You piece of shit. You should be ashamed of yourself."

The girls looked toward the voice down the beach a few yards away. Denise, a full foot shorter than Jack, was pushing the man's chest hard, like she wanted him to fight back. He kept taking small steps in retreat with his hands up. He seemed confused as to who she was.

"Ma'am, please, calm down."

"Don't you tell me to calm down." She was craning her neck to look up at him, but she seemed unconcerned by the size difference. "You watched my daughter get raped."

She waited. She let the word land. Now he knew who she was.

"You are a weak, impotent man."

Denise continued to shove his chest, but Jack was no longer moving backward. Instead, he stood still as she threw curse after curse at him, his dress shoes cemented into the sand.

"You're a pervert," she spat, "a sick, fucking pervert."

Rachel and Fiona remained where they stood and watched silently, shocked and exhilarated by the extraordinary amount of power and adrenaline that seemed to be coming from Denise. Rachel didn't think she had ever seen her mother so strong and so sure. Fiona did not dare to look at Rachel.

And then something happened that the girls would forever after know as one of the strangest, most memorable moments of their young lives. As Denise pushed and cursed at Jack and pushed him some more, seemingly exhausting herself but not slowing down, and as the entire crowd of mourners watched it, Amy Larkin—grieving Amy Larkin, who had just lost her young daughter, who had been bedridden and unable to walk unaided for the past month, who had never before had anything of consequence to say to Denise—standing as tall as she ever had, strode over to Rachel's mother and took the woman by the arm.

At the touch, Denise turned to Amy and immediately stopped pushing. She looked at the woman, bewildered. Amy nodded and took Denise into her arms. Denise accepted the embrace and, in one single moment, fell into it with a low, mournful groan.

Rachel was sure it was the ugliest sound that had ever come from her mother's mouth. "I'm so sorry," they heard Denise saying between sobs. "I'm so, so sorry."

Amy stroked Denise's hair. "I know," she said. Jack stood over the women, perplexed by the scene in front of him. Powerless as he waited for it to be over.

Then Amy looked up at Jack as if she had forgotten, until then, that he was there. She said to him very clearly and very calmly, "I think you should go now."

Who would say no to a mourning mother? Amy seemed to understand this, that all the power in the world suddenly belonged to her. The two women walked away from the shore, away from Jack, and toward the back of the crowd. Once they had settled there, and Denise's sobs had slowed, they watched as Jack ambled onto the trail leading away from the lake and disappeared. The memorial-goers were still standing there, looking around, speaking in low tones to one another, waiting for some sort of order to resume, waiting for someone new to take charge. Jack was supposed to make the opening remarks.

Fiona looked at Rachel and Rachel at Fiona. "I didn't—" Fiona started to say.

Rachel shook her head and took Fiona's hand. Emboldened by their mothers, perhaps, or by what one might call a ghostly atmosphere down at the lake that day, with Helen's memory hovering so close, each girl saw the other fully in that moment.

Later they planted a garden for Helen near the stables at Camp Marigold. The Larkins donated her horse, Dandelion, to the camp, less out of benevolence and more because of the grief that would have come with having to care for her, day after day. And once they decided to donate Dandelion, Fiona wanted Josie to go too; she couldn't bear to separate them.

Helen would never have to realize, years later, what Sarah had had to endure, that clenching her teeth and waiting for the sex with Danny Sheppard to be over wasn't normal or okay. She wouldn't live with a scar from that glimpse of Yonatan in the shed that night, wouldn't ever know why Rachel left camp.

All the girls Helen loved and hated would not be formative in the development of her adult self, would not be discussed in therapy nor play major roles in her future relationships with her roommates, her bosses, her mother-in-law. She would not be threatened by women or seek to defy them.

In her adult siblings' homes, and those of her aging, divorced parents, Helen would remain suspended in the same picture: Camp Marigold, July 2006, half-smiling at the camera, as though taken aback by it, her blond curls fading at the edges into a sun-softened day. Hipless, flat chested, some time before she would have gotten her first period. Downy tanned legs in kid-sized medium shorts. She was perfect. She had left perfect. Though no one admitted it, or outwardly wished it upon themselves, when it came to Helen, they silently agreed: They all thanked God she was a late bloomer.

But in that moment at the beach, when Denise had lashed out at Jack, and everyone was standing silent and confused about what was supposed to happen next, Rachel said to Fiona, "Maybe you should go up there." There was no one else equipped to speak. Fiona knew this too. She nodded, let go of her friend's hand, and made her way to the front of the crowd.

Acknowledgments

Meredith Kaffel Simonoff, my agent, took this project on in its nascent stages and helped me to shape it into something more like a book. Her savvy, generosity, and dedication have been career-making and life-changing.

Andrea Walker is a dream editor: whip smart, incisive, and most of all, kind. I don't know how I lucked into getting to work with her, but I'm so glad I did.

Kaela Myers, my sister in ampersand, has been incredibly helpful throughout this entire process. Janet Wygal's copyediting skills are out of this world. Lucy Silag, Andrea DeWerd, and the rest of the lovely folks in the publicity and marketing departments at Random House have shown nothing but excitement and dedication for *Perennials,* and I am so grateful to them.

Susan Kamil and Andy Ward: Thank you for believing in this book.

To the many more working hard behind the scenes, both at Random House and DeFiore and Company: Thank you.

Kelly Farber is my unofficial guide through this wild world of publishing, and I couldn't get by without her honesty, intel, and humor.

I'm extremely grateful to the Columbia University Writing Program for providing me with two years to write and, consequently, a second home. My teachers, particularly Elissa Schappell and Rebecca Godfrey, helped me to spring *Perennials* into being when it was just a bud. Victor LaValle helped me turn it into a novel. Corinna Barsan's input was instrumental to the revision process. I'm thankful to all of my peers and professors, too many to name here, who read drafts and pushed me to do better.

Katie Abbondanza, Julia Bosson, Kea Krause, and Soon Wiley are brilliant readers, writers, and people. Dr. Matt Cummings called me on his overnight shifts and patiently explained heart conditions and concussions to me. Ellie Hunzinger, my English rose, was my British vernacular adviser. Elise Brandenburg taught me about horses.

My best friends, Laura Ferrazzano, Kelsey MacArthur, Lauren Pagano, and Marissa Danney, live in the girlish heart of this book.

And the greatest thanks to my family, for their love and unwavering support: the clans of Cambridge, Corvallis, Newport, and Whippany; my grandmother, Connie Berman; my brother, Sam Berman; and my parents, Tony Berman and Jill Remaly.

PHOTO: © MARTIN BENTSEN

MANDY BERMAN is originally from Nyack, New York. She is a graduate of the Columbia University MFA Writing Program and now lives and writes in Brooklyn. This is her first novel.

mandyberman.com
Twitter: @MandyBerman